JUN   2003

ARTIFACT

BOOKS BY KEVIN J. ANDERSON
Dune: The Butlerian Jihad (with Brian Herbert)
Ignition (with Doug Beason)

BOOKS BY F. PAUL WILSON
The Haunted Air
Conspiracies
Legacies
The Tomb
Deep as the Marrow
Implant

Available from Tom Doherty Associates

ARTIFACT

A Daredevils Club Adventure

KEVIN J. ANDERSON, JANET BERLINER,
MATTHEW J. COSTELLO, AND F. PAUL WILSON

A Tom Doherty Associates Book
New York

13976543

ARTIFACT: A DAREDEVILS CLUB ADVENTURE

Edited by James Frenkel

Book design by Michael Collica

A Forge Book
Published by Tom Doherty Associates, LLC
175 Fifth Avenue
New York, NY 10010

www.tor.com

Forge® is a registered trademark of Tom Doherty Associates, LLC.

Library of Congress Cataloging-in-Publication Data

Artifact / Kevin J. Anderson . . . [et al.]—1st ed.
    p.   cm.
    "A Tom Doherty Associates book."
    ISBN: 0-765-30063-X
    1. Astrogeology—Fiction.   2. Energy development—Fiction.   I. Anderson, Kevin J., 1962–

PS3600.A1A88 2003
813'.08708—dc21

2002045492

First Edition: May 2003

Printed in the United States of America

0   9   8   7   6   5   4   3   2   1

ACKNOWLEDGMENTS

The authors wish to thank Robert L. Fleck, without whose hard work and dedication this book never could have been completed. Also Laurie Harper, an excellent agent and friend. And finally Jim Frenkel and the staff at Forge Books for making the editorial process smooth and enjoyable.

Additionally, thanks are due to our Grenadian friends Moses Findley, George Grant, and Winston, as well as Rebecca Moesta and Catherine Sidor.

PROLOGUE

Grenada, December 31, 1982

Show time!

Peta Whyte struck a Bob Fosse dance pose in front of the brooding edifice that was Richmond Hill Prison. Despite the tension of the moment, she smiled at the strange juxtaposition. The two-hundred-year-old fortress, with its view of Grenada's harbor and the crystal blue Caribbean, was a perfect symbol of the harsh reality that now controlled her island, an island that had long been considered the jewel of the West Indies.

The U-shaped harbor and surroundings looked like a miniature Monte Carlo. A rainbow of brightly colored tin-and-wooden houses, small hotels, and provision stores which stocked little more than the necessities of life—rum, rice, cigarettes, and beer—meandered from the top of several hills down to the business and restaurant district which fringed the water. Fort George, like Monte Carlo's famed Castle-Fort, crested the top of the right-hand hill. Below it, hidden from view on the far side of the hill, lay the central marketplace. Looming over that, at the top of Church Street, stood a cathedral whose bells pealed melodically and often. At the top of the opposite hill, replacing Monte Carlo's casinos, was a gun emplacement which surrounded and essentially hid the island's only radio station from view.

From where she was standing, Peta could hear her Rasta friend Jimmy and his buddies playing soca on the steel drums that lined the fringes of Tanteen Park, which lay directly below her. In her mind's eye she could see the familiar scene at the bottom of the hill. Across the street

9

from Jimmy, in front of the entrance gates to the docks, a series of booths sold food, smokes, and fireworks. Outside the neighboring fishery, old ladies, unmindful of the country's unrest, were sitting at open grills, cooking corn and jacks, the long silvery fish so abundant in the waters around the island. The jacks looked like overgrown sardines and, even grilled to a crisp and eaten bones and all, tasted like kippers.

Between the bountiful waters and the fruit and vegetables available all year just for the plucking, the only reason anyone went hungry on the island was out of sheer laziness, Peta thought, wishing that she could be among the vendors and musicians, acting like a carefree teen instead of someone with murder on her mind.

Only, if she were, her mentor and friend, Arthur Marryshow, would be as good as dead, and it would be as much her fault as it would be the Communists' who had imprisoned him.

Obedient to her instructions, Jimmy continued to play. His beat wafted up the slope on Grenada's sunset trade winds, heralding the end of the old year and the start of the new. Any excuse was good enough for a party. And why not? Tomorrow would be time enough to return to politics; tomorrow, when everyone had slept off the rum and the beer and the ganja. She had told Jimmy to keep playing loudly for at least an hour or until she returned, whichever came first.

It occurred to her now that he would have played on anyway, and that a more intelligent instruction might have included telling him what to do if she didn't come back, like calling her next of kin.

Such thinking was, she knew, counterproductive. She stopped herself and glanced up at the small window of the cell where Arthur was being held in solitary. His crime: suspected espionage against Grenada's Cuban-backed New Jewel government. If her friend and mentor was watching, her pose would send him a message, a reminder of their trip to New York three years ago. The trip had been her thirteenth birthday present—and his thirty-first.

Peta had been a precocious thirteen. Her mother had been working several jobs since her father's untimely death four years earlier, so Peta was left to take care of her younger siblings. Saved from feeling sorry for herself by natural intelligence and a streak of innate pragmatism, she'd managed to be practical, popular, and a good student.

All of which Arthur rewarded in as many ways as he could, including the trip to New York. They'd seen *All That Jazz,* and declared the movie's risk-taking protagonist to be their hero. Later, they'd eaten dinner at a place called Danny's Seafood Grotto, and vowed to return there every year. On New Year's Eve.

A good plan, Peta thought. Except that someone should have told the Cubans not to interfere with Grenada and told the New Jewel Movement to disband. Instead, a hunger for power and for the blood of the enemy, whoever that might be, had turned her island into a madhouse.

This was a small island. Half the people were related, and the rest knew each other's business. Which was how she knew that William, her cousin's husband, would be on guard duty outside the prison tonight.

She rubbed her shoulder, bruised from the heavy backpack she'd lugged up Richmond Hill for William and his partner. William was a militant, sadistic bastard who for the last few years had hit on her at every opportunity. He'd be happy to see her, and easy to convince that the real reason she'd trekked up St. George's highest hill to spend New Year's Eve at the island's only prison was that he was, finally, irresistible.

And just in case his ego was on vacation, she'd brought ganja and the sweetness of the birthday cake and . . .

It had all sounded so simple in the planning that she hadn't had time to be afraid or to indulge herself in prayers or wishful thinking. Besides, above all else, she was a doer. Even were that not her nature, she'd be a doer now. She was damned if she was going to let them put Arthur Marryshow up against a wall and shoot him.

Dead.

Or take machetes and hack him into pieces as a lesson to others who might be thinking of not toeing the line. Rumor had it Maurice Bishop and his Commie henchmen planned to do one or both of these things on the first day of the New Year.

Tomorrow.

With that sobering thought and the renewed realization that she was the parrot fish, the designated decoy, Peta took a last look at Burns Point and at the lagoon which lay adjacent to the harbor. She could see the *Assegai*, Fredrick "Frikkie" Van Alman's 120-footer, anchored in the lagoon. The schooner rocked gently, and Peta wished that she were there too, lying safely in the warm waters of the Caribbean.

Trusting that her partners in this rescue attempt, Frik and his ex–Green Beret buddy Ray Arno, already had their asses in gear, she put on a dash of lipstick and adjusted the backpack. She hiked her short skirt level with her panty line and tuned in to Jimmy's calypso. Never more aware of her physical beauty, and determined to use everything that good genes had given her, she set her body into deliberately sensual motion. Dancing around the corner of the stone facade of Grenada's fortress prison, she prayed for this exercise to be over fast, as planned. It was one thing to play tease; it was quite another to have to deal with fully aroused male libidos.

"Hey, Joe. You see what I see?" Her cousin's husband and his Soviet-made submachine gun leaned in a triangle against the wall. He touched the weapon as if to reassure himself that it was still there, removed his dark American shades, and grinned at Peta.

"I see it but I don't believe it." His buddy, squat and ugly as a blowfish, grinned back. "Whatchou doin' here, girl?"

Peta danced into the circle of their lechery. She took off the backpack, dug into it, removed the ganja, and threw it to William. "Natalie says happy New Year."

"You telling me you came all the way up here to give me this?" From his breast pocket he pulled out a packet of rolling papers and removed one. Reaching into the plastic sandwich bag filled with marijuana, he removed a couple of dried buds and rolled them between his fingers, which caused the bits of leaf to fall into the paper while the seeds and stem remained in his fingers.

"I need you to do me a favor, Willy," Peta said as she watched him roll the ganja-filled paper into an expert joint.

"Anything." William licked the end of the paper, rolled his tongue at her, and lit the joint. "Almost anything." He drew deeply, then offered it to her. She took it and toked, drawing less deeply than it appeared, and passed it to Joe.

"It's my birthday," she said, taking the boxed cake out of the backpack.

Joe opened the box and pulled matches out of his pocket. He counted the candles. "Sixteen candles," he sang out, jiggling himself. He put his arm around her and kissed her full on the mouth. "You legal now, girl."

Peta pulled away. Grinned. Felt like throwing up. "I got a friend inside."

"You want to go inside and celebrate with him?" Joe asked. "We not good enough for you?"

Willy laughed. "Sir fucking Dr. Arthur Marryshow, right?"

Happy birthday, dear Arthur, Peta thought.

"How about we light a fire under that cocksucker and turn him into a candle?" Joe said.

Animal! Peta thought, deliberately feeding on Joe's callousness to harden herself for what lay ahead.

"Great shit." William took another toke from the joint. "Bring anything else, sweetface?" He rummaged in the backpack and found the beers. "Let's party." He opened one of the bottles and slugged down the contents. "You too good to us, girl." He belched loudly. Joe roared with laughter.

Their noises covered the sounds for which Peta had been waiting, three in succession, Frik's practiced imitation of the distinctive deep-throated howl of the Mona monkeys he'd often hunted for his dinner pot. She looked at the sky. In the way of the Tropics, darkness had suddenly come upon them.

"Tell you what," William said. "We'll save the good doctor a beer and a couple pieces of cake in case he's alive in the morning."

"How about some for the other guards?" Peta asked, ignoring the loud beat of her heart in her ears.

"They's inside. They'll never know the difference. Nobody out here but us."

There was a moment of silence as one man toked and the other opened and slugged down another Carib. Too late, Peta tried to cover the silence.

"What the fuck was that?" Joe said.

"Didn't hear a thing." William put his arm around Peta and pulled her toward him.

"Well, I did."

"Okay, so maybe a dog took a loud dump. If it bothers you, go see what it was."

Beer in one hand, weapon balanced by his forearm and lying across his shoulder, Joe took a step in the direction from which Peta had come. "I think I'll just do that," he said. He bent first to extract a large and messy chunk of birthday cake.

"You'll miss the real party." Peta pressed herself against William.

"I'll be back," Joe said. "Have to take a piss anyway. Might as well do a tour while I'm at it."

He didn't seem particularly worried until the sound came again—the harsh clang of something against metal. He stiffened and moved toward the noise.

Dear God, forgive me, I didn't want it to come to this, Peta thought, as she swung into the action she and Ray had rehearsed.

Quickly, using maximum energy and strength, she removed the scalpel that had been disguised as part of her belt buckle. Imagine Willy's a goat, she told herself; she'd helped kill those often enough before a family feast.

The illusion worked, aided by a massive rush of adrenaline. Before he realized what was happening, William's carotid artery had been neatly slit. Her cousin Natalie's husband.

She turned her attention to Joe, who was just about to round the corner that led to a scene he could not be allowed to witness. For a split second, she diverted her focus to William's submachine gun.

"Don't even think about it, sweetface." Joe turned around, his weapon cocked. "This no toy in me hand, you know. Now, you mind telling Joe what be going on?"

"Sick dog was feeling me up," Peta said, knowing how stupid she sounded after giving both of them the come-on.

"Sick dog?" Joe motioned at her with the rifle. "You sick bitch, if you ask me. C'moverhere." She didn't move. "Be a good girl, sweetface. Drop you knife and come over here. Slowly."

She walked toward him, swaying her hips. She was taller than he was by some inches. As she came close to him, she could see over his right shoulder. Two figures stood behind him, no more than thirty feet away and exposed in the fullness of the New Year's Eve moon.

Watching her, Joe put the remainder of the cake into his mouth. "Want some?" He held two fingers of icing next to her face. "Might as well. Fat won't matter when you's dead and you's going be dead in a minute, you don't tell me what's going down."

He had allowed Peta, encouraged her, to come close enough to implement Ray's lessons. Praying that he had not yet released the safety on his weapon, she struck fast, kneed him in the crotch, and when he doubled over in pain, jabbed her thumbs into his eyes, then struck with the edge of her hand to the back of his neck. The gun clattered to the ground, along with his bottle of Carib. Clutching his balls and whimpering, Joe buckled and fell facedown into the dregs of the beer that had trickled from his bottle.

Thinking of the danger to Arthur, Frik, and Ray, and to herself, Peta did what she had to do.

He's a goat, she told herself again.

In an act punctuated by the repeated clatter of a hard object against metal, she picked up Joe's submachine gun and smashed his skull.

"I—"

"We saw what happened, Peta," Ray said. "Thank you."

"You all right, kid?" Frik asked.

An irreverent thought flashed through Peta's mind. These two men were having fun. Educated, well traveled, experienced, they were not much more than altered, older versions of what William and Joe might have become. Ray, a demolitions expert turned stuntman, had come to Grenada to shoot some scenes for a Hollywood movie, and had stayed on when the revolution heated up. The truth was that he'd rather be shooting a gun than a film. As for Frik, the stocky expatriate South African was an oil magnate whose wealth was exceeded only by the size of his ego. Like Joe, he saw himself as irresistible to women. He acted as if he were Hemingway incarnate, and looked the part, especially when he had a crossbow slung over his shoulder.

"I had to hit the bars first," Frik said, as if there were any way he could have been that accurate.

She looked at the crossbow, which was now in his hands. So the sound that had nearly gotten them killed earlier was an arrow—or a bolt, as Frik called it—hitting the bars of the window of Arthur's prison cell and ricocheting back to the ground.

"Had to warn Art to get out of the way."

Art? It's Arthur, you dumb shit, Peta thought. She looked up at the window. Arthur was looking down at them. Even in the moonlight, she could see that his face was thin and drawn. He was a huge man, almost six feet five. Before his arrest he'd weighed over 250 pounds. By all reports, he had lost nearly a hundred of that during his year of confinement.

Peta waved and smiled at him, trying not to let her body language show how scared she really was, but he seemed to be too focused on Frik to notice anything else.

Frik was preparing to send up another bolt, attached to a nylon fishing line which was in turn attached to a rope.

"Let's get this show on the road," Ray said.

Frik nodded, and this time the bolt found its mark between the bars. Arthur signaled to them, bolt in hand, and immediately began pulling up the rope. Ray checked the small black bag that was attached to his belt. It contained, he had told her, a fine powder, a mixture of iron oxide and aluminum. He patted his pocket, as if to reassure himself that he had the magnesium strips and matches he needed for ignition. Arthur disappeared from her view for a moment, then reappeared, giving a thumbs-up.

Ray tested the rope. "Hold it taut at the bottom," he told Frik as he handed the end to the Afrikaner. Moments later, Ray was effortlessly scaling the wall, working his way upward toward the small barred window.

"Keep your eyes open, my little miss," Frik said, holding on to the rope. "We can't be sure someone won't come looking for those buddies of yours."

"They weren't my buddies," Peta said, more sharply than was necessary. *And I'm not your little miss!* She needed to release some of her pent-up fear and guilt. This was hardly an auspicious beginning to her adulthood. She knew that she'd had to kill to avoid being killed herself, but that didn't mean she liked playing God . . . any more than she liked being patronized.

Above her, Ray had reached the window. First he pulled the magnesium strips from his pocket and wrapped them around the bases of the three bars farthest from the rope. After that, he took the explosive from his belt, tamped some of the aluminum–iron oxide compound around each of the bars, and lit a long match. He touched the flame to a fuse attached to the magnesium strips, then, with the skill of a coconut thief, slid a dozen yards down the rope. A series of crisp sizzles followed, each accompanied by a flash of light. Darkness returned.

When Peta's eyesight had adjusted, she saw that there were huge scorch marks on the masonry below the window, and the bars had been bent out of the way. Ray was already halfway down the rope.

As soon as the stuntman reached ground, Arthur eased his spare frame through the window and followed suit. When his feet touched solid ground, he stopped for a moment as if the physical effort had worn him out. He bent over and took several deep breaths, then straightened up.

"Let's go," he said.

Taking their cue from Arthur, the four of them raced, as fast as his slower pace would allow, down the hill toward Grenada Yacht Services and the comparative safety of the *Assegai*.

The gated compound of GYS was unattended after midnight. Peta watched Frik use his membership key on the entry gate's massive lock. As she walked inside and heard Frik click the lock shut behind her, she became aware of the silence. She realized, with wonder and what was almost a sense of discomfort, that no alarm had been raised at the prison. She was wrenched out of her thoughts by the sight of a large gun emerging out of the shadows.

"Evening, Frik."

Peta breathed a sigh of relief as she recognized the voice and short, slight figure of Emanuel Sheppard, an old friend and freelance boat captain who seemed to live at GYS. "I see you brought some company."

"Actually, amigo, if you know what's good for you, you didn't see anyone," Frik replied.

A sly look washed onto Manny's face and rolled away again with the tide of his easygoing nature. Peta had known this man her entire life, and had never seen a single person rattle him. Everybody seemed to trust him implicitly. She was sure that he knew almost every secret on the island, and just as sure that not one of them would ever pass his lips. If you pushed him, the most you'd get was a sly glance and a tall story about his days in the Organization of Eastern Caribbean States security forces.

The group hurried along the creaking boards of the Grenada Yacht Services piers until they came to the two-masted beauty of the *Assegai*.

Frik's Great Danes, Sheba and Maverick, greeted them ebulliently as they clambered on board, though Peta knew that the animals would not be so friendly were their master not in the group. Frik wasted no time in starting the engines. Still on the dock, Manny cast off the tie lines, and the yacht began a stately drift, aided by the motors, which thrummed to life.

"Happy New Year, all," Manny called out in a stage whisper. Then softer, "It was nice not seeing you again."

As they cleared the harbor, Arthur turned to Peta. He bent down to lift her into the air. Still too weak to do so, he simultaneously hugged and reprimanded her.

"Happy as I am to see you, girl, I want to know what you're doing here." He released her and looked at the others. "This is hardly a child's game."

The warmth Peta had felt with Arthur's arms around her instantly dissipated. "Damn it, Arthur, I'm not a child. Tell him, Ray. Tell him why I'm here."

"This was all her idea," Ray said, somewhat grudgingly. "She planned the operation—"

"And set it up," Peta interrupted. "I killed two men so these *boys* here could play Scaramouche meets Robin Hood," she went on. "Killed. As in dead. William—"

"Natalie's William?"

Peta nodded. "He's lying on the ground up there with his carotid sliced by one of your scalpels. And Joe—" She put her hands over her face.

"I'm sorry, Peta," Arthur said quietly. After a moment he added, "What are we waiting for? I, for one, could use a drink."

In short order, the three men were seated around Frik's large wooden outdoor table, where a bottle of Westerhall rum, a dish of nuts, three highball glasses, and a bottle of guava juice awaited their return. Peta cynically assumed the last was her reward.

Arthur poured himself a short glass, adding juice, rather than his usual straight-up tumblerful. "It's been a long time," he said. "Happy birthday, Peta. Happy birthday to both of us."

No one said much more until the rum was half gone. Peta sat away from the other three, on a locker which, she presumed, held life jackets. The spot was ideal in that she was close enough to see and hear them, yet far enough away from them to deal with the distraction of her own thoughts, which were none too pleasant. Every once in a while, a flying fish arced from the water, its silvery scales flashing in the moonlight, or a star shot across the heavens. She took solace in those signs, telling herself that the universe had forgiven her trespasses against it.

To port, she could see that they were rounding the peninsula of Point Saline. In a few minutes, the lights of the Cuban encampment would be visible, and the great black expanse of the airstrip they were building.

Her mind returned to the events which led up to tonight.

Why had Arthur, her father's godson, insisted upon playing hero and martyr? Sure, he was a Marryshow and thus by nature a political beast, but as much as she adored him, she sometimes wondered about his sanity. Everybody knew he was none too fond of Prime Minister Bishop and his Communist regime, but so what? Arthur was a doctor, for God's sake, not a warrior or a politician. He could have kept his nose clean. Then he wouldn't have been arrested, and she wouldn't have had to kill two people.

She stopped. There was no point to those thoughts. She turned away from the receding coastline of her home and focused on her three shipmates. While they were unique in many ways, and two of them weren't Grenadian, they were typical of Grenada's male population, who were die-hard chauvinists. Arthur was less so than most, at least in their private moments, but in the company of men he acted little better than the rest, who adored females of all shapes, sizes, colors, and ages but believed them to be creatures of service, there to nurture them and to bed them. Like the others, he had no quarrel with women entering nurturing professions. They could become doctors and nurses and teachers. Anything else, law for example, or engineering, was a man's domain.

Like drinking rum, which, too, was some pathetic rite of manhood, she thought as they started on the second half of the bottle. Westerhall was as close as they could get to pure alcohol, so it was none too surprising that their tongues loosened. They began to regale each other with a succession of stories of prior adventures which grew more daring and less believable in inverse proportion to the amount of rum left in the bottle.

By five minutes to midnight, they were well into their next bottle. In their drunken state, they seemed to have completely forgotten that Peta was there.

"We are the best," Frik said, raising his glass.

"The very best," Ray agreed, doing the same.

"Uh-huh." Arthur tilted his glass in their direction.

Frik started to hold forth. Peta stopped listening until the end of his pronouncement. ". . . Daredevils Club," he said. "We'll meet every year. . . . New Year's Eve's a good time. Swap stories. See which of us has taken the biggest risk. Whatcha think, guys?"

Peta glanced at her watch in the moonlight. Thirty seconds and it would be 1983. She rose to her feet and approached the table. "Happy birthday, Arthur," she said.

"Happy birthday, Peta," he echoed.

"And happy New Year . . . everyone." She turned toward Arthur. "Are we all going to meet at Danny's Grotto for our birthdays *and* the Daredevils Club."

"Not you, little Miss Sweet Sixteen," Frik said, grinning inanely. He looked at the others. "You're a succulent piece of meat, but you're a kid. Besides, we don't play women's games."

"S'right," Ray added. "You're just a kid. I'm not gonna be responsible for a kid risking her life on a stupid stunt. Especially a girl."

"What do *you* say, Arthur?" she asked, in a voice so soft that she seemed to be shouting. "Do you also think I have to grow balls to be a Daredevil? You're a plastic surgeon. You could make me some. Or is killing two men enough to prove that I'm as tough as you are?"

"She makes sense, gentlemen," he said, looking at Frik and Ray. They shook their heads vehemently. He turned back to Peta. "I'm outvoted," he said. He had begun to slur his words. "Besides, I promised your father that I'd keep you out of harm's way." Clearly exhausted and more than a little drunk, he put his head down on the table, in the crook of his elbow, and fell asleep.

Peta looked back at the small spot on the horizon that was Grenada. She imagined she could hear music and shouting as, all along Church Street, bells rang out.

"Happy New Year, assholes," she said, loudly this time. Then, disgusted, walked toward the prow of the boat and stared into the vast, dark ocean that lay ahead.

1

After a full day on the platform observing the core samples being raised at the Dragon's Mouth test drill site, what little patience Frikkie Van Alman might have had to begin with had dissipated.

He wouldn't have been there at all, but the crew, skittish to begin with, had been downright nervous since the drill had passed through an undersea cavern. Frik was not renowned for his vast store of patience, but he could not ignore the continuing gloom among his workers. At the other sites there was always music, always someone dancing, someone hiding a joint or a bottle of beer. Here, the only sounds were the wind and the sea, the mechanical whirring of the drill, and the padding footsteps of workers who, morose and silent, moved with the speed of turtles.

"What's eating at them, Blaine? Give me your best guess."

Frik thought of Eduardo Blaine as his wholly owned subsidiary. The Venezuelan ran the only hotel in San Gabriel and managed the ferries that brought workers out to this site in the Dragon's Mouth, the northern channel into the Gulf of Paria. He was also a pretty fair diver and knew how to fly the helicopter which transported the owner of Oilstar to this jack-up drilling rig.

"They don't care for work in the Dragon's Mouth." Blaine made a weak attempt at a smile. "Tell you the truth, I'm not too crazy for it myself."

Before Frik could say any more, the drill returned to the surface and its load of sludge and rock was tipped onto the platform for examination.

He had ordered a core sample of the floor of the cavern, wanting more evidence that there would be oil under it before he went to the trouble—and expense—of having another section of pipe sent down to keep any oil from flowing into this new cavern.

Lying on top of the mud were four irregularly shaped objects such as he had never before laid eyes upon. He had the immediate impression of the turquoise he'd known as a child in South Africa, but these were a bluish green color that he couldn't quite identify.

He walked over to the silt pile and stretched out to touch them.

"Don't touch, Mr. Frik! Bad stuff!"

Frik looked around to see who had spoken and saw the backs of his workers as they scattered, all except Eduardo.

"He's right, Señor Frik. Better not to touch." In a show of bravado, the Venezuelan moved to Frik's side. "See where they come from first. Make sure they're not Obeah, or the Obeahman might get us."

"Don't tell me they've got you convinced about their kaffir bogeyman." He'd dealt with enough shamanistic beliefs in his boyhood on the veldt that he was unimpressed by the men's fear that the objects might be fetishes. Besides, when he'd first been told of the local superstitions, the anthropologist he'd talked to had said that this particular myth predated the arrival of the Africans and their Obeah worship. It was probably, in fact, as old as the first Arawaks to cross the gulf from Venezuela on their migration northward.

Frik got up abruptly and strode over to the drill assembly. The bit looked like a giant apple corer, almost twenty inches in diameter. Hand on the side of the drill, he glanced through the base of the derrick to the water fifty feet below.

"I'm sending the camera down. I want to see the bottom of the bore hole."

He set up the feedback equipment, attached the underwater video camera to a cable, and lowered the assemblage down the well. As it descended, he focused on the small screen that would show what the camera found. Despite the sophistication of the equipment, the image was grainy and cloudy with silt from the drilling process. It got even worse when, about seventy feet below the seabed, the camera passed through the hole in the roof of the cavern.

The light from the camera rig vanished into the cavern, which was apparently too large for the illumination to reach the walls. A large, indistinct fish swam in front of the lens, and the floating debris drifting away from the drill hole made it look as if he had suddenly picked up *White Christmas* on the monitor.

Frik's frustration mounted. There was little chance on this monitor that he'd be able to distinguish any turquoiselike fragments which might have remained in the undersea cavern. The only way to be sure was for someone to dive down and enter the cave. Fortunately, the presence of the fish assured him that there was an entrance other than the hole his men had drilled.

"I'm not going down there," Blaine said, anticipating what Frik had in mind.

"You'll go where I tell you to go," Frik said, "but you're right. I need you around to fly me off this rig." He yelled out the names of the few workers he knew. "You want to be paid?" he shouted when no one appeared.

One by one, the men returned. They clustered in small, silent groups, far from the strange objects.

"All right now. Who's going down?"

Nobody moved. "You. Charles." Frik stared into the man's eyes. "You just volunteered. You, too, Abdul. Get your gear. Find the opening to that cavern. If there are any more pieces down there, bring them up. There's a bonus for each one you find."

The men did as they were told. When they had been lowered into the water, Frik said, "The rest of you bastards, no pay today. Tomorrow you work like men or—"

"They don't want to work here anymore," Blaine said.

"The hell they don't." Frik took his cell phone out of his pocket and dialed the lab.

"Trujold? Frik. Listen carefully. I want you to get the speedboat and bring your ass over here."

"I'm not going anywhere near your boats," Trujold said. "Your dogs'll eat me alive."

Frik thought for a moment. "All right. I'll send Blaine for you. It'll only take him a few minutes in the chopper, so don't mess around."

"What's the emergency?" Trujold asked.

"None yet." Frik looked at the indistinct image on the screen. "But I smell one coming on."

2

The helicopter carrying Paul Trujold moved quickly toward the Oilstar drilling platform where Frik's men had been testing drill sites in the Dragon's Mouth. The passage earned its name from the toothy spears of rock that pierced the surface of the water and connected the dots between Trinidad's Chaguara Peninsula and the coastal range of the Venezuelan mainland. Many a ship's hull had been chewed by those teeth when her captain didn't know the waters, or he was caught by a storm. Given that history, why would Frik think it surprising that some parts of the Dragon's Mouth were also believed by the locals to be haunted or cursed?

"Sorry to pull you out of the lab," Frik shouted over the slowing thump of the blades as he reached up and helped Paul out of the chopper.

Such courtesy, Paul thought. Must be something mighty important. "What's going on?"

"I sent a couple of divers down. Only one of them came back, and he died kicking and screaming on the deck before he could tell us a thing."

"Sounds like a bad case of the bends." Must have shot straight to the surface without a decompression stop. What could spook a diver enough to do that? Paul winced at the thought of nitrogen bubbles fizzing through his bloodstream, ending in an air embolism to the brain. "No sign of the other?"

Frik shot him a look. "I told you. Only one came back. And the other's tank would have run out long ago."

Paul always felt an uncomfortable sense of obligation around Frikkie, to whom he owed a great deal of money, borrowed for his daughter's long years of schooling. The debt forced him to stick around, but it didn't change the fact that he neither liked nor trusted his boss. What's more, Frik always made Paul, younger by a decade, feel like the older of the two. Somehow the older man had maintained the toned body of a man twenty years younger. Piercing blue eyes and even white teeth gleaming from a perpetually tanned face, dark hair just beginning to gray at the temples. Paul was shorter, darker, heavier, and, in the looks department, somewhat further down the evolutionary tree. All the way back to Amphibia class, he thought. A newt—no, a frog . . . waiting in vain for the princess's kiss that would turn him into a Frik. Tough. Single-minded. An expert manipulator.

Like now.

Paul was sorry about the men, but that was hardly a reason for Frik to demand his immediate presence. "You brought me down here because of the missing diver?"

"Not exactly. I need your help with these lazy bastards who are refusing to go on working."

"Why?"

"*You're* a damn Trini. You tell me. They were bringing up a core sample and found some strange fragments," Frik said. "That seems to be what spooked the hell out of them. Blaine here thinks the men may believe they are fetishes—Obeah—and that if we mess with them the Obeahman will hurt us."

"What is it you think I can do?"

"Get someone to dive down and see if he can find Abdul." Frik pointed at four objects lying atop a pile of silt. "Then take those back to the lab and examine them."

Paul walked over to the objects and hunkered down to take a closer look. Though he was far more educated than his average countryman, he was born and bred a Trini. He knew the power of local superstitions. There was nothing he could do about the workers or about Abdul. As a scientist, a chemist, he dealt in atoms and molecules and exchanges of electrons—an unseen realm, but vastly predictable.

Most of the time.

But not this time.

There was something different about the objects. He wouldn't go so far as to say "wrong," because that was a moral or ethical judgment, and in his world, morals or ethics didn't apply to lumps of matter. But he had to admit, if lumps of matter could be "wrong," these four were pretty damn close. In the eyes of many of the Trinidadians working for Frikkie, these trinkets would be a sure sign of wrongness. The Trinis— whose heritage embraced both Africa and India—were an innately superstitious group.

He, on the other hand, was not. As far as he was concerned, what he saw was . . . what he saw.

To him, the pieces looked like the stones he'd seen embedded in Native American jewelry in the States . . . asymmetrical matchbox-size lumps of bicolored turquoise from the Kingman Mine in Arizona, or something very much like it.

He picked one up. It didn't feel like turquoise or any other kind of stone. More like a rather strange form of plastic. There was no specific design to the lumps, but they were definitely not naturally occurring shapes. These were fashioned objects, products of intelligence, though he could not guess what kind of intelligence could have made them.

That, Paul decided, was what had spooked the workers. No one had ever seen shapes like these before, so they automatically shied away from them. As far as he was concerned, it was a typical islanders' response to the new and different.

He didn't consider himself a typical islander, however, and while he couldn't help Frik with his divers, he wanted very badly to take a closer look at these trinkets.

3

Where the hell is he? Paul wondered as he paced back and forth in front of Oilstar's labs.

Frik was late, but what else was new? The man got a charge out of keeping people on hold. He was probably having another cup of coffee and taking his own sweet time getting here just to be annoying. Even if he'd stopped in at his San Fernando corporate office building on the way from his house, he should have been here by now.

If he was certain of nothing else, Paul was sure of one thing: once he had shown his discovery to Frik, the man would wish he hadn't played games this particular morning.

Not that a few minutes, even a few hours, could make a difference. It was just that Paul couldn't wait to share his conclusions. Those "trinkets" Frik's drillers had raised from beneath the ocean bed just might change the whole damn world.

He gazed at the morning sky, a flawless pale blue, promising another perfect day. His lab was a squat one-story white stucco square which lay near the town of La Brea—a short way south of San Fernando on Trinidad's west coast, with a good view of the Gulf of Paria. The sun had yet to crest the lush hills behind him, but it had reached the drilling platforms that studded the still water like ticks on a dog's belly.

Trinidad . . . Paul loved the big, bold island. It anchored the Lesser Antilles to the continental shelf of South America. Nestled into a large depression on the northeastern coast, it played footsie with Venezuela with the extended toe of its southern tip, Punta del Arenal. He was born here and, except for college and postgrad years when he was earning his Ph.D. from Harvard, had spent his life here, lost a wife and raised his daughter, Selene, here. He planned to die here—but not for some time yet, thank you.

He inhaled the morning air. When the wind was wrong, you could smell Pitch Lake, but not today. This morning the air filtered from the northwest, clean, with a briny tang from its journey across the Gulf of Paria. Early morning was his favorite time of the day.

Early? He rubbed his burning eyes. Early for Frik, maybe, he thought, but late for me.

He'd been up all night, feverishly testing and retesting. The key to a true breakthrough in science was reproducibility of results. He had that now. Oh, Lord, he had that indeed. And he was dying to show *someone*.

But not just anyone. He had to keep this under wraps until Frik saw it—then they could tell the world.

To that end, Paul had given the staff the day off—with pay. Frik would squawk at that. If he wasn't already a billionaire, he was knocking on the ten-figure door with champagne and flowers in hand. Yet how he pissed and moaned about the slightest overrun.

Well, once he saw what Paul had, he wouldn't bitch about an extra paid vacation day for the small, bright crew of Trinis who staffed the lab. He'd forget all about it, the way he'd forgotten about the cost of the mainframe and electronic testing equipment Paul had asked for after it became clear that the apparatus had increased the efficiency of Oilstar's refineries more than a hundred percent.

There . . . the rumble of a big engine down the slope. Seconds later, Frik's Humvee hove into view. The roads around here could barely handle a couple of passing Nissans, and he imports a Hummer. Typical.

Paul waved as Frik skidded to a halt and hopped out. His boss didn't wave back.

"This'd better be good, Paul," he said. "I've got a sweet young dancer visiting from Mumbai sleeping it off in my bed. She knows tricks neither of us has ever dreamed of, and I'm looking forward to another demonstration when she wakes up."

"This'll make you forget all about the angle of your dangle," Paul said, turning and leading the way to the lab entrance.

"I seriously doubt that."

Paul smiled. He was tempted to trap Frik into a big bet, but decided that wouldn't be fair. His boss was short-tempered, high-handed, and vain, and brilliant, funny, and loyal as well. Paul alternately loved and loathed him. Right now, he loved him.

Paul led Frik through what he thought of as his lab, though of course it wasn't really his. The Oilstar insignia graced the glass entry doors, the stationery, and just about everything else. Since Frik *was* Oilstar, he owned the lab. But Paul ran it, and he felt that made it his, too, in a way. The lab was a small cog in the giant Oilstar wheel, but an indispensable one. This was where the crude from Oilstar's wells was analyzed before and after its journey through the refinery.

"My patience is wearing thin, Trujold. Let's get this over with."

"Your wish is my command." Paul led his boss into a storeroom he'd converted for his personal experiments—the odds of his creating a new petroleum-based polymer with industrial applications were slim, but he could dream, couldn't he?

"What's that smell?"

Paul sniffed and turned on the lights. Damn, he thought. He knew the odor: ether. He'd been testing that and some other solvents on the trinkets. He spotted the open jar on his workbench. The all-nighter had made him careless.

"I'll get rid of it."

He recapped the jar and started the exhaust fan in the ceiling. As the fumes were pulled away, he turned on the two bench lamps and ignited both Bunsen burners. Then he pointed to the object sitting in the center of the cleared area on his workbench.

"Thar she blows."

Frik stared at it. "What the hell is it?"

"It's those trinkets your men found in that core sample."

"I gave you four objects," Frik said, staring at the assembly.

When Paul had started analyzing the objects, the first thing he'd discovered was that they weren't made of turquoise or mother-of-pearl or anything else he had ever seen. The second was that they were all part of a whole. "And there they are, all four of them," he said. "They click together like pieces of a three-dimensional jigsaw. I'm talking *perfect* fit."

Frik bent and stared at the unified object from different angles. "They look even weirder together than they did apart."

Paul couldn't argue with that. The assembly looked like something from an abstract painting. That was what he found most disturbing: how could objects that fit together with such fine tolerances appear so lacking in functionality?

"*Looks* weird?" Paul said, repressing a grin. "You don't know weird until you see what it *does*. Watch this."

He took a long pair of plastic forceps and grasped the object at what he'd by now determined was its center of gravity. He lifted it and began tilting it this way and that, rotating it back and forth.

Now we fricassee Frikkie's mind.

"Paul," Frik said when nothing happened. "Have you lost it?"

"Just be patient. It never seems to work the same way twice."

Paul kept his eyes on the main piece—at least he called it the main piece. It was the largest and had a vaguely figure-eight or Möebius strip configuration. Telltale piece was probably a better name. He watched its outer edge, waiting . . . waiting. . . .

He felt the now-familiar chill run over his skin. A heartbeat later the motor of the overhead exhaust fan rose in pitch and the room brightened.

Got it!

He moved the assembly again, and everything returned to normal.

"What just happened?" Frik asked.

"Watch that gooseneck lamp right in front of you."

Paul rotated the assembly back, felt the chill again, and then the bulb flared, sixty watts climbing to one hundred. All the lamps in the room seemed to have doubled their wattage. The overhead fan whined and jittered, sounding as if it were about to take off. He'd had to move his computer terminal out of the room because he was afraid the power surge would damage it.

He heard Frik gasp. "What the hell?"

"Check out the Bunsens," Paul said, keeping his eye on the telltale piece.

"They're almost out."

Paul lowered the assembly, and the light dimmed, the Bunsen flames grew.

Frik stared at it. "*That's* doing it?"

Paul nodded.

"What is it? Some sort of rheostat?"

"Can't really call it that—I've never seen it dim the lights, only brighten them. I don't have the equipment to measure how much faster the fan goes."

"But the Bunsens—"

"The Bunsens burn sixty degrees cooler. And did you feel the air temperature drop? That was a full ten degrees. Your skin temperature drops as well. Only the device doesn't change temperature. It appears to be impervious to cold and heat."

Frik looked shaken. He turned, found one of the stools, and eased himself onto it.

"Christ, Paul . . . what is it?"

Paul couldn't maintain his scientist poker face any longer. He burst into a grin. "I don't know, but isn't it great?" He heard an edge of hysterical laughter creep into his voice. "Isn't it fantastic?"

"That it is, but—"

"You think you've just seen weird?" Paul was pleased with himself for having saved the best for last. "Get behind me here and watch."

Frik stood and positioned himself as directed, his hand on Paul's shoulder.

"Keep your eye on the big figure-eight piece while I move this around."

He angled the assembly this way and that, slowly, methodically, until . . . the outer edge of the telltale piece began to blur.

He felt Frik's hand tighten on his shoulder. "What—?"

"Wait."

Paul rotated it a little further and half of the outer loop appeared to dissolve. The chill . . . the flaring lights . . . He raised his free hand and passed his index finger through the empty space where the loop had been. Nothing there but air.

"Christ, Paul!" Frik's grip was painful now.

Paul rotated it back and the loop became whole again. The lights dimmed.

Frik released him and leaned back against the counter, staring at the assembly. His face was ashen under the tan.

"D'you mind telling me what's going on?"

"I don't know." Paul's excitement bubbled through him. He felt like a shaken champagne bottle, ready to uncork. "The edge of that piece doesn't just disappear. It's not an optical illusion—it's *not there*. It goes away."

33

"Goes where?"

"I don't know. But it goes somewhere *else,* and when it reaches that somewhere else, the room gets cold and anything using electricity within a dozen feet revs into overdrive."

"A dozen feet?"

"Give or take a few inches. I spent half the night testing its range, and a dozen feet is about its limit. Do you have any idea what this means, Frik? This little artifact is going to rewrite the laws of physics. Not only does it promise free energy, I'm willing to bet it taps into another dimension!"

"Free energy?" Frik said, still pale. "No such thing as free energy. No such thing as free *anything.* As for other dimensions—"

"All right, maybe not another dimension, but it goes somewhere, and another dimension is as good a hypothesis as any for now."

"A dozen feet is a pretty limited area."

"Doesn't matter if it's three feet, this is a whole new energy source, utterly revolutionary. And there's one more thing you should know."

Frik looked at him bleakly. "I don't know if I can handle another revelation right now. But go ahead."

Why isn't he excited? Paul wondered. He should be dancing around. This is the find of the century—of the millennium!

Paul held up the assembly. "I don't think this is all of it. It looks like there's a piece missing." He pointed to a pair of sockets opposite the figure-eight piece. "Somewhere down in that area of ocean floor you sampled is a fifth piece that fits here."

"What do you think it will do?"

"I don't know. Maybe act as an amplifier that will extend its range. Maybe something even more mind-blowing."

Frik looked away and said nothing. Paul let the silence hang, waiting for his boss to announce the obvious next step: a search for the missing piece.

"Question," Frik said. "Where did that thing come from?"

The question flustered Paul. "From the core sample that you—"

"No. I mean, who made it? That thing was buried in underwater shale. In pieces. Who buried it there? When? And why?"

"I don't know."

Good questions. Paul had been so taken with the artifact's astounding properties, so focused on the impact it would have on the world scientific community when it was made public—he'd gone so far as to picture himself on a dais, the focal point of a thousand cameras, demonstrating the artifact—that he hadn't asked the next question.

"What about your Trini brothers' belief that it's Obeah?"

Paul shook his head. "I don't think this was made by some primitive shaman. I'm not even sure it was made on this planet."

"Then where? By whom? Don't you think we ought to know?" Frik said, eyeing him intensely.

"We can leave that up to others." He waved away the concern like an errant mosquito. "When we go public with this, there'll be experts from every discipline—"

"Public?" Frik said, straightening away from the bench. "I don't think so. Not till we know more."

"We've gone as far as we can with our limited resources. The next step is a university setting, a major research center—"

"No," Frik said, steel in his voice. "Not yet. Not until we've found the fifth piece."

4

"This is not open to debate, Paul," Frik said. "I want absolute secrecy. In fact, I don't want that thing to leave this room. And I want this room locked at all times. Is that clear? This is too important a find to rush into the public eye, especially in an incomplete state. Who knows what that fifth piece will do? For all we know it could transform the artifact into some sort of devastating weapon. No . . . we've got to proceed cautiously and weigh every move. Do you see what I'm saying?"

Paul nodded. He saw what Frik was saying.

Exactly what he was saying.

"Good." Frik thrust out his hand. "Then can I have your word that you will keep everything you've discovered here secret until I decide the time is right to go public?"

"Very well," Paul said, shaking hands reluctantly. He didn't see that he had any other option, but in his raging heart he held back from a true promise.

He's lying to me, so it's only fair that I lie to him.

"Good! After all, Paul, my men found it, so I feel responsible for it."

"Yes," Paul said. "A terrible burden."

In his peripheral vision, reflected in the shiny surface of the stainless steel door of a storage cabinet, Paul glimpsed the angry set of his own jaw. He was reminded of how his daughter had looked the day she'd turned her Ph.D. in physics into a paper boat and floated it off the dock. She'd resembled her mother so much that day, with the latté-colored skin of her mixed French-Arawak ancestry. As he'd stood with her and watched the breeze take away the piece of paper that had given him such pride, she'd announced her intention to go to Caracas and join a small group of like-minded people dedicated to the preservation of the environment, by any means necessary.

Much as he'd tried to dissuade her, much as he'd tried to tell her she'd be wasting her intellect, a part of him was proud of her. And wanted her to be proud of him.

"Keep working with it," Frik said, clapping Paul on the shoulder. "Write up your notes, but do it yourself—no secretaries involved. We'll talk tomorrow and decide our next step."

"Yes." Paul was afraid his anger would explode if he dared to say more than the absolute minimum. He clenched his fists at his sides; resisting the urge to throw something hard at the back of Frik's head, he settled for tossing out the word "Tomorrow."

When he heard the Hummer start up and drive away, Paul pulled out a plaster cast. He had made it to support earlier reasonably successful attempts to duplicate at least the look, if not the feel, of the artifact, which he'd wanted to study without always risking the original. Separating the device into its original four pieces, he used the largest of the authentic pieces as his base and constructed a polyurethane model of the artifact. Then he locked the two smallest real pieces together, put them in a padded envelope, and addressed it to himself.

The third, the one with the figure eight at one end, he packaged separately, along with a letter of explanation to the only person he could fully trust—the only person who, as a physicist, would understand what he was saying—his daughter, Selene. He wrote her name on the package. Nothing else. Since she'd joined that ecoterrorist group, Green Impact, she had given up on conventional addresses. His only route to her was through Manny Sheppard. The diminutive boat captain had been a friend of Paul's wife. When she'd been killed, Manny had helped raise Selene, teaching her the joys of the ocean, and how to be true to herself.

Turning back to the model, Paul checked that it was solid and placed it in the middle of the lab table, as if it were no more important than the beakers and tongs. That little bit of "carelessness" should drive Frik crazy, he thought.

He put the packages in the wide pockets of his lab coat, draped the coat over his arm, and glanced at his watch. It was after four. Manny should be arriving down at the dock, if he wasn't there already. Bone weary, Paul left the lab, making sure he heard the click as he pulled the door shut and it locked behind him.

Once outside the building, he walked to his Nissan, got in, and drove out of the parking lot. He followed the potholed, semipaved road for a few hundred yards, out of view of the labs, then turned onto a side road which wound down to the smaller of Oilstar's two docking areas. In quick glimpses between the hills, fruit trees, and palms, he spotted the *Assegai*'s tall masts. As he turned the final bend in the road, he saw Manny's small cargo boat and something that made his heart leap: Frik's Hummer, parked at the end of the dock.

Paul stomped on his brakes and threw the car in reverse. Using his cell phone, he dialed Frik's ship-to-shore number. What he didn't need was Frik walking in on his conversation with Manny.

He let the phone ring a dozen times. This was an emergency number that Frik always answered if he was on the boat. When Paul was convinced that his boss was not on board, he put the car back in gear and drove down to the dock. He had set up the duplicate device in the conviction that Frik would go back to the lab tonight to find it.

It suddenly occurred to Paul that maybe Frik hadn't answered the phone because he was moving sooner than Paul had anticipated. The Afrikaner could easily have walked the quarter mile from the dock to the lab while Paul was making his preparations. He could have been hiding in the bushes when Paul left the lab, waiting for the building to be empty.

He could be in the lab right now, which made it even more imperative that Paul find Manny and rid himself of the packages in his pocket.

To his enormous relief, as he parked he saw Manny sitting on a piling, a cigarette loosely held between two fingers of his left hand, which also held a Carib. The diminutive seaman waved as Paul approached.

"Good to see you. Get you a beer?"

The chemist shook his head. "I've got something to tell you, Manny," he said, "and a favor to ask. A large favor."

Paul told Manny everything that had happened, beginning with the call from Frik and ending with the Afrikaner's own words: *Who knows what that fifth piece will do? For all we know it could transform the artifact into some sort of devastating weapon.*

"The man's a ruthless bastard, capable of anything."

Paul nodded. "We both know why I'm working with him, but you?

39

You have a choice—" He stopped himself. "I'm sorry," he said. "It's really none of my business."

"I work for Frik for two reasons," Manny said, ignoring Paul's last comment. "The first is obviously money."

"And the second?"

"I'd rather be in a position where I can keep my eye on him, and stay in touch with the few good people who work for him. Now, what's that favor you wanted?"

Paul held out the two packages. "I don't know where Selene is exactly, but I'm sure you do."

"I know how to find her," Manny said.

"I need you to get one of these to Selene and post the other to me. Wait a few days first." Paul paused. "If anything happens to me, make sure Selene knows about it and get the other package from my place. Don't risk keeping it yourself. Give it to someone you'd trust with your life, the way I'm trusting you with mine."

Grinning, Manny replied, "I know just who the doctor ordered."

5

Frik ducked deeper into the foliage as Paul Trujold stepped out the front door of Oilstar's labs. The chemist's lab coat was draped over his arm, and his shoulders sagged. He looked exhausted.

About time he came out of there, Frik thought. He glanced at his Rolex. Four o'clock. Thought he'd never leave. What was he doing all this time?

From the cover of a thick growth of hibiscus, he watched Paul lock the door and head for his car. He felt ridiculous. Here he was, the owner of this whole complex, hiding from one of his employees so that he could steal a piece of property that already belonged to him.

I should have demanded it from him, he thought. Should have stuck out my hand and said, Give it to me, Paul. It's mine.

Much as he'd wanted to, he hadn't been able to force the words past his lips. Had he done so, Paul would have known; he'd have looked down on him from the moral high ground he occupied and seen into Frik's heart. He wouldn't have uttered a word, but the look in his eyes would have said it all.

I know what you're thinking, Frikkie. I know your intentions. You never want this artifact to see the light of day. You want to sail out past the edge of the continental shelf and hurl it into the sea, let the Guyana Current carry it into the abyss.

And he'd have been right, damn him.

That was indeed what part of Frik *wanted* to do. But he wouldn't. Couldn't. He'd never forgive himself for destroying a technological boon like that. If need be, he'd hide it, keep it to himself. Not forever, maybe, but for a long, long time.

He was not a man of science, yet he knew as sure as he knew this morning's spot price on a barrel of sweet crude that the artifact operated comfortably on principles not even suspected by modern science. Just as surely, he knew simply by looking at the thing that it wouldn't give up all of its secrets until it was complete.

When that happened, he would need people he could trust, people like Paul, to help him decode it, decipher its technology and break it down into patentable units to make it Oilstar's technology. He'd call the shots then.

Paul's car cruised out of the parking lot. Frik didn't move. Best to give the man a few minutes on the road, in case he forgot something and decided to come back. He could think of worse places to hide than among these fragrant red blossoms. A little more time in the bushes wouldn't kill him.

The sound of a familiar motor drifted up from the boat dock just down the hill from the lab. Manny had arrived with some of Frik's favorite supplies, the ones he didn't want passing through the sticky fingers of the customs inspectors in Port of Spain. He had left the Hummer down there and walked back up, knowing that anyone seeing it there would assume he was on his boat. When he went back down there to pick up his car, he could also pick up his loot.

The thought encouraged him to pull out his cigar case and remove a long, fat Cohiba Esplendido. He could have a celebratory cigar now without worrying about Paul seeing the smoke.

As he lit up he thought again about that scene in the lab this morning. Christ, what a moment that had been. He had imagined one of those gizmos attached to every car, truck, train, and plane engine, to every furnace, to every freaking dynamo in every power plant across the world. Frik could see his life's work crumbling to smoke and ash if this device were reproduced and oil became as old-fashioned as vinyl records.

Paul had seemed somehow oblivious of the full implications of what he'd found. Yes, he was holding the key to a future free of dependence on fossil fuels. But that key, that odd little contraption he had assembled in there, could make Oilstar obsolete. No . . . obsolete was a euphemism here.

Extinct was more like it.

Let's not forget you assembled that thing from pieces *I* gave you, he thought. It's not about money, Paul. As it is, I've got to rack my brains to begin to find ways to spend the *interest* on my holdings. Money hasn't been the point for a long time. It's the *doing,* Paul. This is my company.

Frik thought back to when he had left South Africa. His family's fortunes in land and gemstones could have kept him in Cohibas and fine scotch for a lifetime, but it would have meant being under his father's thumb. He couldn't stand that. He'd filled the *Assegai* with supplies and sailed alone across the Atlantic to make a life he could control.

I worked as a stinking charter captain for a year to get together a few thousand bucks, he recalled. Hocked my soul for start-up money, sank my first well almost single-handed. Oilstar isn't just a company, it's not some soulless corporate entity. It's *me,* damnit.

He was a bull tyrannosaur now, but that little gizmo Paul had assembled in there was a dino-dooming asteroid aimed straight at the heart of Frik's personal Cretaceous period.

Think what you will of me, Paul, he thought. I'm not ready to become extinct.

Figuring he had waited long enough, Frik stepped out of the bushes. As he strolled down the slope to the lab, he fished a set of keys from his pocket.

Immediately after leaving Paul this morning, he'd returned to his office in San Fernando and put together a full set of keys for the lab building. He just prayed that Paul hadn't at some time changed the lock on his personal lab.

He unlocked the front door and hurried down the central hallway. The key fit into Paul's door . . . turned. He was in.

He crossed to the workbench but stopped halfway there. The artifact sat alone in the center of the black surface.

Christ, Paul hadn't even bothered to stick it in a drawer. This was not something to leave lying about, even in a locked room.

He approached it slowly, cautiously, with the proper respect due a thing of such wonder. He leaned close to the bench top and stared at it. No question—there was something unearthly about this thing. Reminded him of the science-fiction paperbacks he'd read when he was a teenager, the ones with the abstract covers by someone named Powers who squiggled bizarre-looking shapes in the backgrounds of his paintings. This thing would have been right at home on one of those covers.

"Where *did* you come from?" Frik muttered.

He looked around and found the chopstick-length forceps Paul had used earlier. Turning on the bench lamp, he grasped the artifact with the tips of the forceps and lifted. He twisted it, turned it, rotated it this way and that, waiting for the loop of the figure-eight piece to fade away.

Nothing happened.

He kept at it, remembering how it had taken Paul a good bit of trial and error this morning before he'd found the precise orientation that made it work, and he'd had a whole night of practice.

Still nothing.

Frik felt himself starting to sweat. Why wouldn't it work? Had Paul taken one of the pieces? No, all four were there. Then what—?

"I thought I'd find you here."

Frik froze. The words had been spoken without inflection, with far more weariness than heat. And that only sharpened their edge. Clamping his cigar between his teeth, he turned to face Paul Trujold's withering stare.

"Oh. Hello, Paul." Frik maintained his game face and drew deeply on the Cohiba.

"Oh. Hello, Paul," Trujold mimicked. "Is that the best you can do?"

The scientist's dark eyes blazed. Frik fought the urge to step back as Paul stopped two feet in front of him.

"What were you going to do with it, Frik?"

"Put it in a secure place. This room is too vulnerable. I'll feel better if it's in the safe in my office." He held up the artifact, still clasped within the forceps. "Perhaps you're forgetting, Paul. This belongs to Oilstar, and Oilstar belongs to me."

"Yes, *Oilstar*'s yours Frik, but the artifact belongs to the world. One man can't be allowed to keep it hidden."

"Since when do you speak for the world?"

"Since *now,* you selfish son of a bitch."

Frik couldn't say exactly what happened next, what it was inside that snapped. In his mind, the bizarre object he was holding became a meteor, and Paul the inexorable laws of the universe that were propelling it toward Frik's world. He reacted the only way he knew. Sure that the scientist was about to grab for the artifact, he dropped it and lunged at

44

the smaller man. He grabbed Paul by the shirtfront and twisted him toward the lab table.

Paul took a swipe at Frik, knocking the cigar from his mouth instead. The Afrikaner pushed Paul backward into the workbench. It tilted under the force of the impact, and the very air seemed to explode, sending Frikkie staggering in the opposite direction.

When he recovered his balance, he heard screaming. Paul was rolling on the floor, his body bathed in flame.

"Paul! Oh, Christ!"

Frantically looking around for a blanket, a lab coat, anything to beat out the flames, Frik spied the red canister of a fire extinguisher on the wall. He ran to it, ripped it free, and carried it over to the wailing ball of flame on the tiles.

Don't die on me! he screamed inwardly. God, don't die on me. I didn't want that.

It took him precious seconds to find the safety pin, yank it free, find the trigger, and start spraying. The conical nozzle coughed white plumes of CO_2, enveloping Paul and seeming to take forever to douse the flames.

Frik stared at what had been Paul Trujold. He could recognize the face. Though charred, it had miraculously all but escaped the flames. The rest was nothing more than a twitching, man-shaped thing with only patches of clothing remaining. He didn't know whether to retch or sob. With the room ablaze, there was time for neither.

"Jesus, Frik, get yourself out of here. I'll get Paul."

Where Manny Sheppard had suddenly appeared from Frik did not know or, at that moment, care.

Ignoring Trujold's moans of pain, Manny lifted the man onto his back in a fireman's carry. Frik started toward the door, but stopped when the artifact caught his eye. It lay at the edge of the flames, and it was burning.

He reached into the fire with his foot and kicked the object across the floor. The flames were doused by its tumbling flight. As he bent and picked it up, it oozed against his palm, searing his flesh. He cried out in pain that was more than just physical. The device was melting. Ruined. All but its base, which, amazingly, had remained intact and cool to the touch.

Tucking that against his shirtfront, he lurched toward the door.

6

The phone rang two, three times. Frik could not recall ever having felt so frustrated at the hollow ringing of an unanswered telephone.

"Come on," he begged. "Pick up. Be there." But at the end of the third ring, an answering-machine message came on.

"You've reached Dr. Arthur Marryshow. If this is an emergency, please call my service at 212-555-9239 or you may leave a message at the beep."

The number Frik had dialed was Arthur's personal one at the midtown Manhattan apartment where he'd lived for the last few years—when he wasn't away on some mission or another. Had it been on voice mail, which Arthur refused to use because he felt it was too impersonal, Frik might have left a message. But he didn't want to go through the service—not unless he had to. The less anyone knew about this the better.

There was, however, another number he could try, one Arthur had asked him not to use except in dire circumstances.

He dialed Arthur's cell phone number.

The phone clicked and rang.

"Yes."

"Arthur?"

"Who else would it be, Frik? You dialed my number." Arthur sounded annoyed at the interruption. Still, Frik had never been so glad to hear someone pick up. "This had better be important."

"It is. I need help. I need it fast and discreet. There's been an accident at the lab—and—"

"Frik, where are you?"

"Trinidad. Look, I need you to get here fast. Right away. You can use the Oilstar jet. It's at Kennedy."

Excellent chess player that he was, Frik automatically considered multiple options before embarking on any action, like the tone best used in this call. "Could you please" had been easy to discard because it left Arthur with too much of a choice. Offering recompense was out. Arthur, a plastic surgeon who had specialized in burn medicine, years before had pioneered grafting and reconstruction techniques that gave disfigured victims a chance at a normal life. It had made him loved, almost worshiped. It had also made him wealthy.

Of the two alternatives left to him, Frik had chosen the imperative. If that failed, he would take the I-scratched-your-back, you-scratch-mine mental leap which generally got him what he wanted. You owe me, Marryshow, he thought, picturing the prison escape in Grenada and the half dozen times he had saved his fellow Daredevil's life in the intervening seventeen years and conveniently dismissing the equal number of times the roles had been reversed.

"What is this about, Frikkie? What happened?"

Frik sighed with relief and outlined a carefully edited version of the night's events.

"You must get Paul and yourself to a hospital. You—"

"No." This was the hardest part: telling Arthur only enough so that he'd come and help with their wounds—especially Paul's. The scientist's skin was dotted with great blackened patches, as though someone had taken a brush laden with tar and swiped at it. "I can't."

Frik could hear Arthur's fury. "Call the hospital, get an ambulance, and . . . I'll . . ."

Frik took a deep breath and chugged Lagavulin straight from the bottle. A friend had sent him the bottle of his favorite single-malt scotch from Argyll, Scotland, and he'd kept it for a rainy day.

As far as he was concerned, it was storming.

He couldn't tell how bad his own burns were, but he could see only hazy fog through his left eye, and the left hand felt like it was being prickled by a hundred poisonous black sea urchins. His whole body was an archipelago of pain, the little islands only occasionally blurring together. A flash here, a flash there.

The alcohol was keeping the isles from connecting into a continent

48

of agony, but it was also getting him drunk. He had to stay clear enough to make Arthur understand.

"We found something, Arthur. And if Paul spoke about it, at the hospital, under drugs, it would be bad—"

"You are one stubborn bastard. I should hang up. What have you done for him?"

Saaliim, Frik's assistant, a native of Honduras who wore a perpetually thoughtful look, stood by the door, waiting to see what would happen. Frik relied on Saaliim for everything and anything. He was about the only person in the world, other than the members of the Daredevils Club, that Frik fully trusted.

"I gave him morphine from one of the kits. He's either asleep or unconscious, I'm not sure which. I think he'll be okay for the three, four hours it would take you to get here."

"Sooner. I'm in Grenada. Your call was transferred here."

Thank you, Lady Luck, Frick thought.

"If I cancel tomorrow's appointments, if I drop everything and run to you, I could fly myself over and be there in an hour, maybe less," Arthur continued.

Being the man of integrity that you are, you'll do exactly that, Frik thought. "Thank you," he said, without waiting for Arthur's full agreement. "There'll be a car waiting for you and I'll be sitting at the window, watching the road."

"You expect me to work in your house?"

"I can get you anything you need."

"Right. Like a burn center?"

"Mount Hope Medical Center has an HBO chamber but nothing for burns." Frik had to make his friend understand. "You have to trust me, Arthur. What we found, it's too important to risk having anyone learn about. It could change the world."

"And changing it could use. All right, Frik, I'll come. But I'm warning you, this had better be damn good."

7

To Frik, the next hour seemed like a lifetime. Arthur had called on his way to the airport and issued instructions for what would be needed. Frik jotted them down and repeated each one, a slur creeping into his voice. When he put down the phone, he handed the list to Saaliim and told him to go out and collect everything Arthur wanted.

Saaliim was also given a second mission.

After showing Saaliim the piece of the artifact that he'd rescued from the fire, Frik ordered his assistant to search the remains of the lab and Trujold's house and car for the three missing components of the strange object.

Reluctant to leave Frik alone for long, Saaliim returned in less than an hour. He had gathered everything Arthur needed, but he'd found nothing that in any way resembled the pieces of the artifact. Maybe he'd made the wrong choice, not taking Paul directly to the hospital. Chances were, they would have ignored his babblings there, but they could have done something to keep him alive—at least long enough for Frik to extract from him the whereabouts of the missing pieces.

Then again, he'd learned to trust his first instinct, which in this case was to keep things under tight control.

Leaving the matter of the artifact to be dealt with later, Frik settled down to wait for Arthur. Every car he saw on the road had to be his . . . until it was swallowed by the balmy night. He cursed himself for not arranging to have a helicopter waiting for Arthur at Piarco. The airport was only forty or fifty kilometers from the house. Marryshow, an accomplished pilot, could have been here long ago. Christ, how he hated inefficiency, especially his own, he thought, as the pain came back and he gulped more scotch. He couldn't risk taking morphine and losing control of this situation. Have to make Arthur help me, he kept telling himself.

Car lights cut through the darkened room.

Paul, finally knocked out by the drugs, didn't stir. Frik turned on a light. Seconds later, Arthur came into the house.

"Frikkie, I've just sent Saaliim to get some more things. I need you to tell me exactly what happened. By the way, you look like hell."

Frik realized that he hadn't done anything to clean himself up. "Like I told you, there was a fire. I——"

Arthur was already standing beside Paul. He pulled back the sheet exposing the black splotches where fire had seared the skin. "My God. If you're up to it, hand me my bag."

Frik handed him a medical bag that looked more like an oversized attaché. "We have to talk," he said.

"Let me check him first. I'll listen to what you have to say later."

Arthur checked Paul's vitals. "His pulse is thready. His breathing's ragged at best."

Frik ventured closer. To his astonishment, Trujold had opened his eyes. Clearly, he was struggling to say something, but what emerged from his scorched lips was little more than a series of croaks. He seemed to be saying "Anny."

"He's trying to say Manny," Frik said. "Manny carried him out of the flaming building."

"Easy, Paul," Arthur said. "Don't try to speak." He motioned Frik to follow him out of Paul's earshot. "He's a mess. Chances are he's not going to make it. His only hope is to be moved out now."

"No."

"Excuse me? Paul needs things I can't do for him here."

Frik glanced over at Paul. He had closed his eyes and seemed to have fallen unconscious again. "Listen to me, Arthur," he said.

"We're talking about the man's life." Arthur's harsh whisper held both contempt and anger.

"You have to know there's a reason I didn't take him straight to Mount Hope," Frik said. "Not only *a* reason, but one that's more important than Paul or you or me."

"I must move him to the hospital right away, Frik," Arthur said. "And I should take a look at you, too."

Frik shook his head. "We found something, Arthur. In the deep test drilling area. I wanted to hide it, but Paul had already—"

Arthur looked over at Paul. *"Found something?"*

Frik nodded. He described—as best he could—the indescribable, and watched Arthur's eyes narrow. This had to be a strange night for him. Flying here, seeing both of them burned, now this. Frik anticipated a barrage of questions, but when he'd finished, Arthur only asked, "Where is it?"

Frik shook his head. "That's the point. I thought I had it. I thought I was bringing the device out of the lab. When it started melting in the heat, I knew most of it was only a goddamn replica Paul had made. Only one piece of the real thing was left. It's right over there." Frik nodded in the direction of a side table. On it, under a lamp, sat the one piece of the artifact Frik had. It reflected the artificial light with an unnatural eeriness. From the confused look on Arthur's face Frik concluded that he sensed it too.

Saaliim came into the room with some ice and glasses and a small pitcher of water. Arthur grabbed the bottle of Lagavulin and poured himself a few fingers' worth.

"Tell me . . . what did you plan on doing with the . . . whatever it was?"

Frik moistened his lips and looked over at Paul. Best-case scenario, the man regained consciousness long enough to disclose the whereabouts of the fragments to Frik—and then died. If he lived, the truth would come out. Or at least Paul's fantasies of the truth.

"What were you going to do with this incredible device?" Arthur asked again.

"If I couldn't figure out how to replicate it . . . control it? I was going to hide it. For as long as I could," Frik said.

As if he had heard Frik's words, Paul groaned slightly. An intake of air. Arthur walked over to him, looked at Paul, then at Frik. "I must move Paul now. There's nothing more I can do for him here. Have Saaliim call for an ambulance."

At that moment, Frik's assistant returned to the room. "I took the liberty, Dr. Marryshow, of ordering Oilstar's medevac chopper. It should be here shortly." His words were punctuated by the *thump thump thump* of the emergency helicopter approaching.

Frik said, "Most efficient of you. Thank you, Saaliim," but his words lacked true conviction, and the younger man averted his eyes.

Arthur turned back to Paul and rechecked the burned man's vitals. The thumping outside became a torrent against the side of the house, and then quieted.

Two EMS techs ran into the room pushing a gurney. Frik watched them gently shift Paul from the small daybed.

"Careful," Arthur said.

The techs looked from Arthur to Frik. One asked, in accented English, "You 'kay, Mr. Van Alman?"

Frik nodded.

"Get him on the chopper." Arthur indicated Paul. "I'll be right out." The tech nodded, and they wheeled Paul out.

"Frikkie, you need medical attention too. You need to come with us to the hospital."

Frik poured another scotch. "Arthur—I want our club to find those pieces. The Daredevils."

He turned toward his old friend. Arthur's face showed consternation, even anger. "I have a patient to deal with, Frik. We'll have to have this discussion another time."

"But—"

Arthur cut off Frik's response by turning on his heel and walking through the door. Over his shoulder he called out, "If Paul has any relatives, I suggest you contact them."

Frikkie downed the scotch and reached for the bottle. As he sank back into the cushions of his leather sofa, the torrent of noise outside returned. Small twigs and leaves battered the windows and walls of the house as the medevac chopper took off.

Frikkie snapped awake at the sound of the telephone. His first sensation was pain, searing, aching pain. He reached for the bottle of Lagavulin and knocked it over, but nothing poured out. Empty.

"Master Frik, you're awake." Saaliim's voice was soft and full of concern. "Dr. Marryshow is on the line."

"What time is it?"

"Half-four. Should I bring you the phone?"

Frik waggled his head to try to clear it. It took a few moments for all of the previous day's events to return to him. "Yes," he said at last. "Also some coffee and anything you can find for this pain, short of morphine."

As Saaliim left, Frik tried to stand. A wave of nausea passed over him and he dropped back onto the leather sofa he'd been sleeping on. His left hand was a mass of pain. His mouth tasted as if he'd washed down the embers of a campfire with a bottle of whiskey, which he supposed wasn't far from the truth.

Suddenly the receiver of a telephone appeared in front of him. He picked it up and croaked, "Hello, Arthur?"

"You don't sound good, Frik."

"I'm fine if you discount the pain, and the aftereffects of a bottle of scotch. The important question is, how's Paul?"

There was a pause on the line, and Frik knew the answer to his question.

"He died twenty minutes ago."

"Damn it. Wasn't there anything you could do?" As soon as he'd asked the question, Frikkie knew it was a mistake.

"Had he been brought straight to a hospital instead of your house, maybe. But—"

That line of discussion wouldn't get them anywhere, so Frik cut in, saying, "His wife died years ago, as did his parents. Saaliim is trying to locate Paul's daughter." The smell of fresh coffee wafted into the study.

"I think I've got that taken care of," Arthur said. "Manny stopped by to see how Paul was doing. He just left. He said he can get a message to . . . Selene, right?"

Frik inhaled deeply of the comforting coffee aroma. "Yes. Selene. She's not particularly fond of me. She's one of those environmentalists." Saaliim returned with a cup of coffee and a Vicodin. Frikkie washed down the pain pill with a swig of the liquid, which his assistant had cooled just enough with the addition of milk.

"I'm sorry to bring it up at a time like this, but . . ." Frik paused and took a deep breath. "The Daredevils Club meeting is less than two weeks away. Tell me that you'll support me in this, Arthur. We have to find that device."

"We'll talk about it tomorrow."

Frik took another swallow of coffee. He couldn't wait. The sense of dread that had seized him in the lab was eating at him, trying to get another grip. "Tell me you'll help, damn it. You're my friend."

Arthur would have to back him in this. You owe me, he thought again, but as they had done right after the accident, the words remained unspoken. There was silence on the line. Were it not for the background murmur of the nurses at the station from which Arthur was making the call, Frikkie would have thought that his friend had hung up.

"Your answer?"

"No, Frik. I don't think so. The club has never been for the aggrandizement of any individual member. Besides, there's something unsavory about all this—"

"You don't understand. You could be throwing away the key to the universe."

That made Arthur laugh. "Some lids are meant to remain locked, Frikkie. I'm not willing to be Pandora, here."

"Damn it, Arthur—"

"Over my dead body, Frik. The whole thing smells wrong to me. I suppose you can bring it up at the meeting New Year's Eve, but I'll fight you on it."

This time, the silence on the line was absolute.

Frikkie put the receiver in its cradle and lay back on the sofa. The alcohol he had consumed had not fully left his system and the narcotic was beginning to numb his extremities. He tried to focus on the events of the day, and on how to proceed, but things quickly got hazy. One diaphanous plan melted into another, until he passed out cold.

At around midmorning, Frik awoke again, stiff and groggy and in his own bed. He assumed he'd been carried there by Saaliim. Wouldn't be the first time, he thought. He didn't know which was worse, the pain in his hand, the tightness in his chest from the smoke-filled lab, or his pounding hangover headache.

"Saaliim!"

His call instantly brought his assistant into the room.

"Coffee, my man. And something for this pain."

"Dr. Marryshow, he sent you some medicinals," Saaliim said. "Right there on your nightstand."

The younger man left the room and Frik picked up the white paper bag with a note in Arthur's handwriting stapled to it. Inside the bag there was antibacterial ointment for the burns and a small bottle of painkillers. The note contained cursory instructions about how often to take them and a warning not to drink alcohol while he did so. At the end of the instructions, Arthur had added:

I'm leaving the island. Take it slowly for a few days, Frikkie, and don't overdo the medication. By then you'll have come to your senses. Arthur

Or maybe you'll have changed your mind, Frik thought, and promptly swallowed twice the recommended dose of pills. By the time Saaliim returned with coffee, he was falling back into blackness.

For three days, Frik remembered little except pills, coffee, pain, and Saaliim's quiet presence floating in and out of the room. By the fourth morning, he was up and trying to dress when Saaliim knocked on the door.

"Telephone, Master Frik."

"Who is it?"

Arthur, he told himself as the events of the past few days returned to him. He's changed his mind.

"Missy Selene. Yesterday I told her you can't talk. Today she don't sound too good."

"I'll talk to her." Frik sat down on the side of the bed. Saaliim plugged in the extension phone, which he'd apparently kept unplugged for the last few days.

"Hello? Selene?"

"Frik." Selene's voice was like an ice cube.

He shivered, despite the heat of the morning. "I'm sorry about your father, Selene. He was a good man."

"Sorry? I'll bet you are. You lost a major workhorse, not to mention his discovery. You've never given a damn for anyone's safety but your own, you bastard."

"Selene—"

"You and your fucking oil drilling," Selene yelled. "By the time we're finished with you, Oilstar will be nothing but a memory."

The phone went dead in Frik's hand.

He pieced together what he knew about Selene. It wasn't much. She was bright, attractive, and had a Ph.D. in physics for which he had paid.

The penny dropped.

Green Impact had to be the "we" to which she had referred.

That was when the second penny dropped.

She knows, Frik thought. Her father must have sent her the pieces of the artifact. But how? There was no way she could have received them yet unless they'd been hand delivered. But by whom? Manny?

No. That was laughable. Manny was too smart to bite the hand that fed him.

How then? Maybe she hadn't received them yet. Maybe her father had told her he was sending them but—

It doesn't matter, Frik told himself. All that matters is that she knows. If Paul had told her about the artifact, then even if he hadn't sent them to her, he might have told her where he'd hidden the missing pieces. In order to find out, he'd have to capture Selene, and for that, he'd need some help.

The Daredevils Club remained his only choice. He'd have to convince them, whether Arthur objected or not. Whatever it took, Frik needed the club. He wasn't going to go into extinction quietly, damn it. He was no dumb tyrannosaur, he was Frikkie Van Alman, head of Oilstar, man of adventure. Nothing would stand in his way.

Nothing.

8

Shivering from the cold, Peta pulled open the door to Danny's Seafood Grotto. She had made eighteen visits to New York, trips punctuated by high school and college graduation, the beginning and end of medical school, and taking over Arthur's Grenada practice during his long visits to Manhattan and his absences when he sojourned to destinations unknown. By now she should have expected it to be cold, but she was never quite prepared for its reality.

"Peta! Welcome back." Danny's maitre d' took her coat. "Stunning as ever." He hugged her like an old friend. "Lucky man, Arthur. He's waiting for you over at the piano. I'll take care of your coat."

It didn't surprise Peta that George greeted her by name, not after this many visits to the West Forty-sixth Street restaurant. On the one hand, she thought, it was boring to be that predictable; on the other, to be welcomed so effusively in a city like this made her feel rather like a celebrity.

Arthur sat at the piano bar, his back to her. To her surprise, he was engaged in earnest discussion with his buddy, Raymond Arno. She felt a spark of annoyance. This was her time, her part of the evening. Bad enough that she was excluded from their damn Daredevils Club meeting that started at midnight every New Year's Eve.

She felt herself pouting and stopped. With Arthur, there was no use making a fuss. Ever. He did what he did, and generally for what he believed was good reason.

At that moment, the piano player looked up and saw her. Grinning happily, he switched gears into "Happy Birthday to You," played a few bars of "Hot, Hot, Hot," then segued into a lively rendition of "Dollar Wine."

Peta broke into the sensual steps of the Caribbean soca. There was a round of applause. Arthur looked up and waved. Even at a distance, his expression softened. If only he looked that way more often, she thought. She moved to the rhythm for a moment longer before pushing her way through to the piano.

"You two look as if you're plotting a world takeover," she said.

"You're early." Arthur kissed her. "And beautiful."

"I'll second that," Ray added. "You're a lucky man, Marryshow." He pecked her on the cheek.

Ray and Arthur exchanged a quick glance, then Ray gestured in the direction of the men's room. "Too many beers," he said, though his tough, firm body belied the statement. "Think I'll leave you two to conduct your annual birthday meeting and slip out the back way when I'm done. Happy New Year, Peta. Nice to see you again. Quick, take my seat before someone else does. Happy birthday—to both of you. See you later, Arthur."

Arthur patted the seat. "Don't be angry with me, Peta. Ray and I had some things we had to discuss. Seemed like as good a time as any to do it."

Peta watched Ray disappear into the dimly lit passage that led to the rest rooms and the storeroom in the back. She knew the layout well: a right into the alcove with the two rest-room doors; a door straight back to the "family" exit through the storeroom and into the back alley. Turning to Arthur she said, "Get me a drink and you're forgiven. I was surprised, that's all. I didn't think he'd be here at all this year. Isn't he supposed to be opening a new casino in Vegas about now?" She snuggled up to her mentor and friend. "In case you don't know it, it's cold as a witch's tit out there."

Though he was more than half again her age and a little craggy, Arthur was a handsome man, very tall and, like her, elegantly dressed. They blended seamlessly into the crowd as Danny's grew dense with New Year's Eve partygoers. The bodies around the piano bar were two and three deep and it took influence, bribery, or a very loud voice to so much as order a couple of drinks.

"I see you wore it," he said, fingering the exotic pendant he'd given her earlier in the day. She wore it around her neck, a smooth and somehow oily-looking irregular blue-green disk, bezel set and hung upon a twenty-four-carat gold chain.

Peta placed her hand over his and pressed it against her. She could feel the pendant against her skin. It was as if it were sucking the heat from her body, and yet it didn't feel uncomfortable. "What the devil is it, Arthur?"

"That's my secret. Just take good care of it."

"You and your secrets."

He smiled. "Call it a lucky piece. That's what I call mine." He opened his hand and showed her his stone. "I use it like a rubbing stone."

An hour passed with Arthur and Peta sometimes silent, often animated, always affectionate. Yet despite her best efforts, something was making Peta uncomfortable. Searching to find a reason for her discomfort, she noticed that Arthur was playing the time-conscious physician's game of glancing a little too frequently at his watch. When he did so twice within two minutes, Peta covered the face of the watch with her hand.

"You just looked," she said. "You'll have plenty of time to get to your meeting at midnight. This is *our* celebration. I get you for another hour."

While Arthur had many mysterious missions in his life about which he said little to her, the Daredevils Club bothered her more than the others. She resented the fact that he would say nothing about the club's activities and that she was not welcome there. After all, she had been the instigator of the adventure that created the club. Her exclusion seemed personal. *Was* personal, all the more so since at least one woman had been admitted. And died.

"You're a bunch of nasty little misogynists," she said, knowing he would understand the reference.

"I've told you over and over that I swore to your father I would not ever knowingly encourage you to endanger your life. Not while I was alive. So stop thinking about it, darlin'," Arthur said. "The meeting is something I do and you don't. It's that simple." Yet one more time, he glanced at his watch.

Peta sipped her wine. "If it's that simple, what are you so nervous about?"

As if he'd made a sudden and difficult decision, Arthur said, "I'm going to tell you something, but you have to promise me that you'll keep it to yourself."

She nodded. It seemed odd for him to be telling her secrets in public, but she knew that sometimes an anonymous crowd made for more privacy.

"There's new trouble brewing in the Middle East," Arthur continued. "Big trouble. After the meeting, I'm going to Israel. I'll be teaching medics about frontline emergency burn treatment. God knows I've had enough experience. There'll be danger." He leaned toward her and stroked her cheek. "I'm getting tired, Peta," he confessed. "Tired is bad in my business."

Peta was thrown by Arthur's serious tone and flattered that he would risk the implicit danger of taking her into his confidence. She'd known for some time that he occasionally worked with some secret branch of the American government, but he'd never so much as whispered any of the details until well after the fact.

Not wanting to trivialize what he'd told her, yet knowing he would not want her to be melodramatic, she said, "Make sure you're back here next year, Doctor—if we don't cross paths again before that."

"I promise." His smile returned playfully. "In fact, I've already made reservations for dinner, instead of just drinks. Five o'clock won't be too early for you, will it?"

"Are you sure you can spare seven whole hours? Or does that mean you'll be leaving early for your meeting?" She tried to match his humorously sarcastic tone, but the words came out sounding petulant.

Immediately the smile faded from his lips. "I won't have to be there until midnight. Promise." He downed the rest of his rum and stood up. "My turn for the men's room." He took out his wallet and handed it to her. "Do me a favor, settle the bill."

To Peta's surprise, he kissed her hard on the mouth. He was a private man, and such overt displays of affection were not his norm. She watched him turn on his heel and head in the same direction as Ray had gone earlier. Fighting jealousy about his anxiety to get to his "meeting" on time, she counted out the money and handed it to the waiter. She stuffed a fifty-dollar bill in the piano man's glass, blew him a kiss, and wished him a happy New Year. Having retrieved her coat from the coatroom, she put it on and stood near the exit door, people-watching while she waited for Arthur.

He should have come out of the rest room by now, she thought. It occurred to her how much simpler it was to check on an escort in Grenada, where most bathrooms were unisex. She was seriously considering asking George to check on Arthur's welfare, when there was a flash in the bathroom hallway and a concussive blast shook the restaurant.

In an instant that seemed to last an hour, a man who had been walking toward the bathrooms staggered out, a gash on his forehead pouring blood. The fire sprinklers burst to life, like a sudden tropical storm trapped inside the restaurant.

Immediately everyone was in motion. Men and women alike screamed as they rushed for the exit.

Panicked bodies pressed Peta out of the door into the small foyer. She fought against the current, finally sidestepping into an eddy created by a *Variety* dispenser. "I'm a doctor," she called out. "Let me through!"

By the time the flow of people eased enough for her to get back into the bar, she could hear sirens approaching. Even under the circumstances, the thought flashed through her mind that the police and fire department were responding astonishingly fast.

Inside, she stumbled around the overturned furniture. As she made her way toward the hall to the rest rooms, George blocked her way. "You don't want to go in there, Miss Peta."

Stomach clenched with a painful sense of knowing, she moved past him into the cramped passage. Chunks of the bathroom door lay in the small alcove, covered with gore. Within the bathroom itself, she saw a portrait of blood and mashed body parts. One thing told her irrefutably that the victim was Arthur Marryshow: lying in the midst of the grisly evidence was the stone matching the one around her neck.

Her knees failed her and she sagged to the floor. Seemingly with a will of its own, her hand reached for what Arthur had called his lucky piece.

"Hey, lady. What do you think you're doing?" A policeman took her by the arm. "You have something to do with this?"

"I'm a doctor." Peta used all of her courage to stem her emotions. "The . . . victim . . . is a friend of mine. Dr. Arthur Marryshow."

"I'm sorry about your loss, ma'am, but there's nothing much you can do for him now." The cop took her arm and helped her to her feet. "Come on."

The torrent from the sprinklers had been shut off. The police officer led Peta across the wet floor to a chair at the far side of the bar. "I hate to intrude, ma'am, but I need to ask you a few questions." He took out his notebook. "What did you say your name was?"

"Whyte." Automatically, she spelled it.

He wrote it down. "Dr. Whyte. And you said the deceased was named Marryshow?"

"Yes. I . . ." Her voice trailed off into silence. George appeared at her side with a glass of scotch, which she downed in a single motion.

"No offense, Officer, but I really don't think she's in any condition to answer your questions right now."

"Yeah," he said. "Sorry. Is there somewhere we can get in touch with you, Doctor?"

Mechanically, she pulled a card out of her purse and handed it to the officer. "I'd like the piece that matches this." She held up the pendant she was wearing. "It's in there with . . . with—"

"If it's with the . . . it's evidence, ma'am. When we're done with the investigation we'll get in touch." He glanced at the card. "Grenada," he said, mispronouncing it Gre-nah-da.

"Hey, John," a fellow policeman called out. "We need you over here."

"We'll be in touch, Doctor." The cop named John turned to the maitre d'. "Get her out of here. Now."

9

Numb with shock, Peta found herself relegated to the street outside the restaurant. She stood there unmoving. Rooted to the concrete.

"Peta! Peta, are you okay?" The familiar face of Ray Arno forced itself through her stupor. "I was on my way to the apartment. What happened in there?" He stared at the flood of gawkers and the half dozen camera crews that had been drawn away from the New Year's Eve action in Times Square. "Where's Arthur?"

"Ray!" Peta leaned against the man she'd known for seventeen years, since together they'd saved Arthur's life. "There was an explosion. Arthur's . . . he's dead, Ray."

Ray looked stunned. "What the hell are you talking about?"

Peta at last let go. Tears streamed down her cheeks as she described what she had seen.

Ray gripped her shoulder. "I'll find out who did this to him. I swear I will."

"Did this to *him*?" Peta repeated. "You think someone was out to murder Arthur?" Somewhere at the back of her presently fuzzy mind she remembered Arthur telling her about his mission to the Middle East. Was this a directed act, connected to the trouble in Israel he had mentioned, rather than a random act of violence?

"He was into a lot of dangerous stuff. You know that." Ray paused. "I'll miss him too," he said, more gently. "He was one of my oldest and dearest friends, Peta." His eyes filled with tears, and for the first time since she'd known him, he looked middle-aged.

"Look, I don't mean to sound callous but there's nothing we can do for Arthur. Not right now. It's not going to be easy to get through the crowds, but I have to be at the meeting by midnight. So do you." He put his arm around her. "Arthur said he wanted you to take his place if something . . . permanent . . . ever happened to him. There has to be a vote and it has to be unanimous, but—"

Peta shook off his arm. She was stunned. Angry that Ray could even consider such a thing right after Arthur's death. "You're still going to have the meeting? After this?"

"Yes." He buttoned up her coat, took off his scarf and wrapped it around her neck. Then he put his arm back around her. "Listen," he said. "Before we go, there's something I should warn you about. No matter how much we loved Arthur, you won't see us mourning his death, not in any conventional way. It's an agreement we made after our first member died. The meetings go on and we grieve privately, each in our own way."

Peta felt her temper rise, but pragmatism and emotional exhaustion won out. There *was* nothing else she could do right now. She allowed Ray to lead her through the drunk and rowdy New Year's Eve celebrants to Arthur's Manhattan penthouse, a one-bedroom apartment that sat squarely in the middle of the flat roof of the Time Hotel.

The prewar hotel was on West Forty-ninth, half a block from Broadway in the heart of the theater district. At the Ambassador Theater next door, a performance was just letting out. Peta didn't see the people, didn't notice anything but her sorrow. She couldn't think beyond Arthur: his mentoring and friendship; their first visit to New York; their first lovemaking, on her twenty-second birthday, and the evolution of that night into an abiding, all-encompassing love.

She was oblivious to the greetings of the doorman, who knew her from her annual visits and waved them inside, seeing in her mind's eye the pieces of Arthur's tortured and scarred body. She followed Ray into a small, antiquated elevator. On the ride up to the sixteenth floor, she remembered the first time she'd used this elevator, the first time she'd stayed overnight with Arthur, their pillow talk about his dangerous work as an undercover plastic surgeon for a small outcropping of the CIA that sent its people on *Mission: Impossible* jaunts into the firing line—including surgeries on the famous and the infamous.

The elevator opened into Arthur's apartment. Frik stood on the rooftop, his back to her, staring down at the city. Three more men waited inside. She recognized them as acquaintances of Arthur's.

Stone-faced, Ray poured brandy into two glasses and handed one of them to her. "Drink it," he said. He downed most of the contents of his own glass. Then he turned toward the others and told them that Arthur would not be at the meeting that night, or ever again.

Each of the men reacted in his own way. One stood up and began to pace. Another, whom she'd known for some time, had tears in his eyes. He put his face in his hands, as if he did not want the others to see his weakness. The third man yelled out "No!" His cry brought Frik to the doorway.

"What's happened?" he asked, standing in the half shadows.

"It's Arthur," Ray said quietly. "He's dead."

Frik stared at Ray. "Here," he said, reverting to his native Afrikaans. "God." After a moment he asked, "How did it happen?"

As Ray began his recounting, Peta felt on the edge of hysteria. In emotional self-defense, she fell into the habit born of years of training. She looked at the members of the Daredevils Club and cataloged what she knew about them and their activities.

While he'd kept the details a secret, Arthur had told her small things, nonspecific things. She knew that they gathered every New Year's Eve to exchange tales of the past year's most daring and death-defying adventures, that they were all people who, by inclination or profession, risked their lives on a regular basis. They sought out trouble, took on jobs that nobody fully sane would do, and put their lives on the line at every opportunity. The playground for their adventures was the world—be it in military installations, deep undersea trenches, or just on the mean streets of New York. They risked their lives for the thrill, the glory, or the money, and they came together to share their adventures because half the fun was telling the tale.

Peta tried to remember what specifics she could about the three men sitting in Arthur's living room.

The one she knew best, outside of Frik and Ray, was the man who had cried and called out. He was Simon Brousseau, a Miami-based inventor of scuba-diving gear, a womanizer, and an underwater junkie. Judging by his pallor, he had a bad heart condition. Were she his physician, she'd be warning him to take it easy.

The other two men she'd met only briefly, over dinner during one of her trips to New York. The burly one was Terris McKendry, a freelance security specialist. She remembered him as a thorough, stoic, and patient man—the type who could probably sit unmoving for hours when concentrating on something, a man who always had a Plan B thought out in advance. He was trained as a civil engineer but had spent many years working for a large personal-security firm that hired him out as a personal bodyguard. According to Arthur, Terris had received a huge bonus when he'd saved one of his clients, a foreign diplomat, from an assassination attempt. With his reward in hand, he'd set off on his own.

The last man, the pacer, was Joshua Keene, McKendry's "partner in insanity," according to Arthur. Keene was McKendry's opposite, a wild man who placed great stock in his instincts and his intuition. He had a quick and winning smile and was the guy who always bought the next round of drinks. He'd dropped out of college after a succession of majors and was mostly self-taught, a voracious reader and learner who bounced from one fascination to the next and lived in and for the moment. He seemed to have succeeded in life by always doing the unexpected.

Peta had not found McKendry's gruff manner particularly appealing. Keene, however, she'd found to be gregarious and likable.

"That's all I know," Ray said at last. In the ensuing silence, he added, "You're all aware that Arthur wanted Peta to be his successor if something happened to him."

Frik, who had stayed in the doorway listening to the details of his old friend's death, stepped into the light. Peta immediately noticed burn scars on his face. He was wearing gloves, but she could see the traceries of more severe scars on his left hand in the gap between the sleeve and the glove.

"Peta's entry fee for membership will have to be the same as it is for any man," Frik said. "Proof of participation in a new adventure that makes her worthy of inclusion in the club."

"Damn all of you." Peta hurled her brandy glass in Frik's direction. It hit the wall closest to him and splintered, leaving behind a golden brown trickle. "Your friend is dead. Dead. And why? For all I know, it's because of some stunt he pulled to impress you."

She pushed past Frik and went out onto the rooftop. In the distance, she could see the lights of a vessel making its way up the Hudson. Closer and down below, people streamed around the corner toward Times Square to wait for the ball to drop and for the new year to be upon them.

As if it mattered what year it was, she thought. The days and months—and years—would march on. Gradually the pain would leave her. For now, tending her island patients and Arthur's was all she could think of doing to get herself through.

She looked up into the cloudy sky. "Happy New Year, Arthur," she whispered as her tears once again rolled freely, "wherever you are."

In the heat of her fury at the callousness of the men inside the apartment and despite the depth of her sorrow, she considered Arthur's last wish—her inclusion in the club. She wasn't willing to go out *looking* for life-threatening stunts so that she could prove herself to the Daredevils. Her own line of work brought her into more than enough danger all of the time. Life-and-death decisions were her stock-in-trade. Then again, if the original members hadn't considered the rescue of Arthur from prison dangerous enough to overcome the fact that she was female, these idiots certainly wouldn't agree that what she accomplished daily was suitably perilous.

Behind her, inside the apartment, someone turned on the local news, apparently to see if the aftermath of the explosion was being televised. Peta moved close enough to see the screen.

Her timing was impeccable, although whether impeccably good or bad was, she thought briefly, up for grabs. Though she'd been unaware of it at the time, it seemed a cameraman had picked her out of the crowd. There she was, a full shot first, then her face filling the screen.

She walked into and across the living room and entered the small bedroom she'd so often shared with Arthur. She stared at herself in the small mirror she'd used to put on her makeup, took off the coat she was still wearing, and fingered the pendant Arthur had given her. Taking it off, she placed it lovingly in her handbag, and began to pack her things.

10

In the living room, Frik leaned forward, staring intently at the television screen. The announcer said that a lone Muslim extremist had claimed responsibility for the blast, and the camera closed once again on Peta. Encircled by a gold bezel, suspended from a gold chain, was a fragment of the artifact.

Filing away the certainty that she knew everything Arthur had known, he turned his attention to the people in the room. "Meeting's in order," he said. "You go first, Ray."

With visible reluctance, Ray pulled a videotape out of his coat pocket and slipped it into the VCR. It began with Channel 8 hype about the preopening advertising for his hotel.

"Ray Arno, owner of the new Daredevil Casino, is much more than a wealthy investor in a business suit," Paula Francis of *Eyewitness News* began. "He's a well-known Hollywood stuntman, an Evel Knievel, if you will. You're about to see him perform a spectacular, death-defying stunt to highlight his new adventure hotel, with its theme park full of thrill rides and its high-stakes casino."

"Behold one of those stupid macho stunts Peta was talking about," Ray said. "You will notice that there is no safety net."

Followed by cameras and reporters, Ray could be seen climbing to the top of Las Vegas's Stratosphere Tower—the tallest observation tower west of the Mississippi. He smiled, took a deep breath, and leaped into space. The camera tracked his shrinking figure until a rectangular skydiver's parachute unfurled behind him.

The camera angle changed to a shot of a wedge-shaped building with what looked like a space shuttle jutting from one side. A large neon sign in front of the structure proclaimed THE DAREDEVIL. The image panned up to show Ray in his bright jumpsuit, expertly gliding toward the roof of the casino.

The report switched to a cameraman on the Daredevil's rooftop helipad. As Ray stuttered to a stop and removed his parachute, he said into the camera, "Follow me to the Daredevil. *You* may use the front door."

The screen filled with snow as the tape ended. "That'll do," Frik said. No one disagreed. "Who's next."

Briefly, as if they were reading Cliff's Notes, each of them, including Frik, added a tale of derring-do. Frik summarized an African man-faces-rhino ecoadventure that sounded like an outtake from Hemingway's *Green Hills of Africa*; Keene and McKendry gave a précis about having infiltrated a white-supremacist group to rescue a black professor who had been taken hostage; and Simon described a shark attack during the exploration of a wreck near the Bermuda Triangle.

"Listen, everyone," Ray said after Simon had finished. "Why not talk about next year and call it a night? We obviously won't be able to meet here from now on, so how about my place in Vegas?"

"Your place?" Joshua Keene looked amused.

"My new hotel. Look, I realize this apartment was Damon Runyan's home, which made it perfect for us, and the Strip isn't Times Square—"

"But it's the next best thing to being here." Keene lifted his glass in a mock toast.

McKendry chuckled, appreciative as always of his friend's sense of humor.

"Someday I'm going to buy this place and turn it into a casino," Ray said. "But that's not happening quite yet. Meanwhile, why not some desert R and R away from the . . . um"—he glanced at Arthur's bedroom—"the memories?"

The venue was readily agreed upon. Glasses were refilled, and a few people munched on pretzels and nuts.

"About next year." Frik got ready for what needed to be a convincing performance. "I have something to propose. Something urgent that I cleared with Arthur, on condition the rest of you agreed."

He too glanced toward the bedroom where Peta had gone, then sat back and put forth his proposal. He went over what information he wished to divulge: the discovery of the artifacts; the fire that had killed

Paul Trujold; a description of how he had sustained third-degree burns on his face and left hand.

Having gained the group's attention, he went on to talk about his suspicion that Selene Trujold had at least one piece of the device, sent by her father, and he recounted her threats to destroy Oilstar. Of course, he said nothing about his true purpose, making it easy for everyone to agree upon a treasure hunt for the missing pieces of the artifact.

"I don't mean to minimize what you're suggesting, Frik," Keene said grimly, "but shouldn't we be putting our energies into finding out who killed Arthur?"

"You're right, Josh," Ray said quickly. "Given the relative skills of the rest of you, you'll have no difficulty divvying up Frik's search. I'll handle Arthur's death on my own. I can always call on the rest of you if I need help. Sound reasonable?"

Frik held his breath.

There was silence while the others thought everything through. "Sounds more than reasonable to me. I'll dive for the piece that was left behind," Brousseau said, not mentioning what Frik already knew—that his doctor had warned him that his heart condition made deep-sea dives not just dangerous, but potentially suicidal.

Frik said nothing about it. Simon's reaction was perfect, imperative to his plan. The only risk was that Simon could mess things up by dying underwater before retrieving the piece, but that was a chance he was willing to take. "You can fly back with me," he said.

Simon shook his head. "I have to take care of some things in Miami first. Tell you what. Bring the *Assegai* to Grenada. I'll fly in there in a couple of weeks and you can sail me to Trinidad. I could use a good sail, a little time on top of the ocean."

Keene and McKendry volunteered to track Selene Trujold and her gang of ecoterrorists. From her father's notes and earlier comments, Frik knew that she had tended to focus her Green Impact activities in the main Venezuelan oil fields, near Maracaibo. If he was right, that was about to change. Now Oilstar's large new *Valhalla* rig, just beginning production in the Orinoco Delta, would become her prime target.

"There is something else *you* can do," Frik said to Ray. "Correct me if I'm wrong, but I seem to remember that you told me you were building a state-of-the-art laboratory adjacent to your penthouse."

"Yeah. In my guilty moments I tell myself that I built it to develop a new means of detecting and neutralizing land mines and live shells in war zones. Really, though, I'm just a kid with a four-million-dollar chemistry set," Ray said, grinning.

"A useful one. If you don't mind, I'll have Trujold's computer models and results transmitted from our mainframe in Trinidad to your computer in Las Vegas. I need you to study them and determine if his findings were correct."

"Okay with me," Ray said. "Now if you'll all excuse me, I have to check on preparations my people are making for an important guest at the Daredevil."

He left the room to use the phone in Arthur's kitchenette. By the time he returned, Peta had reentered the room. Frik could see her closed suitcase standing upright on the floor near the open doorway.

"Fly back with me in the Oilstar jet," he said to her. "I'll divert and take you to Grenada before going on to Trinidad. Sure you won't come with us, Simon?"

Simon shook his head. "Aside from anything else, there's some diving gear I want to pick up in Miami."

"Diving gear?" Peta sounded shocked. "Are you *trying* to kill yourself?"

"What are you talking about?" Ray asked. "He's been diving forever."

"I'm a doctor, remember," Peta said. "I don't need to do an EKG to see that he has a heart problem."

"Is that true?" Ray looked at Simon as if he hadn't really seen him before.

"Leave him alone, both of you," Frik said, more brusquely than he had intended. "He's over twenty-one."

"Yes. Stop fussing over me. I'm going to do this." Simon crossed his fingers, put his hand behind his back, and grinned like a little boy. "Tell you what, though. I promise you, this will be my last dive."

11

"We're hanging out in the wrong places, Terris. Let's go get dirty."

McKendry grunted in agreement. He didn't need to comment further; he and Keene had been working together long enough that they often seemed to read each other's mind. For that reason, they had hardly spoken about Arthur's death. Each knew how much the other would miss him, but since no amount of talk would bring their friend back, they mourned him in silence. Having lost friends before, McKendry understood his own process. For him, acceptance would come slowly, but come it would, ultimately turning the open wound of loss into one more scar on the body of his life.

"The sooner we get out of Caracas, the better." Keene slurped the last of his *michelada,* a concoction of lime juice, beer, ice cubes, and salt. He had taken a great liking to the drink, which he compared to a *cerveza margarita.* "We need to start sniffing around the oil operations. I'm betting Selene's moved from Maracaibo and is headed east to focus on Frikkie's operations near the Orinoco Delta."

McKendry knew that at any other time, Joshua Keene would have enjoyed hanging out in nightclub after nightclub, where the dancers were topless and the salsa music too loud. Not now. "You just want to get into the jungle," McKendry said.

"And you don't?"

McKendry gave a small, unintelligible response which seemed to satisfy his partner. In any event, Keene was right about Caracas. Someone like Selene was unlikely to be here by choice. Besides, at this moment in their lives, the city was far too civilized a place for the two of them. Yes, it was magnificent, the jewel of Venezuela, but a postcard would have sufficed. Shining buildings and upscale restaurants, sidewalk cafés with bright yellow awnings, lavish marble-and-brass hotels and wild nightlife never had been his idea of a good time.

Still, McKendry thought, the search for Paul Trujold's daughter needed to start somewhere. This had seemed to be as good a place as any. He hadn't actually expected to find her here—Frikkie's information said that Green Impact worked primarily in the western oil fields of the Maracaibo Basin—but this was where he had contacts in Venezuela. He knew people who could potentially lead them to Green Impact, or lead them to someone who could lead them to someone. . . .

People like Rodolfo. The Spanish action-film star, one of McKendry's former employers, was very popular in South and Central America, though his career had gone nowhere in the United States. He had hired McKendry as a bodyguard and tough guy, a brawny piece of furniture to hover behind him every time he went out, even when they went where nobody knew who Rodolfo was.

The work had been a profitable and not unpleasant contract job. The star was less obnoxious than several full-of-themselves celebrities McKendry had guarded in the past. But when the six-month contract came up for renewal, he politely declined further service and moved on to another freelance assignment. He preferred to provide real protection rather than testosterone-filled eye candy.

When the two Daredevils were arranging to fly down to Venezuela and begin their search for Selene, McKendry had called the action star and asked what connections he might have, what help he could offer.

Rodolfo seemed delighted to hear from him and offered to do what he could. At Simón Bolívar International Airport, in glistening tropical sunshine, the star had welcomed them both with all the enthusiasm of a long-lost Italian uncle. During their first few nights in Caracas, the grinning and too-tanned film star showered them with free champagne and front-row tickets to all the hottest nightclub shows. He took them to dinner at Tambo, Il Cielo, and other jet-set favorites, and provided them with a spacious suite in the Eurobuilding Hotel, far from the outlying shanties and slums and the lush jungle-covered mountains that rode high on the horizon; they were further yet from the political, economic, and natural disasters that inevitably piled one upon the other in various parts of the South American continent.

McKendry played along for five days, asking questions and enduring the pampered treatment. Five long days; five noisy nights in nightclubs. They had been seen by all the local celebrities, by important political people in Caracas, by hotel managers and casino owners. Rodolfo was doing his best and glorying in the doing of it.

For a different assignment, perhaps, McKendry might have been able to use these new connections he had made, to pull strings and apply leverage. But not this time. No self-respecting member of Green Impact would ever hobnob with such people.

"We're getting nowhere," Keene shouted across at McKendry. He pounded on the table, signaling the nearest waitress for another michelada; so far, they had experienced no difficulty meeting the nightclub's expensive minimum-consumption requirement.

The music picked up tempo. Several topless showgirls jiggled coffee brown breasts as they danced past the table en route to the small central area cleared for occasional performances. "Nice," McKendry said. "Very nice."

Keene ran his fingers through his curly hair. He smiled appreciatively but said nothing. When his fresh michelada arrived, he slurped salt from the edge, tasted it with an extravagant flourish, and handed the waitress a large tip.

The dance number finished with a brassy finale followed by a shower of applause from well-dressed Venezuelan businessmen and their various foreign guests.

"If Selene Trujold is an ecoterrorist, self-proclaimed or otherwise, she wouldn't be caught dead in Caracas," Keene said. "She wouldn't let any of these bozos so much as buy her a drink."

McKendry drained his too-sweet drink and stood up. "Get a good night's sleep. We'll check out tomorrow."

"Not quite yet." Keene made a motion with his hand and forearm, parrying with it as if it were a sword. "Zorro the Gay Blade approaches."

McKendry turned toward the door. He really does look like George Hamilton playing Zorro, he thought, watching Rodolfo weave his way through the crowd.

"So soon you leave me?" The star arrived with his latest accessory. "But I have just found a wonderful man for you to meet. Quite a coincidence. I have brought him over here to you."

A stranger accompanied Rodolfo, a small, wiry man with quick eyes and a feral smile. His mode of dress, not glamorous but prosperous, made it clear that he was in the Venezuelan government, and well placed at that. More important, as far as McKendry was concerned, the man's furtive glances and calculating stare showed him to be in a security field—police, military, or something even more useful.

"Don't think of it as leaving you, Rodolfo." Keene rolled the *r* and lengthened the vowels. "Think of us as lost sheep and know we'll find our way home."

McKendry stifled a laugh and thought, not for the first time, that his partner should have been in movies.

Keene went on, "But who is your friend here? We haven't had the pleasure." He thrust his hand toward the official.

Rodolfo responded as the perfect host. "Ah, my manners. Terris, Joshua, this is Juan Ortega de la Vega Bruzual, *ministro de la seguridad*. Juan, these are my friends whom I told you about."

Señor Bruzual's lips twisted up on one side of his face. "My pleasure," he said, shaking first Keene's hand, then McKendry's.

Music blared from the sound system as more scantily clad dancers rushed onto the stage behind them. Keene leaned in and shouted, "We can't hear ourselves think here. Why don't you join us in our suite for a nightcap?"

McKendry considered that a very good idea, now that Rodolfo had finally brought in someone who might have information for them, or at least suggestions on how to proceed. He noticed that Rodolfo seemed very pleased at Keene's offer and motioned his muscle man to clear them a path out of the nightclub, but Juan Ortega touched the star's arm and gestured back toward the table where he had been sitting. "But my own guests, Rodolfo. I can't simply desert them." The minister looked genuinely stricken, then brightened. "Perhaps . . . I hate to impose, my friend, but could you entertain them until I return?"

Well maneuvered, McKendry thought, nodding good night to his former employer, who bravely went to join Señor Bruzual's guests.

The ride up in the glass-enclosed elevator was fast and filled with chitchat between Keene and Señor Bruzual. McKendry, lacking their obvious gift for inane chatter, kept silent.

When they reached the suite, one floor below the top of the towering hotel, the minister got right down to business. While Joshua poured drinks, Bruzual said, "I can tell that you are not men of leisure, that you would prefer to be direct. I have heard of your interest in Green Impact. Why do you seek this terrorist group?"

"We're actually only interested in one of their members, Selene Trujold." McKendry took a scotch and water from Keene. No reason to beat around the bush. Bruzual had been apprised of their search.

"Well," the Venezuelan said, sipping his own drink, "Selene Trujold is not just a member of Green Impact, she is the leader."

McKendry didn't want to get sidetracked. "That complicates things a bit. I suppose now you're going to tell us that Green Impact is no longer operating from the Maracaibo Basin."

Bruzual's lip twitched up into his crooked smile, but instead of answering, he asked, "Why do you seek Señorita Trujold?" He sipped his own scotch, obviously savoring it. During the headiest days of the oil boom, Venezuelans had consumed the highest per-capita amount of fine scotch in the world, and their taste for it had not declined despite higher tariffs and import restrictions.

McKendry nodded to Keene, who said, "We're working with Oilstar. She may have information about a sensitive . . . item stolen from Oilstar's labs. We're here to recover it."

The security minister nodded. "I have had a task force keeping an eye on Green Impact's troublesome activities for many years. For the most part, their terrorism has amounted to nothing more than an annoyance. However, two months ago their former leader was found shot along with several security guards at the site of an attempted sabotage in Cabimas. None of the guards had fired their weapons.

"A week later, we received reports of sabotage campaigns in the east led by a woman. Our information shows that Green Impact has gone at least as far as Maturín, and it is said they have an encampment in the Delta Amacuro."

Keene looked at McKendry. "Just like Frik thought. Not far from Oilstar's operations between Trinidad and the Venezuelan coast."

"That is all I can give you." Bruzual downed his scotch and stood up. "It's been a pleasure, gentlemen."

McKendry stood and extended his right hand. "Thank you, Señor Bruzual. We will return the favor."

"Just bring me Selene Trujold's head. One of those dead guards was my nephew."

As the door closed behind the Venezuelan, Keene grinned. "You pack," he said. "I'll see about getting us a ride. Should I bring an Enya CD for mood music? *Orinoco Flow*, maybe?"

"Very funny." McKendry grimaced at Keene, pulled out his suitcase, and started to pack. His friend was well aware that Terris had turned down a lucrative assignment with the New Age star because he couldn't stand to listen to her music.

Keene chuckled. "I didn't think so," he said, and picked up the phone.

12

Sitting directly behind the pilot of the Cessna they'd hired to fly them from Caracas to Maturín, McKendry had a clear view of the gray ribbons of pipe forming stripes through the woven tapestry of green and brown and tan that was the coastal range. The pipelines delivered crude from the rich Orinoco oil belt in the south over the mountains to refineries in Puerto La Cruz and other cities to the north, on the Caribbean coast.

From his seat, he couldn't see the vast central plains and forests of the Venezuelan interior, but from Keene's bored expression and constant attempts to find something to talk about over the growl of the engines, he knew there couldn't be much excitement down there.

McKendry instead used the time to review their plans. The pattern of Green Impact's movements made it clear that Selene was attacking targets of opportunity as the terrorists relocated for their campaign against Frikkie and Oilstar. The obvious place for them to hide was the maze of the Orinoco Delta, which lay due south of Trinidad on the east coast of Venezuela. The delta, a vast fan of swampy streams and dense jungles that covered nearly eight thousand square miles, emptied into the ocean across more than a hundred miles of coastline.

The northwestern curve of the delta fan flowed into the Gulf of Paria—where Frikkie had most of his oil wells—and the nine-mile-wide channel known as the Boca de la Serpiente, or Serpent's Mouth, which separated the southern tip of Trinidad from the Venezuelan mainland. On the map, McKendry thought, the island's southern peninsula looked like the head of an adder set to strike the giant body of South America.

The snake analogy was not appealing. For all of his daredeviltry, there were two things McKendry preferred not to face: snakes and sharks. There was little he could do about the latter except avoid them, to which end he confined his swimming to lakes and pools. As far as the former were concerned, he habitually wore heavy boots and always carried a fresh snakebite kit in his backpack.

Pausing in his review, he checked to make sure the kit was there.

Deciding that the scenery held no further interest to him, he leaned back, closed his eyes, and napped for the remainder of the trip.

Upon landing, McKendry and Keene hired a truck and a driver to take them from Maturín across the Tonoro River to the Mánamo, on the western edge of the delta.

They kept to the lowlands, to the less-inhabited villages, where they considered it most likely Selene Trujold had gone to ground. They paid with worn bolivar notes to take guided boats up and down some of the delta riverlets—called *caños* by the locals. In U.S. terms, the money they spent amounted to little, but McKendry was aware that their frequent hiring of the poor boat pilots helped the local economy a great deal.

Everywhere they went, Keene and McKendry asked about Green Impact, trying to uncover secret support for the environmental group. They moved in a "drunkard's walk" pattern across the coast, one day heading up a caño into the interior, the next doubling back down another, tending in an easterly direction, but occasionally circling around to see if their earlier questions had raised any alarms behind them.

They met with no success. Oilstar's work was the salvation of the local economy. The local Warao Indians did not seem to have much of a global perspective, and it was clear they would not have joined Green Impact's cause. The same was true of most of the villagers who lived in thatched huts atop stilts in the muddy marshes. They cared little or nothing about protecting the ecology. In fact, many of the taro and yucca farmers were in the process of hacking down rain forests and slashing and burning the land so they could plant crops.

Time trickled by like the water in the languid river, but just like the river, the current of days was deceptive. McKendry, perhaps because he understood the people less, was growing impatient. It annoyed him that his partner seemed perfectly content to go on sitting in dockside cantinas, looking out toward the ocean, or sometimes just under over-hanging foliage beneath an awning on a dock beside the river, drinking *micheladas* and asking questions. While they both understood the language, McKendry freely admitted that his partner seemed far more comfortable with the culture.

Eventually, they began to pick up word of a group of radicals headquartered in some unnamed village farther south, a group led by a young woman. Unfortunately, no one seemed to know exactly how to find them.

More likely, nobody gave a damn.

"Damn bugs," McKendry said as they sat in yet one more cantina eating yet one more plateful of black beans and spicy empanadas filled with an unknown meat from the jungle.

"To them, you're a necessary part of the food chain," Keene said, grinning.

Terris pushed the rest of his meal aside and reached for his beer. He was about to make some rude comment when two newcomers entered the cantina.

The owner sat in a chair behind the bar and paid no attention to the strangers, but instinct born of long experience told McKendry to take note of the young white man and his companion. The man marched into the restaurant as if he belonged there. He wore his hair in a long ponytail, a floppy leather hat, and a plaid shirt, and had a guitar in a case slung over his shoulder. His *india* girlfriend, a short dark-haired beauty, held a tambourine, and spoke not a word.

The young man slipped his guitar case off his shoulder, opened the case on the floor, and eyed McKendry and Keene the way a con man eyes his marks.

McKendry did not change his expression, but Keene sat forward and stared with intense interest. With a preliminary strum of the strings, the young man played and sang, though not particularly well, a Beatles song followed by an old Bob Dylan tune.

"Hey," Keene called out to him. "Why don't you play one of those old activist songs, like how the oil companies are wrecking the environment?"

He raised his eyebrows and looked over at his partner. McKendry cleared his throat and nodded.

"How 'bout 'The Wreck of the *Exxon Valdez*,' sung to that old Gordon Lightfoot tune?"

The young man laughed and strummed his guitar. "Well, I'd have to make up the words."

"That's all right," McKendry said.

Joshua Keene fidgeted, but could not contain his impatience. After the young man struggled through half a song, Keene clapped loudly. He tossed a handful of coins into the guitar box. "Say, you wouldn't know anything about Green Impact, would you?"

The young man stiffened. "That's a terrorist group, and they're not terribly welcome around here. Why would I know anything about them?"

"Not saying you do, amigo," Keene said carefully. "It's just that we're looking for Selene Trujold. She's supposedly one of their members, maybe even their leader."

"I know of Selene," the young man said, equally carefully.

"We were friends of her father's," McKendry said. "He died a little while ago."

"Didn't Selene's father work for Oilstar, the one with that big faulty rig off the coast between here and Trinidad?"

"The big rig in the Serpent's Mouth?" McKendry played dumb. "Oh, yeah, the *Valhalla*. What's wrong with it? I heard that it's at the top of its form."

"It—" The young man caught himself. "Well, I hear Green Impact has been claiming the rig is a monstrosity, unstable, a disaster waiting to happen." He shrugged, flashing an embarrassed smile; his india girl-friend still said nothing.

"Selene's father was killed by the oil company," McKendry said. "Paul Trujold was a friend of ours, so we're not big fans of Oilstar either."

"I can't tell you where you can find them in the jungle. Nobody knows that. Only official members. But I hear she's coming out of hiding real soon now. You'll see it on the news." He adjusted his guitar on his knee. "That is, when we *get* news out here. Green Impact wants to strike back, hit that platform out in the Serpent's Mouth or an oil tanker in the vicinity or something like that. You know, make a spectacle." He seemed to catch himself, looked embarrassed. "But other than that, I couldn't tell you how to find her. Just keep your eyes open."

"We will," McKendry said gruffly.

The india girl shook her tambourine in impatience, and the young man looked down meaningfully at the few coins in his guitar case. "Now, do you guys have any other requests? I mean, for a song instead of for information?"

Keene threw another hundred bolivars into the guitar case and requested "Stairway to Heaven."

McKendry looked at him over their warm cervezas.

Both men knew where they were going next.

"Looking good." Keene took stock of himself in the bathroom mirror. He ran his fingers around his clean-shaven chin. "You could use a shave yourself, buddy."

McKendry grinned and elbowed his friend out of the way. He hadn't shaved since leaving Caracas. His beard, which had always grown fast, was already beginning to take shape.

"Tell me you're not thinking about growing it again. Remember last time? The good guys took one look at you and thought we were the bad guys. . . ."

Reluctantly, McKendry picked up a razor. It had taken them two days to get back to Caracas. Amazing, he thought, how it always feels like it takes forever to get somewhere and no time flat to get back. Like shaving a beard. Takes forever to grow and comes off in a minute.

When they looked fully presentable again, McKendry called Rodolfo. The actor willingly gave him what he needed—a way to contact Security Minister Bruzual. The minister in turn connected McKendry with the harbormaster in the major refinery city of Puerto La Cruz, where Oilstar's largest tanker, the *Yucatán,* was currently moored.

The rig actually produced more oil than Frikkie's facilities on Trinidad could handle, and the refineries at Puerto La Cruz were the closest place he could use to turn a profit from the excess. The complex had been built to take crude from the long pipeline that extended through the deep jungles from the inland Orinoco oil belt. Oilstar had arranged with the Venezuelan government to use the refinery facilities—which had been nationalized in 1976—in order to prepare the offshore crude and send it up to the United States through the Caribbean and the Gulf of Mexico.

Keene—the better linguist—called the captain and made an appointment for them to speak with him, privately and in person.

"Perfect timing." He put down the phone. "We see Captain Miguel Calisto tomorrow morning while the *Yucatán* offloads. By afternoon she'll be on her way to refill at Oilstar's offshore rig, *Valhalla,* in the Serpent's Mouth."

"Now all we need is a way to hitch a ride. Any suggestions?" McKendry sounded dubious.

"Piece of cake," Keene said. "I'll explain over breakfast."

With no further explanation, Keene placed two calls. The first was to Bruzual. All McKendry gleaned from the conversation was that his partner had asked the security minister to send them a fax care of their hotel.

The second call was to Frik on board the *Assegai.* Again, Keene asked that a fax be sent to them at the hotel, one that urged Captain Calisto to give them all possible assistance.

"Frikkie's in Grenada," Keene said after he'd completed the call. "Simon's flying in today."

13

Peta was pleasantly surprised when Simon called her before leaving Miami to ask her to pick him up at Grenada's Point Saline Airport and transport him and his equipment to the *Assegai*. Given the fact that she had made it so clear that she believed he was risking his life to dive again, now or ever, she had thought he would slip quietly onto and off the island.

Simon was one of the last people to debark. He looked pale and tired.

"How was your flight?" Peta asked.

"Fine until we landed. The pilot must have had a hot date the way he stopped short on the runway."

"I guess he didn't want to taxi very far. Lord knows there's no lack of runway. The Cubans saw to that."

Simon laughed. "As I recall, they were building it long enough to handle bombers. That's one of the real reasons why our forces took the revolution seriously, no matter what the president said about the medical students."

Nodding, Peta said, "Eventually they took it seriously, but not before a lot of good people were killed. Arthur was almost one of them." She stopped talking and waited for the sudden wave of nausea to pass. Simon was respectful enough not to try to say anything more.

When his gear was loaded and they were pulling out of the airport, Peta said, "I'm going to keep trying to talk you out of this madness, you know."

"I know, but I'm going to do it anyway, so you might as well stop nagging me about it."

"If that's how you feel, Simon, why did you let me know that you were coming?"

"Tell you the truth, I don't know. Maybe I really did want you to talk me out of this." He looked at her and sighed. "Or maybe I just wanted to have the most beautiful woman in Grenada chauffeur me around. Not doing too much else with women these days, not even the ugly ones."

"That's hard to believe," Peta said, though in fact she did believe him.

Simon changed the subject. "I'd like to see the Rex Grenadian," he said, referring to a large resort near the airport, one of the newest on the island. "Could we stop in for a drink?"

Peta hesitated. Simon's color was awful. Positively gray. "You probably shouldn't be drinking."

"You're not my nursemaid," he said. He sighed again, loudly. "Look, I'm sorry. I didn't mean to snap at you." He thankfully paused a moment while she negotiated one of the dangerous roundabouts along the two-lane strip of concrete called the Maurice Bishop Highway, and headed down the side road that would lead them to the nearby resort.

When they were safely driving through the small patch of palms and mahoganies that separated the northern beaches of Point Saline from the airport, Simon said, "It's about Arthur. I didn't have a chance in New York to tell you how sorry I was, not really. We're sailing tonight. I'd like to talk about him a little. Have a chance to—"

"You'll have Frik around. You can do that with him." Instantly she was angry with herself for her tone.

"Frik doesn't believe in mourning the dead."

"You're right. I'm sorry. I guess it was my turn to get snippy." Peta swerved to the left to avoid a water truck heading back to the main road, and turned onto the Rex Grenadian's driveway.

The resort fronted on two beaches. One of them had no name that she could recall. The other was Parc a Boeuf Beach. Where they had found such an ugly name for so magnificent a stretch of sand was a mystery to Peta and everyone else. The hotel was frequented mainly by rich Americans; the Europeans preferred to be on Morne Rouge Bay or Grand Anse Beach. The Rex boasted a man-made, lushly landscaped three-acre lake, complete with aesthetically placed islands and waterfalls, as well as three restaurants, and an attentive staff.

All in all, it was an excellent facility for the traveler who was looking for a place to enjoy the tropical climate without having to interact with the people who actually lived there. Because it was too expensive to be a local hangout, it was not so Grenadian that you couldn't shut your eyes and imagine yourself on almost any tropical island.

Sitting at the resort's poolside bar, staring out over the Caribbean, Peta listened to Simon talk about his memories of the man she loved. She didn't nag him again about the dive or the drinking. It was obvious that he was feeling his own mortality very acutely.

A couple of hours later, she delivered a considerably more mellow Simon into Frikkie's hands.

14

"Port of Spain is busier every time I see it," Simon said, admiring how gracefully Frik eased the sleek 120-foot *Assegai* into its berth at the private docks. Despite the residual effects of the lab accident to his left hand—and with the help of twin screws which made maneuvering easier—he operated the throttles with surgical skill.

Frik turned and grinned through the shade under the brim of his battered Panama hat. Barefoot, in white slacks and white shirt, he looked every inch the patrician yachtsman. "The busier the better," he said.

"Do I take that to mean you own a piece of the action?"

Another grin. "A big piece."

Just what Frikkie needs, Simon thought, looking around at the tankers and container-laden freighters that clogged the harbor and dwarfed the yacht. Another revenue stream.

In contrast to his host, Simon wore torn sneakers, raggedy cutoffs, and a profoundly ugly red-and-orange Hawaiian shirt—the uglier the better was his rule. With his bull frame and short silver hair, he'd been mistaken all over the world for Brian Keith by people blithely unaware that the actor had killed himself back in 1997. Thanks in large part to satellite TV, old shows and old stars seemed to live forever. He never disabused these folk of their mistaken notion, especially if they were female. Amazing how free women became with their favors in the presence of celebrity.

Simon tipped up the brim of his olive drab boonie cap, a concession to the skin of his face and ears, which was proving a gold mine for the dermatological profession, some of whose members were putting their kids through school as a result of all the little cancers they'd carved from his hide. Well, what could you expect after a lifetime in the tropical sun?

That sun hung hot and bright in the immaculate morning sky; the water lay calm below; a gentle briny breeze kept them cool on the afterdeck: a day to savor. But then, every day was a day to be savored when you'd been told time and again that you wouldn't have too many left unless you changed your ways. And what changes were those? Oh, not many, simply eliminate everything that elevated daily life from mere existence to something worth looking forward to.

Simon caught the eye of Frik's man Friday and held up his glass, rattling the cubes. "Another Bloody, if you please, Saaliim. There's a good lad, and make this one light . . . on the tomato juice, if you get my drift."

Saaliim grinned as he took the glass. "I hear you clear, Mr. Brousseau."

"How many is that?" Frik said, staring at Simon.

"I haven't been counting."

"Aren't you supposed to be cutting down?"

"Where'd you hear that?"

Frik pursed his lips. "I have my sources."

"Find new ones," Simon grumbled. "Yours are full of shit." He hid his annoyance by accepting the fresh Bloody Mary from the silver tray Saaliim proffered. He sipped, savoring the tang of the beef bouillon Saaliim always added to his pepper-laden tomato juice, and toasted the Honduran. "My compliments to the chef."

Three doctors now, four if you counted Peta, had told him the same thing: Take your prescriptions, cut the booze to two drinks a day, watch the saturated fats, drop thirty pounds, limit yourself to less energetic sex, and substitute snorkeling—which Simon had always thought of as *snore*keling—for scuba.

In other words, live small.

Simon didn't know how, nor did he wish to learn. Unless medical science took several giant leaps, he was going to die anyway, so why not go the way he had lived.

"Hell, Frikkie, just because I'm fifty-eight doesn't mean I'm ready for a nursing home."

"You're sixty-two, Simon, and I didn't mean—"

"I'm fine," he said, taking another gulp of his drink. "Fit as a fiddle—a frigging Stradivarius."

Yeah. One that's been run over by a truck.

According to the docs, he might be in his early sixties, but he had the heart of a man in his early eighties, and had to act accordingly—not run around like a guy in his thirties. He was suffering from a bad case of the ups and downs, with everything going in the wrong direction: his cholesterol, blood sugar, and blood pressure all up, his erections down. If he took his nitroglycerin on schedule, he could get through most activities, even sex, without chest pain; trouble was he couldn't get it up for sex without a dose of Viagra, but mixing Viagra and nitro will kill you. So what he'd do was skip the nitro and pay for an orgasm with the sensation of a bull elephant camping on his chest.

Getting old sucked.

"At least you stopped smoking."

Simon nodded. "Wasn't easy, but it got so every time I lit up it felt like the Marlboro cowboy's horse was taking a dump in my lungs, so I tossed them."

Frik laughed. "Simon Brousseau, ever the epitome of earthy."

"Yes, well, I've always believed in calling a spade a shit shovel," Simon responded, though he wasn't entirely sure how to take Frik's comment. At times like this he wished he'd had a little more education. Not that he regretted for an instant dropping out of Florida State, but when he was around people like Frik and Arthur and even Peta, and they'd mention the title of a book or recite a line from a play or a poem that he'd never read, he felt left out. He'd been boning up on Shakespeare—had a book of the Bard's plays in his duffel, in fact—but he was a long way from feeling comfortable with the strange sound of centuries-old English.

Maybe that was why he found the underwater world so alluring, and kept returning to it as often as he could. No subtexts with undersea life: if you're not looking for a meal you're trying to avoid becoming one.

He guessed growing up in Key West was a contributing factor too. He'd spent his youth living half a dozen feet above sea level, surrounded by reefs teeming with a mind-boggling array of life in a dazzling variety of shapes and colors that drew people from all over the world. Graduating from snorkeling to scuba at age eight, he was guiding tourists on a dive boat by the time he was twelve. Working as a salvage diver between his frosh and sophomore year, he along with a buddy found the wreck of the *Santa Clara*. The long-forgotten galleon wasn't a treasure ship, but Simon's share of the salvaged jewelry and doubloons was enough to set him up in his own salvage business and make returning to college seem like a waste of time.

He'd kept going after deeper and deeper wrecks, and when the available equipment and gas mixes weren't up to the job, he made his own modifications. Over the years the income from the patents on those innovations had left him a wealthy man. At age thirty he'd sold his business to become a scuba bum, hiring out for diving jobs that challenged his equipment and his nerve, and exploring the diving meccas of the world: off Yap, in the South Pacific, he'd gazed up in wonder from the sea floor at the schools of manta rays parading above; he'd hitched rides on the whale sharks of Ningaloo Bay; and, until two years ago, he'd held the deep-sea depth and endurance records.

Along the years he'd done a number of extreme dives for Frik, which eventually led to his induction into the club.

"Okay, down to business," Simon said, placing his empty glass on Saaliim's silver tray. "What haven't you told me about these doodads and the contraption they're part of?"

"Not much. And I think you'll better appreciate them if I show you rather than simply tell you."

As Frik led the way down the dock toward the parking lot, Simon heard quick footsteps padding up behind him.

"Excuse me?"

He turned to find a thirtyish brunette wearing a well-stuffed CCNY T-shirt and a bikini bottom.

"Mr. Keith," she said, smiling as she thrust her right hand forward; she held a pen and a cocktail napkin in her left. "I'm *such* a big fan of yours. Would it be too much to ask you for your autograph?"

Simon glanced around as he shook her hand. He leaned close and spoke in a half whisper. "I'd appreciate it if you didn't let this get around. I'm here scouting locations for a hush-hush project."

She lowered her voice to his level. "Really?"

"And when Stevie gets here, he'll want a little space."

"Stevie Wonder?"

"No." Simon lowered his voice further. "Spielberg."

"Ohmygod!" Her pale blue eyes widened as her hand flew to her mouth. "Oh! My! God!"

"Shhh!" he whispered, glancing around again and taking the pen and napkin from her. "Mum's the word." He scribbled something that might pass for "Brian Keith" on the napkin and passed it back to her. "Here. Write your name and number on the corner there and I'll give you a call when I get back in a couple of days."

"Sure." Her hand trembled as she wrote. She tore off the corner and handed it to him. "Really. Call me."

He glanced at the scrap, then gave her a lopsided grin. "Will do, Lori. Talk to you soon."

At the end of the dock he found Frik waiting by an idling dark green Hummer. "Who was that?"

"Just another of my many fans." He feigned astonishment as Frik slipped behind the wheel. "What? No driver?"

"Like with my boats, I prefer to drive my own cars," Frik said. "And besides, with no extra set of ears around, we can talk."

"Can it wait? I'm not in the mood for talk right now." The potent Bloodies had relaxed him into a deliciously dreamy haze.

The Afrikaner nodded, and Simon leaned back into his seat to watch Port of Spain's squares, parks, and surreal mix of Catholic churches, Muslim mosques, and Hindu and Jewish temples slip past the window. By the time they drove into the wooded uplands, he had tugged his cap down over his eyes and leaned back in the seat for a little siesta.

He awakened with a start as a loud thump was followed by Frik's shouted curses and the feel of the seat belt cinching across his chest. The Humvee jerked to a stop.

"Goddamn bastards!"

Simon straightened himself and looked around. They were on the outskirts of a little village. The reason for the sudden braking was splattered all over the hood and windshield. At first he thought they'd hit a small animal, but he soon realized what the yellow-orange pulp dotted with black BB-sized seeds really was. Someone had pelted them with an overripe papaya.

The Hummer's heavy-duty wipers and windshield washers made

quick work of the mess, and soon they were on their way again. As they roared through the village, Simon noticed an occasional raised fist and more than a few angry looks.

"I take it that piece of fruit didn't drop from a tree."

"Superstitious Trini clods," Frik said, eyes straight ahead.

"May I also assume it's not Humvees they're superstitious about?"

"It's the drill site. They've got some local legends about the Dragon's Mouth. They think drilling into the bottom there will offend the Obeahman and bring bad luck to the island."

Simon nodded. His years in the Caribbean had taught him a little about Obeah, though it was a much less well-known superstition than voodoo or Santeria. An Obeahman was a kind of sorcerer or shaman who controlled spirits which he could put into objects, like fetishes, and make them do his will.

Simon's one memorable encounter with an Obeahman was on Jamaica, where a buddy had almost hit one of them walking along the side of the road. The man threw something, which hit the car, and a moment later the engine sputtered and died. No matter what his friend did, the car wouldn't start. He had a mechanic tear the damn thing apart and put it back together like new, but it still wouldn't work. Finally, he tracked down the Obeahman and gave him two dozen chickens as penance. After that, the car never so much as backfired.

"Did you know this beforehand?"

"Of course."

"But you went ahead and drilled anyway."

"This is the twenty-first century, Simon. About time they moved into at least the twentieth, don't you think?"

"And you're going to move them?"

"My civic duty."

Simon smiled and shook his head. Typical Frikkie logic. If he wanted something, he could always find a rationale for why he should have it. The rest of the picture was coming into focus.

"So that's why you need me: the local boys say no way, José."

"I could find somebody," Frik said. "Haven't met a superstition yet that's proof against the right amount of cold hard cash. But I need someone comfortable in deep water. And most of all I need someone I can trust implicitly."

Simon appreciated the last remark, but he was more interested in the one before it.

"How deep?"

"Not sure. The drill broke into the cavern about seventy feet below the floor, and the floor is an average of one hundred and twenty feet down."

Simon nodded. That meant an operating depth of two hundred or more, at over eight atmospheres of pressure—just the kind of dive the docs had warned him against. But what did they know? They weren't divers. He'd done it before.

"I'll need mixed gases, a tri-mix."

Frik glanced at him. "What's that?"

"A deep-diving nitrox mix that lowers your oxygen for the bottom time, and raises the other gases. You have to know what you're doing, lowering one gas, raising the other. You couldn't breathe that mix at the surface. . . . It would kill you."

"I'll have all the tanks you'll ever need waiting on the platform."

Frik turned off the road and stopped before a heavy wrought-iron gate with "Oilstar" arching above it. The guard waved from his narrow kiosk as the gates swung open, and they were on the move again. He swerved the vehicle to a stop before a row of low white stucco buildings, and led Simon into the first.

After rattling off a string of orders to a male secretary—one of them arranging for tri-mix at the drill site—he motioned Simon around behind his large mahogany desk. A few taps on his keyboard popped an array of thumbnail photos onto his computer screen.

"These are scans and three-D models of the artifacts," Frik said, clicking on each to enlarge them.

Four objects filled the screen in succession, each more bizarre than the last. The final scan showed all four locked together into some weird-looking shape. Frik hit a key, and the shape began to rotate in three dimensions. Simon didn't know much about art, but this looked like something Picasso might have pieced together. Or Dali.

"Why scans? Where's the real thing?"

"The one piece I have of it is under guard."

"It's that valuable?"

Frik shrugged. "Not sure yet. I won't know until I have all five pieces and fit them together."

"And the fifth is somewhere in an undersea cavern." He shook his head. "Christ, why don't you fly me to the Chesapeake and ask me to find one particular oyster."

"Oh, come now," Frik said, grinning. "It's not that bad. This will be a piece of cake for someone like you."

Simon stared at the rotating assemblage. Something about each piece had bothered him, but the aggregate was even worse. He had a feeling that finding the final piece might not be such a good thing.

15

Simon checked his depth gauge: the arrow lay just a hair to the far side of the 130 mark. Even at this depth he was comfortable in a 1.5-mm dive skin.

He looked around. The light level was decent, typical for this depth, though the true colors of the fish and coral were washed out. Sunlight's spectrum got pretty well bleached out after struggling through 130 feet of water.

He'd hoped he'd be diving the cavern through the bore hole, much like descending the limestone cenotes in the waters of the Yucatán, but the hole was too small and there was no hope of widening it any further. So he went hunting for the natural entrance to the cavern. He found it, a dark, narrow, anemone-fringed opening in the wall of a rift in the continental shelf. The wall was encrusted with sponges, guzzling the fringe of the Guyana Current as it swept nutrients up from Venezuela's Orinoco River.

Simon also found the missing diver, Abdul. A rock the size of a Porsche Boxster—loosened by the drilling, perhaps?—had slipped from the wall above the opening and crushed him. The crabs and yellowtails had been snacking on his exposed flesh, but his mask was still fastened around his head, sparing his wide-open, milky eyes. Their empty gaze brought back a few lines he'd just read in *The Tempest*:

> *Full fathom five thy father lies;*
> *Of his bones are coral made;*
> *Those are pearls that were his eyes. . . .*

Simon shuddered and looked away. A sight like that could make you believe in the Obeahman. Empty sockets would have been better.

The stone had also partially blocked the mouth of the entrance. The opening that remained might admit a child but never an adult, especially one of Simon's girth.

Which meant the stone had to be moved. And since the local labor pool consisted of himself and one curious green sea turtle, that meant it was up to him.

After a thorough inspection, he found a spot where he could wedge himself between the rock and the rift wall. It meant disturbing some sponges and dislodging some of the smaller clinging sea life, something Simon loathed doing. The Caribbean reefs took enough abuse without his adding to it.

But he had no choice.

With knees bent almost to his chest, his flippers against the rock and his back against the wall, he took a deep breath and kicked out with everything he had. After half a minute of straining, he felt the rock move. Heartened, he found a little extra strength and increased his effort.

Slowly, moving a fraction of an inch at a time, the rock began to tilt away from him. Simon squeezed shut his eyes and, shouting into his regulator's mouthpiece, pushed even harder.

And then he stopped, gasping as a crushing weight slammed against his chest. He opened his eyes and wouldn't have been surprised to find that the rock had fallen back on him, pinning him to the wall. But no, the rock was falling away, tumbling end over end in slow motion toward the floor of the rift. The pain was coming from his heart. He could feel that battered old pump pounding out an irregular beat, thudding in his ears as his vision wavered.

He slowed his lungs, taking deep, measured breaths, hoping his heart would follow suit, and cursing himself for being so careless as to have left behind his backup nitros, the fast-acting sublingual tablets for when his angina broke through the extended-release pills.

As he prayed for the pain to ease, proving this wasn't the Big One, motion to his left caught his eye.

Abdul, free of the entrapping rock, was pulling away from the wall and gliding toward Simon. His face came closer, his dead wide eyes staring into Simon's as if to say, *Join me . . . Join me. . . .*

With his face close enough to kiss, Abdul turned away. His bloated body began a slow ascent, belly first, arms and legs dangling behind, returning at last to the world of air and light it had departed.

Just as slowly, the crushing weight lifted from Simon's chest. His heart slowed. Just angina. A bad attack, but the 40 percent oxygen in his tanks had helped.

He pushed away from the wall and stared at the now wide-open passage into the cavern. No way. Not today. He didn't have the strength. He'd make up an excuse for Frikkie, tell him about the stone, tell him he'd used up too much daylight moving it, tell him he'd finish the job tomorrow under the high morning sun, tell him anything except the truth about his heart.

Not that his health would prompt Frik even to consider calling off the dive. *A shark bit off your left leg? So? The right one still works. Get back down there and find me that fifth piece!*

No, it was no one else's business.

Tomorrow. Tomorrow he'd find Frik's damn doodad with no problems, no complications.

Right now what he needed was a drink.

Weak, tired, and perhaps even a little depressed, Simon shot a bolus of air into his vest and began a controlled ascent.

16

McKendry and Keene walked confidently along the docks in Puerto La Cruz, fostering the impression that they knew where they were going. At the terminal, the giant tanker *Yucatán* rested far enough offshore that the long walkway looked like a tiny bridge that extended hundreds of yards out into the muddy green water. Pipes paralleled the walkway, heading from the port and the tank farm, the fractionating towers, and the smelly refinery equipment that had turned what must have been a beautiful jungle coastline into an industrial nightmare.

Bleed-off gas flames burned and hissed from the tops of derricks, and gasoline trucks drove around, taking a small fraction of the production to Venezuelan markets. Other tankers came into the port to fill up and redistribute the petroleum products, but the *Yucatán* used the facilities in reverse. It brought fresh crude from the offshore rig to the refineries, rather than hauling separated petroleum of different grades away from the port and to other customers.

Passing a poorly guarded chain-link gate, McKendry strode behind Keene down the walkway, listening to the water lap against the pilings—a peaceful sound compared to the chaos of inland refineries.

"Let's get this set up as soon as we can," Keene called out. "We've got better things to do."

McKendry marched forward with determined strides. He saw his partner look back and cover a smile, doubtless Keene's response to the way he always took everything so seriously.

On the way out to the deck of the tanker, a bored-looking security guard stopped them, probably more suspicious of the two because they were white-skinned Americans than for any other reason. Keene invoked the only name that would matter to the man. "We have an appointment with Miguel Calisto. El capitán? Comprende?"

The guard scowled, but waved them onward.

After they had walked across a deck as big as several football fields and climbed six flights of rickety metal stairs that led up alongside the crew housing and habitation areas, McKendry and Keene stood on the bridge deck.

Within moments, the first mate approached them. "You are not allowed up here."

Keene said again that they had a meeting scheduled with the captain. Eventually, the mate conceded and led them to the captain's quarters.

Miguel Calisto was a ruddy-skinned man whose long pointed chin was graced with a scouring pad of a beard. A rim of dark hair surrounded the gleaming bald spot on the back of his head like a crown. He listened to what the two men had to say, but exhibited no patience with them whatsoever.

"Your request is most audacious," the tanker captain said, choosing to speak English. He narrowed his eyes and sat down at his small desk in the cramped ready room off the bridge. "The *Yucatán* is not a passenger ship. We don't give rides to curiosity seekers. My crew is not here to pamper Americans."

"On the contrary," McKendry said, remembering the too-soft beds and too-garish nightclubs they had endured in Caracas. "We don't want to be pampered."

"Amen," Keene muttered.

"In fact, we don't even want the rest of your crew to know we're aboard. We'd rather find a corner down in the pump room or the engine control room. Keep ourselves out of the way where no one can see us. We're investigating a potential . . . threat."

"Top secret," Keene added.

"I'm afraid that is not possible," the captain said. His lips became thin and hard, like the slash of a scowl. "Yes, indeed. Most impossible."

McKendry looked at the man, trying to discern whether he was opening a door to a large bribe or if he simply enjoyed playing hard to get. Calisto seemed honestly indignant, with no interest in providing passage for the two men, regardless of the circumstances.

Keene stepped in, speaking in the man's own language. "We understand your position, Captain. However, this is a serious political matter. I'm sure that you understand the delicacy of the arrangements between Oilstar and the Venezuelan government. If anything should happen to interfere with that . . . relationship, many people could be out of jobs."

"Show him the faxes," McKendry said.

Keene took out letters from Juan Ortega de la Vega Bruzual for the Security Ministry, and Fredrick Van Alman for Oilstar, both of which firmly requested cooperation "in whatever these two gentlemen desire."

The captain sighed. "Politics!" He practically spat out the word.

"If you wish, we will pass on your reluctance to Minister Bruzual"— McKendry could see by his flinch that Calisto recognized the security minister's name—"and arrange for you to discuss the matter with him. However, he's a busy man and may not take too kindly to being disturbed."

"I'd prefer to know more about your . . . activities," the captain said. "What are you trying to do?"

Keene's nostrils flared. "I will have Señor Bruzual contact you. You will be able to ask him as many questions as you like, provided you still have a job."

The captain gave best. "What is it you want of me?"

McKendry saw his partner's relief. "We need to go with you to the *Valhalla* platform and return here, if necessary."

"Why?"

"Yours is not to reason why."

McKendry shot Keene a look to tell him to let up a little.

"After we load from the *Valhalla* platform, I'm going up to the Caribbean next," the captain said. "Not back to Puerto La Cruz."

"Wherever." Keene shrugged his shoulders. "We'll manage."

"There's a utility closet down in the pump room. No one goes there except for maintenance, and we're not due for any. You're welcome to stay there. Sleep if you can." Calisto reached up to point at a chart on the wall, a large and detailed map of the Venezuelan coast and the Caribbean.

"We'll head out of here in an hour and make our way around the Araya Peninsula between the coast and la Isla Margarita"—the captain's finger traced a line along the northeastern coast of Venezuela—"around the Paria Peninsula through the Dragon's Mouth"—his finger passed through the narrow patch of blue between the point of the Venezuelan coast and the northern edge of Trinidad—"down the Gulf of Paria and into the Serpent's Mouth to the *Valhalla* platform."

"Sounds reasonable to me," Keene said.

The captain looked at him as if he believed he was not all there. "Remember the map well, because you won't have a view. There are no windows in the pump room."

"We're not tourists," McKendry said.

The captain nodded. "Very well. There will be a new moon tonight. We will arrive at the pumping station at approximately ten o'clock. Most of my crew take a boat over to the *Valhalla* for their replacements. Until then, you are to stay in your quarters. Around midnight they should all be out of the way and you can safely come out on deck."

17

After countless hours hidden in the cramped metal-walled crawl space down in the *Yucatán*'s pump room, Keene's idea of what was and wasn't reasonable had undergone a 180-degree change. The passage so far had been long and dreary, with nothing to see, no creature comforts, and too much time for reflection. He would have liked to play a card game or even do something as simple-minded as tic-tac-toe.

Anything to keep himself from thinking about Arthur. By now, after so many years and so many adventures in the Daredevils Club, it should have been easy to accept the death of a member—par for the course. But it was never easy. Were it not for this confinement, the loss of Arthur would have come in sharp stabs of pain, engendered not so much by memories as by sights and sounds that reminded him of his friend. Out of deference to his partner, who was perfectly content to spend the time in silent contemplation, he did not suggest any trivial amusements.

The droning engines stopped a little after eleven-thirty as the tanker pulled up to the *Valhalla*'s secondary pumping pier. Keene glanced at the luminous dial of his watch. "Nearly two hours late. Our Captain Calisto seems to be a true Venezuelan. Mañana, mañana . . . What do you say we give them half an hour to anchor themselves and get the crew off before we wander up and take a look around?"

McKendry didn't answer.

"Hey, Sleeping Beauty," Keene said.

This time, McKendry's answer was a light snore.

As Keene fidgeted impatiently, an idea began to take form. By midnight, it had become a plan. He tore a page out of the small notebook he carried in his pocket. Using a red felt pen he'd found on the floor, he wrote *midnight* at the top of the page. Then he wrote a brief note to McKendry, who would be awakened soon enough by the silence of the engines:

> *Always wanted to piss into the wind from a great height so I'm swimming over to the rig to play King of the Hill. If you can't see me swimming back by 2 a.m., start worrying.*

He threw the pen aside, placed the note where McKendry was sure to see it upon waking, and, groping his way up the metal staircase, left their quarters. Practiced in moving stealthily without losing time, he made his way up the seven decks to the bulkhead door that opened onto the sprawling main deck of the tanker.

Once outside, he took a welcome breath of fresh, albeit humid, air and looked around.

The empty supertanker *Yucatán* was anchored under quicksilver starlight in a calm black sea, about a quarter of a mile from the monolithic offshore oil-production platform. The rig itself stood like a skyscraper on the ocean, raised up out of the water on four enormous concrete piers like stilts. The platform's tall derrick, numerous cranes, helipad, and flare boom rode several hundred feet above the water. The long shaft through its center plunged down into the sea bottom like the proboscis of a voracious mosquito.

Keene had once invested a small amount of money in offshore drilling. The investment had led to a significant amount of reading for which, he thought, he was presently grateful. Without that, he would not have had the vaguest understanding of what was going on. Because of it, he knew that the *Valhalla* rig pumped crude oil from strata deep beneath the sea, but did not bring it up into the big platform itself; instead, the fresh crude was shunted to a pipeline laid across the ocean floor toward a separate derrick, a stand-alone pumping station to which the oil tanker was secured.

On a crane high above the secondary platform, heavy nozzles dangled downward. With the cargo holds of the *Yucatán* open beneath them like the gaping mouths of hungry birds, the crude oil from the *Valhalla* rig gushed out of the nozzles, filling the numerous interconnected but compartmentalized chambers that made up the bulk of the tanker.

The *Yucatán* had a double hull, an outer shell to avoid punctures of the inner compartments—extremely conservative efforts designed to prevent disastrous oil spills. The crude petroleum poured out from the pumping platform at an enormous flow rate, but even so it would take many hours to fill the supertanker. The respite gave plenty of time for most of the *Yucatán*'s crew members to shuttle over to the relative metropolis of the *Valhalla* rig.

Keene was struck by how much the tanker's deck looked like the Great Plains, only uglier. The expanse was dirty and stained, a long series of riveted metal plates studded with hatches and vent chimneys. Lines of different colors—red, blue, and yellow—were painted in patterns across the deck, zone demarcations of some sort. The hieroglyphics were too large for anyone to make out at this level. He figured that they were something like the lines and roads Incas had made in the South American plains, depicting giant shapes visible only from high-flying aircraft.

The crane holding the hoses from the pumping substation extended down into the prow's main hatch, pouring into the primary tank holds. Behind them, the tall nine-deck structure of the bridge housing and habitation levels looked the size of an office complex. Lights blazed from the windows, gleaming up on the *Yucatán*'s radar mast and the long cable of the radio antenna.

Keene fixed his gaze on the huge structure of the *Valhalla* platform a quarter mile away. Holding the tanker's deck rail, he stared at the rig—a dazzling cluster of lights riding high above the gentle Caribbean waves. A torch of natural gas blasted from the end of the flare tip which extended on a long derrick far from the rest of the structure. A tall derrick stood like the Eiffel Tower in the center of the airport-sized deck.

When he saw a challenge like that, he had to go for it. The central derrick was the highest thing around. He wanted to touch it, the way a kid reaches for the star on the top of the Christmas tree. McKendry would say he was thinking crazy—which was true. On the other hand, that was what he was good at.

Keene stripped to his shorts. He climbed down the metal ladder on the outer hull of the *Yucatán* and plunged into the tropical waters. The water was calm and warm, and the tanker and the production rig were huge landmarks even under the pallid moonlight. A powerful swimmer, he estimated that he could relax and cross the distance in less than twenty minutes.

Just enough to work up a little sweat, he thought, interrupting his steady, gentle strokes to tread water so that he could look up at the star-studded night sky. Neither the weather nor the distance concerned him. Unlike McKendry, he didn't have a problem with whatever critters inhabited the depths of these Caribbean waters.

He recalled one time on Lake Tahoe. A couple of dancers had taken the two of them on one of those boat tours around the lake. About halfway around, one of the women took it into her head to move to the rail and yell, "Shark!"

To give him his due, McKendry hadn't been the only one to go on automatic and suspend disbelief. However, while the others moved to the rail on a shark watch, McKendry paled and moved farther away from it.

Time to get over it, buddy, Keene thought, laughing out loud. As far as he was concerned, if he couldn't outswim a shark for a mere quarter of a mile, then he wasn't much of a swimmer.

Stroke after stroke after stroke.

Doing nicely, Keene thought, a little surprised despite himself. He was feeling the effort in his muscles, but that was to be expected. It had been some time since he or McKendry had done any serious exercise. His partner would feel the strain every bit as much.

Closing in on the *Valhalla* platform, thinking about his partner, Keene became aware of the sleek death of sharks swimming below. The idea, he admitted to himself, was not exactly pleasant. He wanted to believe that the noise and chemical leakage and higher temperatures from the offshore structure would drive away such predators, but he knew differently. Part of his education as a short-term investor had taught him that the environment around oil platforms was a boon for fish, and with the increased schools living among the concrete support pillars, he supposed that sharks might also hang out in the better feeding grounds.

He increased his speed, and was happy to reach the shadow of the platform and pull himself up to the metal rungs alongside the fat elephant leg of the pier. Better not rest here, he told himself. You look like somebody's midnight snack. He grasped the rungs and scrambled up, not stopping until he was ten feet out of the water.

Access ladders led up the concrete support legs to the main platform. He looked at the long line of rungs waiting for him. It was quite a way to climb, especially if he wanted to make it to the top of the central derrick in good time.

He climbed higher, to the underpart of the main platform. It hung like a broad airplane hangar above him. Lifeboats dangled under the deck; in an emergency, they could drop a hundred feet down to the sea. Keene recalled having read somewhere that more people were killed during oil rig safety drills testing out the hazardous systems than had ever been hurt in other kinds of accidents on oil rigs.

He listened to the waves echoing in the superstructure, looked at the immense core of the *Valhalla,* and found himself awed that something this huge could be built in a harbor and towed out to sea to be anchored elsewhere.

"Moving on up," he said into the wind.

He began to climb again. Once he reached the undercarriage of the main platform, he followed catwalks, ascended metal steps, ducked through hatches until he stood on the main deck.

A helipad covered a large, flat circle atop the main platform. Next to that was an oil-processing area filled with huge tanks and a nightmare maze of piping. Radio masts and cranes protruded like spines from the rig.

At any moment, Keene expected to be stopped by a security patrol, but the platform supervisors were ridiculously complacent in their security. The pumps and generators hummed and clanked, making loud sounds in the night, but he met no one. Most of the blazing lights he had seen from a distance seemed to be for decorative purposes only, except for the natural blowtorch off to the side; the flare tip hissed and blasted its perpetual flame, removing excess natural gas from the operations.

Keene sprinted across the platform deck toward the central derrick, which stood like a skyscraper in the middle of the *Valhalla.* He could have taken an elevator, of course, but that would have been too easy. And too noisy. Even sleeping security guards could be awakened if the noise was loud enough. Instead, he took the winding ribbon of metal stairs around and around the iron latticework of the structure, heading toward the narrow tip that supported the rig's central production shaft and pipe.

Panting heavily, dripping with sweat, he reached the top platform. The sultry breeze brushed his sweaty chest. Between breaths, he could hear the whispers and clatter of the rig's superstructure, the thrumming guide wires and anchor cables holding the various portions in place. A searchlight beacon flashed around and around in a slow strobe, signaling low-flying aircraft of the danger.

He stood in silence, grinning at the night and gripping the rails. Under stormy seas, he thought, this place must dance like a hiccuping marionette. He looked around the top level. Like a crow's nest on an old sailing ship, it was adorned with the spikes of lightning rods and radio towers.

He raised his fist in the air and gave a short yelp of triumph. "I'm King of the Hill."

Good as that felt, it was not enough to gratify Keene. Still needing completion, he went to the edge, pulled down his shorts, and urinated. Then, grinning and satisfied, he sat down, leaned against the rails, and fell asleep.

The sound of an insomniac seagull woke him from his nap. Not until the third successive squawk did it occur to him that the gull was McKendry, at the bottom of the derrick.

Keene's watch read one-thirty. Unable to believe that his light-hearted infiltration had gone so smoothly, he descended slowly and carefully into the shadows.

"You dumb son of a bitch!"

McKendry's words and fist hit Keene simultaneously. Keene reeled and swiped at his nosebleed. "Are you crazy, McKendry? You've probably broken my nose."

"You have about as much sense as a centipede," McKendry said, clinging fast to the iron rung Keene had used to descend the derrick.

"At least now we'll have a story to tell next New Year's Eve."

"You'll have a story to tell. I probably won't make it." McKendry let go of the rung and sank to the deck. He held one hand over his left ribs. With the other, he pointed at his foot. "Shark," he said, his voice reduced now to the slightest whisper.

"Oh my God!" Keene fell to his knees. In the dim light, he could see huge, red blotches, leaking around the protection of his partner's hand and running across his ankle. "McKendry, I'm so sorry. Oh my God!"

"Could you . . . could you kiss it better," McKendry whispered.

Keene looked up and into his partner's eyes.

"And while you're at it, Joshua, could you . . ."

McKendry's voice was so close to being inaudible that Keene had to lean into it. "Anything, buddy."

"Good," McKendry said, whimpering. "Then you can kiss my ass." He wiped one of the red blotches vigorously. It paled as it left a stain on his fingers.

"The red pen," Keene said.

"The red pen, *buddy*."

"You scared the shit out of me," Keene said.

"I meant to."

"I'm sorry I . . . um . . . pulled your leg."

"We're supposed to be looking for Selene Trujold, not running around at two in the morning playing King of the Hill. As long as we find her, we'll call it even." He paused. "Since we're here, I'd like to take another look around. But first, would you mind telling me what possessed you to pull off this dumb stunt and jeopardize the whole mission?"

"I pissed on the world from up there," Keene said halfheartedly.

"Was it worth it?"

For a moment Keene was quiet. "Yes, it was." He decided to give an honest answer, though he didn't expect McKendry to fully understand. "Listen, we're out here and we're ready for whatever happens. Right now, everything's quiet. We've already spent weeks sitting around in Caracas, taking canoe trips through the Orinoco Delta, drinking beer in dockside cantinas. I had to do *something,* Terris."

He raised his eyebrows and spread out his hands innocently, indicating the ghost town of the oil platform.

"Had to find myself a story to tell. Just in case."

18

Two black Zodiac rafts filled with commandos sped across the channel of the Serpent's Mouth. They had eased out of one of the many mouths of the Orinoco Delta at midnight; after two hours Selene Trujold could just now make out the shape of the *Yucatán* near the gleaming beacon that was the *Valhalla* platform. There was half an hour's worth of water still to cross, the last of it with engines off, moving in silence.

Around her in the rafts, the commandos wore dark suits and carried a stash of black-market weapons, rifles, hand grenades, and explosives. They had night-vision goggles to enable them to direct night operations, but she knew that the Caribbean stars would give them all the illumination they needed.

Her Green Impact fighters were well trained and high-strung, keyed up for this assault, which had been a full month in the planning. Their information had proved correct: the tanker *Yucatán* was lashed to the *Valhalla*'s separate pumping platform during the darkest hours of the night. Though the normal complement of crew members aboard the tanker outnumbered them, Green Impact had both weapons and determination.

And they had a plan, not the least component of which was the element of surprise.

Selene narrowed her eyes and looked around. "We have to time this properly," she said. "We know their routine. During the day, the *Valhalla* needs all of its two hundred crew members aboard. That's why the company gives them time for R and R at night. When the tanker pulls up and begins filling, most of the crew will go over to the *Valhalla* to party with the other workers. During the dead of night, there's only a skeleton crew aboard the tanker. That's when we strike."

Quiet and intent, the members of her force nodded and listened, though they had heard this briefing several times already.

"We are going to hijack the *Yucatán,* get rid of the remaining few aboard. We'll take them prisoner if possible, but don't waste any precious time. Then we disengage the pump and head out. The load should be mostly full by the time we're ready to go. Enough to cause the kind of disaster that *nobody* will be able to ignore. If you have any questions, ask them now."

Selene fingered the relic that hung from her neck, wondering yet one more time what it was. Nothing in her knowledge of physics or the related sciences provided any inkling as to its origins. She'd had it embedded in bark and suspended from a strip of leather soon after Manny Sheppard had delivered it and told her of her father's death. The pendant's smooth, irregular edges bit into the joints of her fingers. She rubbed the fragment's slick, strangely greasy surface. It seemed to have a unique combination of heat and ice deep inside it.

Manny's delivery had also contained a note from her father, telling her of the importance of the contents of the package—and of how Frikkie Van Alman meant to abuse his connections and the resources of Oilstar to exploit the secrets it held. Her father's words had left her under no illusion as to who had been responsible for his death: he had dared to defy Van Alman, and had paid for that defiance with his life.

While this assault fit well within the parameters of Green Impact's agenda, she was doing this for him. She was about to cause a financial disaster, a public relations disaster, and an ecological disaster. And it would all be blamed on Frikkie Van Alman. The media would need a scapegoat, and the pompous CEO would be led to the slaughterhouse.

In comparison, the *Exxon Valdez* spill would become a mere footnote in history. And her father would rest more easily.

The Zodiacs roared forward, plowing through the open waters of the Serpent's Mouth. The charcoal black sides of the rafts were large inflated tubes, big enough that even her largest man would have trouble getting his arms all the way around. The tubes angled up and together in the front, forming a point. Between the tubes, a hard fiberglass hull gave the riders a place to sit, and at the rear, the outboard motor was mounted to the squared-off aft of the hull.

Relinquishing her hold on the pendant, Selene balanced against the rubber eyelets of the black raft. Through the hum of the powerful outboard motor and the whisper of the waves, she could hear her father's ghost laughing.

She herself wouldn't laugh until the bloodshed and the horror of the next few hours were done.

Soon enough, the bulwark of the Oilstar *Yucatán* loomed up out of the water, surrounded by starlight. Selene and her assault team switched off the motors of their dark Zodiac rafts. From that point on, they approached cautiously and in silence.

The garish display of the monstrous production platform sparkled like the contents of a treasure chest. Selene wished they could do something against that target—the *real* target—but her small group had no chance against something as big as the *Valhalla*. There were two hundred people on board. Her group could cause some damage, but they'd all be killed.

On the other hand, if her information was correct and the timing worked out properly, Green Impact could get aboard the tanker and deal with the skeleton crew. Her group would have a chance of survival—and the oil-laden *Yucatán* would certainly make a sufficient statement for their cause.

With whispered commands and information communicated through gestures, the two Zodiacs approached the tanker from the rear. The *Yucatán* sat far from the towering offshore platform, drinking deeply of the crude petroleum that poured down into its holds from the pumping station.

They coasted closer to the stained hull of the ship. Next to her, one of the men stifled an outcry and lunged away from the side of the Zodiac. The large inflatable raft jerked and bumped as something struck it from beneath and swam away, a shadow disappearing into darkness.

"Great white," the man said.

"Fortunately, we're not going swimming," Selene said. "Our business is aboard the tanker."

A couple of men chuckled quietly.

The commandos lashed their two rafts to the lower rungs of the metal ladder on the tanker's hull. Moving like shadows, they climbed to the deck, all but one man, whose task it was to tie the rafts together and move them around to the bow in readiness for the planned escape.

If nothing untoward happened, they could all make it back to the encampment.

In deciding which Green Impact members to take with her from their primary jungle compound, Selene had selected the most dedicated ones, those most ready to follow orders and do what had to be done. These people would be called upon to kill. In an operation like this, she couldn't risk someone flinching or hesitating at the wrong moment.

The Green Impact commandos had studied detailed blueprints of the Oilstar *Yucatán,* memorizing every cranny, every deck plate. They had a fairly good idea of where the tanker's remaining crew members would be. Most would be snoozing in their cabins, perhaps grumbling that they couldn't go to the *Valhalla* platform like the others. Captain Calisto would almost certainly be in his private stateroom taking care of small details and reveling in the peace and quiet. He loved his ship and would not be the least bit interested in leaving her for R and R.

The assault team carried their packs of weapons, ammunition, and explosives. Upon reaching the deck, they stashed the more fragile items they wouldn't need until after they'd dealt with the crew. Then they split up, moving in small groups with separate, well-rehearsed objectives.

Selene and three companions marched up to the officers' quarters while the others entered the lower levels of crew cabins, rec rooms, and mess hall. The first muffled gunshots rang out as she reached the captain's private stateroom. The door was partially ajar, so she could see his expression as he whirled around, astonished to hear the weapons fire from below.

Her three companions held out their assault rifles and Selene took a step forward. "I'm sorry about the disturbance, Captain Calisto." Her voice was quiet; commanding. "We need to have a word with you."

19

"At least you didn't suggest climbing out there to roast marshmallows." McKendry pointed at the jet of flame coming from a pipe extended away from the rig, burning off the waste gases before they could build up and become a danger.

Keene managed a soft chortle. It blended into the murmur of music and laughter that came from the complex of living quarters. "They seem to be having a party down there," he said.

"Another egregious security lapse. Oilstar could certainly use our services as security consultants," McKendry said.

"I'll consider making the offer to Frik." Keene touched his nose, which had begun to ache from McKendry's punch.

From what he could tell, so many people worked on the rig that it was like a condominium complex. He imagined what it must be like to live in a small cabin, to share common rooms. "Not the life for me," he said. "Hard work, long hours, boredom—"

"None of which excuses the lack of security. *Nobody* tried to stop you?"

Keene shook his head. "I didn't see a single human being. This place is wide open to an attack." They strolled around the platform, looking in all directions. "I can't believe Frik Van Alman is so blind. If Selene Trujold means to strike this rig, she won't have much trouble."

"Especially if she shows up tonight." McKendry glanced at his watch. "It's almost two-thirty. We should get back to the tanker before the replacement crew decides to do its job and head over there. We can talk to Calisto in the morning and maybe get him to call Frikkie and set up some better security here."

"I'm all for that, buddy. Let's go."

They climbed back down the leg of the platform as quickly as possible, not pausing to admire the view of the tanker a quarter mile away. As they swam across the placid water toward the *Yucatán,* Keene thought he sensed movement below him. Despite his professed lack of fear, he got set to defy the laws of motion if he encountered any contact with an undersea creature.

"Hey, McKendry," he called out. "Did you ever read any of those Peter Benchley books? You know, *Jaws, The Beast, White Shark?*"

"Idiot," McKendry yelled back, but he put on some speed. Keene was impressed by how little fear there was in his partner's response. See, he said to himself, it was for your own good, Terris.

"I hope the replacement crew hasn't come back yet," McKendry said, climbing out of the water and scaling the tanker's hull ladder.

Keene was right behind him. "If they have, we might have a harder time sneaking back to our presidential suite down in the pump room. Let's see if the captain's awake. Maybe we can talk ourselves into a decent meal."

They had reached the deck. Keene could see a group of people at the far end of the tanker, disengaging the long hose that had been filling the *Yucatán*'s hold for hours. The shadowy workers made no noise, quietly going through the motions with all the finesse of a Green Beret squadron instead of a crowd of roughnecks.

"A meal sounds fine to me. I'm so hungry I could eat a shark." McKendry grinned.

"Better than the other way around," Keene responded. He yawned. "It's after three in the morning. Asleep or awake, Calisto's likely to be in his stateroom."

They entered the crew quarters, climbed up another level, and reached the larger rooms where the crew and officers slept. McKendry sniffed and frowned. "Do you smell that? Gunpowder. Cordite . . . blood."

"Looking for trouble, McKendry?" Keene said. They had reached the captain's stateroom. The door was not entirely shut and light spilled out. "Captain?"

Keene tapped lightly on the door. McKendry pushed it wide open. Both men froze.

Captain Miguel Calisto lay dead in his chair, shot three times in the chest. Pools of blood seeped along the floor.

Keene looked at McKendry. "I get the feeling," he said, "that we just found Selene."

Before McKendry could respond, the powerful engines of the Oilstar *Yucatán* roared to life. With a lurch, the supertanker began to move. The deck vibrated as the tanker crawled away, detaching itself from the pumping station and heading out into the Caribbean.

"Okay, genius. What now?" McKendry raised his voice above the noise of the engines.

"We arm ourselves." Keene swiped his knuckles across the sweat on his forehead. "He's got to have a gun here somewhere."

He was talking as much to Captain Calisto, slumped in his wooden desk chair, as he was to McKendry. The captain's corpse was still cooling. An occasional drop of blood oozed from his gunshot wounds, playing counterpoint to the groan of the tanker engines that shuddered through the walls of the bridge superstructure and the crew housing.

"I'd settle for a baseball bat," McKendry said. Keene knew that his partner was too intent on the imminent crisis to waste words. He moved from cabinet to cabinet, methodically opening cupboard doors, sliding the front panel on an old metal credenza.

Though he could smell the sour blood and the bitter residue of gunfire in the air, Keene, like McKendry, ignored the carnage and ransacked the captain's office. Unlike his methodical partner, his mode was to rifle the captain's desk with all the organization of a squall at sea. He found nothing useful: two well-watched Spanish-language porn videotapes, three battered paperback novels, some paperwork, a stack of photos that variously showed a grinning Calisto with what seemed to be six different women. The wide middle drawer held pencils, office paraphernalia. A few thin ledgers contained uninspired captain's logs.

The bottom left desk drawer was locked.

"This must be it." Keene tugged on the metal handle and pried into the crack without success, making a loud rattling noise that he knew would put McKendry on edge. When the drawer didn't open, he reached into the central desk drawer and withdrew a letter opener. Though he snapped the blade off in the hasp of the drawer lock, he finally succeeded in jarring it open. "Now we're getting somewhere."

He slid open the drawer and rummaged inside. "Nothing but crap!"

McKendry came forward, looked down, and frowned. He pulled out a half-empty bottle of cheap scotch whiskey. "I guess the captain was more worried about someone stealing his booze than his—"

He melted back behind the metal cabin door as footsteps resounded in the corridor outside. A man entered, clearly one of the terrorists. He had high cheekbones, dark hair slicked back with seawater, and a gray jumpsuit with plenty of bulging pockets. His wide black belt was studded with the handles of several weapons or tools.

"Damn," he said. He stared at Joshua Keene. "Looks like we missed one."

Keene tried to grin disarmingly. "I'm looking for the gents' room. Can you direct me, please?"

The terrorist grabbed for a weapon at his belt.

"I don't think so." Terris McKendry sprang out from behind the cabin door. Holding the heavy bottle of scotch, he swung it down with the force of a sledgehammer. With a solid crunch of impact between skull and booze bottle, the stranger's cranium lost the duel. The golden brown liquid sloshed in the bottle as, head bloodied, the terrorist crumpled to the deck.

Keene dragged the man deeper into the cabin and closed the door with a kick of his heel. The fallen terrorist did not let out so much as a groan, and Keene didn't bother to check whether or not he was alive.

McKendry nudged the motionless form with the toe of his shoe. "Green Impact." There was no question in his voice. He wiped off the scotch bottle and set it next to the man, as if to offer him a good stiff drink to send him to the underworld.

Raising an eyebrow at his friend, Keene said, "You didn't spill a drop." He looked down at the body. "I don't see a badge or anything, but I believe you're correct. We can make the assumption that Selene Trujold and her goons decided to hit this tanker instead of the *Valhalla* platform, like Frik thought."

"Frik isn't always right."

"Maybe she considered this just a warm-up exercise."

McKendry reached down and pried the dead man's hand away from his weapon. Instead of a handgun, the terrorist had been trying to draw a large knife, well sharpened, good for throwing or filleting. McKendry took it, examined the wide blade, and shook his head. "Damn macho South Americans. Can't they carry a regular firearm like everyone else?"

He slid the knife into his belt just as his partner found the ship-to-shore phone behind the captain's desk.

"Who do we call? Rescue? Venezuelan military? Trinidad's coast guard?"

"It's gotta be Frik," McKendry said. "He's not gonna want this to be handled by anybody but his own people."

Keene punched in the numbers for Frikkie Van Alman's private phone on board the *Assegai*. He listened to it ring until a recording kicked in. "It's a friggin' answering machine," he said. "Pick it up, Frik! We've got a crisis here!"

With a clunk and a burst of static, the answering machine cut off and the phone picked up, carrying Frikkie Van Alman's familiar voice and familiar impatience. "I'm here. Who is this? What kind of crisis?"

Keene rapidly summarized what they knew so far. He heard the Afrikaner curse and what must have been him punching several buttons on a keyboard or alarm-control panel. "I'm sending in reinforcements to help you mop up. The *Yucatán* won't get far." In a clipped voice, loud enough to be heard by both of the men, he reminded them of their primary goal. "While Selene Trujold is on board, you have one mission that takes precedence over all others. Acquire that artifact she got from her father."

"Instead of stomping terrorists? You've got weird priorities, Frik," Keene said. "Your tanker's been hijacked and the crew's been killed, and all you can think about is a hunk of jewelry?"

"I'm sending help," Frik said. "You two just stay on top of it there."

Keene shrugged. "It's your problem, Frik. Call up whatever cavalry you want."

"Who do you think he'll send?" he asked his partner, setting down the receiver.

"Frik?"

"No. The avenging angel. Of course I meant Frik." He looked around the cabin. "Maybe we should have told him to call in a cleaning crew while he's at it."

McKendry shook his head. "I think you've been sniffing blood long enough, Joshua. Let's get some air."

Keene opened the cabin door. Bowing slightly, he waved his partner into the passageway and followed him until they reached the football-stadium-sized deck of the oil tanker.

Working silently against the thrum of the tanker's equipment, they circled around the *Yucatán*'s white-painted bridge. Behind the bridge house loomed the radar mast with swiveling radar antennas and satellite dishes. The superstructure bristled with navigation and communication arrays. Foam monitors and fire-fighting stations stood unmanned. A third of the way forward from the bridge house, hose-handling derricks protruded skyward like stripped trees, and numerous pressure and vacuum-relief valves studded the deck like dark warts.

White metal rails ran like a spine down the center of the wide deck, flanking the catwalk connecting the fore and aft gantries. The two Daredevils avoided the catwalk and kept to the shadows of bulkheads, vent pipes, and clusters of fifty-gallon drums that held lubricants and waste oil, dirty rags, and powdered absorbents for deck spills.

Beneath the square tank hatches, the tanker deck throbbed as the big engines pushed the *Yucatán* through the calm water, heading into the open straits. Far in the distance to the west, Keene could make out the Venezuelan mainland—a dark line with few marks of civilization. Even without a moon overhead, the billions of stars were like pinprick spotlights; the sparkling wire-caged bulbs scattered around the expanse of the giant ship shone down like guard posts around a prison, and the tall and bright *Valhalla* production platform was like a lighthouse towering over the water.

Looking at the receding platform, Keene figured that by now the disembarked members of the tanker crew, the lucky ones who had drawn R and R time aboard the *Valhalla,* would have noticed that the ship had pulled away from the loading derrick and lurched silently out to sea.

High up, in the center of the top deck, fore and aft walls of windows glowed with yellow light, showing the ship's main control rooms. Keene looked up and saw shadows moving in the otherwise quiet bridge, two silhouettes inside the control deck, backlit by the fluorescents. One was the trim and compact figure of a woman, directing the show.

The woman leaned forward. Her voice came out of the 1950s-era public address system, old bell-shaped metal loudspeakers stationed along the deck. "Everything is secure. The crew has been eliminated. Dump all the bodies overboard. When Oilstar finally catches up with this ship, I want it to look like the *Marie Celeste.* They'll never know how many of their crew members were part of our operations, and they'll waste time and effort looking for traitors among their own employees."

"That must be Selene," Keene said. He had expected her to have a French accent, but what came through the speakers was a flattened version of Peta's Caribbean lilt with a few hints of Spanish.

Lucky for Green Impact that the production rig's efficiency stopped short of security, he thought. She didn't know that they had called Frik and that Oilstar had its security response on the way, but she must know that her group didn't have much time. "She's gotta act fast. It's not like you can hide an oil tanker, and these things don't get up a lot of speed."

Hunched in the shadows of one of the derrick brackets, McKendry nodded again, which was the usual extent of his conversation during an operation.

"I am afraid the oil load is not what we expected," Selene continued. "Apparently, the *Yucatán* docked at the platform two hours late, so there wasn't enough time to fill the storage chambers to the level we had hoped."

From his vantage point, Keene saw several members of Green Impact pause in their furtive duties by the equipment bunkers to look up at her. Before groans could ring out from her team members, she raised her voice. "There's enough to send a message around the world. Oilstar will never get this stain off its shoes!"

20

Following McKendry's lead—which was mostly to remain flexible and mobile until something better came up—Keene worked his way into the shelter of the thick deck manifold tubing. There, safely hidden, they watched in angry horror as the terrorists emerged from the bridge housing and crew cabins, dragging limp bodies toward the railing as if they were out-of-fashion mannequins.

"Cleaning up their mess. The sharks will take care of the rest," Keene muttered as Selene Trujold's followers went to the white deck rails and, one at a time, wrestled the bloody forms overboard into the sea.

McKendry looked even more concerned. "They're going to get the captain, too. When they enter his cabin, they'll find the guy we left on the floor."

"Crap! They'll know we're aboard. Let's go."

McKendry put on a burst of speed, sprinting forward to where one lone man had wrestled the uncooperative body of a thin dark-haired crewman to the side. The terrorist used his shoulder to push the victim up and over and waited for the splash. He turned just in time to see McKendry and Keene closing in on him from both sides.

As if they had coordinated it ahead of time, Keene punched the terrorist in the jaw while McKendry smashed a pile-driver fist into his gut, making the man retch. Then the two men picked him up and dumped him over the tanker railing to join the dead bodies he had dropped into the calm water.

Keene looked at his partner. "Pity he didn't have a chance to take off those bloody clothes. With so many hungry sharks around tonight, I'm sure he'll be quite the dining attraction."

Moving at its top speed, the tanker soon left the floating bodies behind.

They heard the bass chatter of helicopter blades, fast dark aircraft coming in from the main Oilstar complex on Trinidad. They saw lights in the sky drowning out the stars above the dark and quiet channel.

"Party's over. Good old Frikkie to the rescue," Keene said.

On the bridge, Selene's silhouetted form stood straight, like an empress surveying newly conquered territory. "Time to go. Set the detonators for twenty minutes."

With a click, she switched off the loudspeaker system. She and her companion on the bridge disappeared from the lit windows and came around the bridge housing, running down the outer stairs to the main deck level.

Once again hidden from sight, Keene and McKendry watched Green Impact troops drop packaged, blinking explosives through the flung-open hatches for the below-deck storage chambers. Top hatches led down into the crude-oil storage chambers, a honeycomb of tanks that comprised the Yucatán's cargo space. Keene and McKendry saw the terrorists link the timers and detonation cables, rigging everything together on a small cluster of timers outside the top hatches.

"I thought the point of Green Impact was to protect the environment." Keene shook his head in disgust. "Some conservationists."

The Green Impact members began to scramble toward the bow of the tanker. Selene gestured urgently for her team to hurry. Apparently the terrorists had boats tied up to the hijacked oil carrier. As each man finished, she signaled him to go over the side and climb down ropes tied to the anchor windlass. When only one of her group remained, she waved to him and grabbed the rope herself. He gathered the wires from the explosives by the petroleum cargo hatches and ran back to the detonator.

That's some piece of work, Keene thought, watching Selene go over the side, moving with the sleek grace of an otter. At that distance, he could make out cinnamon-colored hair, cut short and practical, and skin the color of burnt sienna. He couldn't really see her face, but judging by her narrow frame he would guess that she had delicate features.

Dangerous, beautiful, tough; doubtless a challenge for any man. "There goes our chance to get Frik's Cracker Jack prize."

"I'm more interested in saving this tanker," McKendry said. "No matter what Frik tells us."

"Looks like now or never, Terris." Keene scanned the tanker deck frantically for a means to get to the linked detonators before all the bombs went off.

"Any ideas?"

"Got it." Keene pointed to two old company bicycles leaning against the fifty-gallon drums; the bikes were used for traversing the long deck on regular inspection runs. "There's our mode of transportation." He grabbed one, holding the handlebars as he swung himself over and began to pound the pedals. McKendry mounted a bicycle of his own. The dented wire basket rattled between the handlebars as they closed the distance.

Keene's sense of the absurd made him wish he had a little bicycle bell to ring. "Not exactly James Bond style," he said, hunched over and gripping the handlebars. "More like Encyclopedia Brown."

McKendry grinned. "I vote for Harry Potter."

"We could sure use a bit of magic right now."

The thin tires hummed across the oil-stained plates of the deck, ignoring the painted boundary lines that made the *Yucatán* look like some child's board game.

"Here comes Evel Knie—." The chain slipped on Keene's bike. He skinned his ankle on the pedal but kept pumping until the bicycle got moving again. McKendry passed him, saving his breath and using his stronger legs to push the bike for all it was worth.

They both picked up speed.

The lone terrorist at the front hatches heard the buzz of tires and looked up. He dropped the detonator box and slung the rifle off of his shoulder. Like an experienced professional, the man didn't call out, but simply aimed the weapon.

Keene ducked and swerved the bicycle, but the terrorist shot twice, coolly confident. The sharp crack of the high-powered rifle sounded simultaneously with Terris McKendry flying backward, as if someone had hit him with two sucker punches. Blood spurted from his back as he flipped off of the padded seat. The bicycle coasted forward another five feet and crashed into a set of fifty-gallon drums.

McKendry's body bounced once on the deck and lay still.

Keene shouted his friend's name and skidded on the bike, wiping out as the terrorist fired one more shot and missed. The bullet punctured one of the big metal drums and spilled a harsh-smelling solvent.

Though he had seen his partner tumble to a bloody halt on the deck, Keene didn't watch to see if he moved or not. Though the terrorist had a rifle, he had no choice except to charge forward recklessly, yowling like a madman.

The chattering helicopters came closer, searchlights shining onto the tanker in the water. The terrorist, fixed on completing his mission, glanced upward, then at Keene, measuring the distance between them. Scuttling backward toward the bow and his escape, the man grabbed a grenade from his belt, yanked the pin, and chucked it like an inexperienced baseball player down into one of the open hatches of the small forward oil-storage chambers. He was reaching for his gun when Keene barreled into him.

The man's hands tangled in the rifle's shoulder strap.

Moving in a blur, Keene wrapped a powerful forearm around his throat and yanked backward as he leaped up, pressing with his knee. He pulled back with all the strength in his shoulders until he heard the man's neck snap.

Keene grinned a feral snarl that wasn't at all a look of triumph. "There—"

The grenade went off inside the oil chamber.

Sealed by bulkheads, the explosion wasn't enough to rip through the double walls of the tanker. But the fire and the pressure wave vomited upward, a powerful geyser slamming like a hot avalanche and hurling Keene and the broken marionette of the already-dead terrorist off into oblivion.

As he flew into the black void over the sea, he wondered if he would be meeting Satan or Saint Peter. Whichever way he went, he hoped that Arthur and McKendry and the other departed Daredevils would be there.

The afterlife would be way too dull without them.

The Oilstar security helicopters came closer, but McKendry knew they would arrive much too late. Selene Trujold and Green Impact had already gotten away.

He dragged himself forward on his elbows. He couldn't breathe. Red-hot bands of pain tightened around his chest like a medieval torture instrument, and he could feel the gaping wet gunshot hole in his chest, the raw crater of the exit wound in his back. His right side seared where the other shot had grazed his ribs. Shock had diminished most of the pain—that would come later, if he survived long enough—but he could hear the gurgling when he breathed that told him his lung had probably collapsed. He couldn't tell how much he was bleeding, only that it was too much.

The curtain of fire from the grenade exploding in the storage tanks had nearly blinded him, but he had seen it throw his friend and the last terrorist overboard.

There was no time to grieve.

The most important job right now was to save the tanker. He might die in a few moments from the gunshots, but that would be better than becoming part of the funeral pyre of an exploding oil tanker.

With his eyesight focused more by sheer determination than because of the quality of light, McKendry crawled forward. The terrorists had left the detonators behind. He had seen the man adjust the timers. At any moment, the explosions would go off, engulfing the *Yucatán* in flame.

Every movement was the greatest effort he had ever made in his life. Leaving a long trail of blood, like the markings of a scarlet garden slug, he reached the open fuel hatches and the hastily rigged box of detonators and timers that connected all the explosives dropped into the storage tanks. He felt dead already. Hoping to hang on for just a few more seconds, he made one last, impossible effort.

His outstretched hand touched the connected detonator boxes, and he saw the last few seconds ticking down: fifteen . . . fourteen . . . thirteen . . .

He worked with the big knife he had taken from the terrorist in the captain's cabin. The wide macho blade severed the first couple of wires. So weak he could barely lift the knife, he brought it down as if he were chopping onions, again and again.

Another wire cut, and another.

In his state, he could not tell how many connections there were, how many remained, but he couldn't bother with details. His vision was failing, and the blood did not seem to stop pouring out of his wounds.

The bright orange glare from the explosion at the bow continued to blind him.

Joshua Keene was gone, blasted far out into darkness.

Hoping he had done enough, McKendry raised the big dagger, point downward, and stabbed the central detonator box, skewering it like a bug on the end of a pin. A few sparks erupted, then died.

It was absolutely the last he could manage. Seeing the helicopters circle for a landing, he collapsed on a deck that smelled of oil and blood as the unmanned *Yucatán* continued to drift into the Caribbean night.

21

January crawled toward February, and suddenly, unaccountably, Peta had been back in Grenada for three weeks.

The first week was spent informing Arthur's friends and relatives, and her own, about the explosion that had taken his life. The island buzzed with the news. Cried over it. Then, since the Marryshows were townies, they organized a mass at the cathedral in St. George's.

The second and third week, Peta kept to herself in her house in St. George's. She ate sparingly, slept little, and spent much time on her balcony staring down at the town and the shallow waters of the U-shaped inlet known as the Carenage. The small bay was filled with the movement of fishing boats, small yachts, water taxis, and the occasional ferry. Periodically, a cruise ship or schooner anchored in the deeper waters or sailed the edge of the horizon beyond. When she did go out to buy food or go to the bank or simply to take a walk, she found herself annoyed that life in Grenada continued as usual. Preparations for February's annual Independence Day celebrations were in full swing. People loved and laughed, and fought and died, as if nothing had changed.

And for them it hadn't. At least not much. They had lost a hero. Some of them had lost a friend. She had lost so much more than that. Arthur had been her best friend, her mentor, a father figure after her own father's death; her lover. He had taught her to drive a car and fly a plane, to perform surgery, to live with losing a patient, and to feel humble when she saved one.

By the end of the fourth week, Peta was able to pull herself together enough to reopen her rooms and reassume the work of caring for her patients and Arthur's at the small clinic they'd shared. She asked the locum they had left in charge to consider a permanent position—something to which he readily agreed, provided a possible partnership was in the offing—and buried herself in work.

Now, standing at the end of Quarantine Point, she watched the sunrise brighten the rocks and the sea, and wondered if her life would ever return to a semblance of normalcy.

She remembered the day her family's house had caught fire when she was a girl of twelve. Her father had come back into the house and saved her, but his own clothes had turned into wicks that burned him like a giant candle.

That's when she'd first met Arthur Marryshow. He fought so hard to save her papa, but there was nothing anyone could do except promise that he would take care of Peta and see that no harm came to her.

What of your promise now? she thought. How can you protect me when you're dead?

Every week since her return, she'd checked in with the Manhattan precinct which was holding Arthur's few remains while—so she was told—they investigated the accident. Yesterday, they'd told her the investigation was officially closed.

Her fury knew no bounds. Arthur was gone and she'd never know why or by whose hand.

Below her, the Rasta who lived behind Bronze House tucked his dreadlocks into his turban and strode into the Caribbean for his morning bath. He must have felt her presence and turned to look upward and wave.

"Peta."

"Ralphie." She waved back at her old friend. He was a little older than she, but not much. An Oxford-educated geologist and son of a former deputy prime minister, Ralph Levine chose to live as a Rasta. He slept in a cave, ran a rudely built hut that he called his geological museum, and carved black coral into jewelry to sell to the tourists.

Beyond Ralphie, Peta could see the luxury of the Spice Island Hotel, and beyond that the medical school, which occupied the choicest piece of oceanfront property in Grenada. In another week or two the American students would return, and she'd resume teaching there. Those kids had better watch out, she thought. This semester she would brook no unruliness from those spoiled brats.

Holding her sandals in her hand, Peta footed it back to where the real road came up from Morne Rouge Bay. She walked past Mahogany Run and the Grandview Hotel, crested the ridge, and continued toward her rooms, which lay a mile or two down the road. Along the road she passed several paw paw trees—papaya, as the Americans called them. The fruit on the plants was still small and green, but it reminded her that she was hungry.

She passed Tabanca on her left and thought about going there for breakfast. *Tabanca.* Unrequited love. Great view and excellent coffee, but the owner was a perpetually sullen German woman whose lover had sailed away and never returned. She lived there alone, growling at everyone except her large German shepherd. She was a downer, which God knew Peta didn't need in her life. Not today.

Reaching the Flamboyant, she made a left turn into the grounds, descended the few steps that led to the Beachside Terrace, their patio restaurant, and breakfasted on papaya and fresh bread and honey. She sweetened her coffee with condensed milk and drank it slowly, watching a small bird enjoy the crumbs at the far edge of the table. The Flamboyant was named after the scarlet trees that dotted the island. It provided its guests with a magnificent view of the three-mile horseshoe of Grand Anse Beach, with its white sand that extended almost half the distance from where she sat to St. George's.

This being a Monday, the manager came out to greet her and invite her to come to his regularly scheduled rum punch party. She did not answer him but merely shook her head, so as to discourage communication. After that, for a few minutes, perhaps even an hour, she felt more at peace than she had since New Year's Eve. Reluctantly, she walked the rest of the way up Camerhogne Park Road to her rooms at the Marquis Complex, put on her shoes and lab coat, and saw her first patient of the day.

Within minutes, she was absorbed in the work.

The telephone rang as she was leaving.

"Peta? Frik."

For one misguided moment, Peta thought Frik might have called to see how she was doing. He soon disillusioned her. Wasting no time on pleasantries, he told her that Terris McKendry had been severely injured in a battle to save one of Oilstar's tankers.

"He was shot and burned. He's in bad shape."

"Where is he?"

"He was medevac'd here, to Mount Hope Medical Center. Unless Arthur's plane is fueled and ready, I'll send my jet to get you and have a car waiting for you at this end."

My plane now, Peta thought, since the reading of his will.

Because she was Arthur's student in his lifesaving burn techniques, it stood to reason that Frik would turn to her for help, Peta thought. Still, a "Would you mind coming?" might have been nice.

"Mount Hope's a good place," she said. "I'll call and let them know I'm on my way."

Pleased with herself for having made the arrangements she had with the locum, Peta called him in from his day off. She had left her Honda at the clinic, so getting home to pack a small bag would be no problem. Nor would getting to the airport be a problem, even with a stop first at the closest Barclays Bank for some cash to see her through.

Standing in line at the bank, she fiddled with the pendant around her neck. When she reached the counter, on a whim, she took off the necklace, sealed it in an envelope, and asked to be escorted to her safe-deposit box.

Frik's jet beat her to the airport; his car was waiting for her upon her arrival at Piarco International. She was pleased to see Saaliim behind the wheel and not Frik. He got out and opened the back door.

"You're not my chauffeur, Saaliim. I'll sit in the front with you, if that's all right."

He grinned and she smiled back. She had always liked the Honduran, and the feeling was clearly mutual. "Mr. McKendry in bad shape," he said when she was settled beside him.

"I assume Frik's with him."

Saaliim shook his head. "He with Mr. Brousseau out at Dragon's Mouth."

"Simon? He's not diving, is he?"

"Yes. As we speak."

"Assholes," Peta muttered. Simon had no business diving in his condition, and Frik had less business encouraging him. She'd have a few things to say to the two of them later. Right now, her focus had to be Terris McKendry.

Twenty minutes later, Saaliim swerved off the Uriah Butler Highway and into Mount Hope Medical Center's parking lot. "You want me to come inside, Miss Peta? Or maybe wait outside?"

Peta thought for a moment. In all likelihood she'd be fully occupied with McKendry for the rest of the day and, by the sound of it, for several days beyond that.

"You go to come back," she said, using the Grenadian colloquialism. "I know my way around this hospital all too well. Tell Frik I'll call him later with a report."

The charge nurse, to whom she had spoken several times en route, ushered Peta into McKendry's private room in the hospital's small intensive-care section. The last time she'd seen him, not that long ago at Arthur's apartment, he'd looked fit and well. Now he looked as if he probably wouldn't make it through the night. He was barely conscious. According to his chart, he had presented in shock, a mess of mud and oil and blood. Her initial cursory examination confirmed that he had been hit by two rifle bullets and that he had sustained some surface burns.

The burns might leave some scarring but were not enough to be life-threatening. The bullet wounds were a more complex problem. Where a hollow point or frangible round would have pureed the contents of his chest cavity, he had every chance of surviving these wounds.

The flesh wound along the right flank would heal, even without medical attention. The second shot was less simple: a full-metal-jacketed slug had made a through-and-through penetration of his lower right chest. Fortunately for McKendry, the bullet had not hit a major artery on the way through or a rib on the way out. The former would have exsanguinated him in minutes: the latter would have deflected the bullet, causing major, possibly catastrophic, collateral damage. The through-and-through FMJ chest wound had collapsed the lung, but some bright medic or ED doc along the way had inserted a chest tube and hooked it up to suction; that no doubt had saved McKendry's life until the local thoracic surgeon got to him and closed the entry and exit wounds.

Peta discovered further evidence of McKendry's dumb luck when she examined the exit wound and found it just low enough to miss ripping up his posterior shoulder girdle. An inch higher and he'd be looking at permanent disability. Talk about charmed lives.

Telling the nurse to set up a bed for her in one of the little rooms adjacent to intensive care, she washed up and put in a call to Frik.

"It'll be a while before his next escapade, but with good care and exquisite attention to antisepsis, he'll make it. His lung's not reinflating as quickly as I'd like, so I'm going to stay here with him for a few days."

Frik sounded relieved. "Thanks, Peta. I'll be in to see you later this evening. I can't leave the office right now."

"I heard about Simon. Is he all right?"

"Why wouldn't he be?"

"I warned you both that he shouldn't be diving, Frik."

"Well for your information, he's fine. He had to come up because he used up most of his tank clearing debris from his entry point. I wish I had half his energy. He's down in Port of Spain now, pretending to be some TV star, but he's going back to San Gabriel tomorrow to complete the dive."

"Alone? No dive buddy?"

"He seems to prefer it that way."

Idiot! Peta thought. She was fed up with all this macho bullshit. When she had stabilized McKendry, she would hitch a ride to San Gabriel. If Manny was in the area, he would take her there; if not, she'd use one of Frik's speedboats. Not that she particularly wanted to delay her return to Grenada, but in all good conscience she had to take one more shot at warning Simon that his heart probably couldn't take another dive. If she couldn't convince him to stop, she would insist on going along. Barring unforeseen setbacks, she should be able to leave McKendry in the hands of the hospital staff in three days, four tops. She would mention it to Frik when he came to see McKendry.

If he came to see him.

22

Thus far, Frik had called several times, but he had not yet made an appearance. Peta was hardly impressed by his lack of compassion and admitted to herself yet one more time that the Oilstar chief was not among her favorite people.

Two days later, by which time McKendry's condition had been stabilized, Frikkie showed up at the hospital. He was not a pretty sight. His one eye hadn't yet fully healed from the explosion that had killed Paul Trujold, and his hand looked as if it had a long way to go before it was good for more than gross manipulation. His visit was short, their conversation brief and more about Simon than Terris; in neither case were his emotions involved.

"Simon's in San Gabriel. He hasn't gone down—in the water—again yet. The weather's not been conducive. Too much rain, too many currents stirring things around."

"You shouldn't let him—"

"Let him? May I remind you again that he's an adult. What he chooses to do is his own business."

There was obviously no point in arguing with the man. None at all. "I'd like to see him," Peta said. "I think I'll head out to San Gabriel for a day or two. I could use the rest."

"What about McKendry?"

"Terris is a long way from full recovery, but he's doing well. Barring unforeseen complications, the hospital can manage fine without me. When they think he's ready, they'll send him on to rehab. He won't need me for that, either. If they have to reach me, they can call me in San Gabriel."

Something in Frik's expression told her that this was the last thing he wanted her to do. For whatever reason, Simon's dive was of enormous importance to him. Well, that's just too bad, she thought. It was not only a man who had to do what a man had to do.

Leaving Frik at McKendry's bedside, she went outside for a smoke. It was the last American cigarette she had brought from New York. From now on, it was back to the local 555s, which were milder and cheaper anyway. I'll give up again soon, she told herself, lighting up. After having given them up for three years, she had fallen into old habit the night Arthur was killed.

"Got another one?" Saaliim asked.

Peta jumped. "Didn't know you were here, and no, this is my last one."

She handed it to him and they shared it the way they would have shared a joint.

"I'd like to go to San Gabriel this afternoon." She waved away the end of the smoke. "Think you can take me there?"

He drew on the butt, then crunched it underfoot. "I have to take Mr. Frik to the *Assegai*," he said. "After that we maybe go to the site. Mr. Frik say maybe Mr. Brousseau come dive today. Maybe not." He looked up at the sky. "Maybe later it storm."

"Could be." Eighty-four degrees. Humid. Sultry. Not a cloud to be seen. A tourist would have laughed, she thought. "Is Manny on island?"

"I think so."

"Good." Peta glanced at the Hummer beyond them in the physician's parking lot, unsurprised that Frik would feel it his right to park there. "I'll get my things and make arrangements with the charge nurse. Don't leave without me."

When she was ready to leave the hospital, Saaliim was half asleep behind the wheel of the car. Frik paced impatiently back and forth next to it.

"One more minute and we'd have been out of here," he said.

Peta didn't answer; in fact, she said little en route to Frikkie's dock, and only waved a passing good-bye as Saaliim turned the Hummer around.

To her delight, the first person Peta saw at the dock was Manny

Sheppard, inevitable Carib in hand. He was clearly happy to see her.

"Hey, beautiful. What's up?"

She hugged him. "You first, Manny. What's up with you? Which way you headed?"

"Which way you want me to head?"

"I need to get to San Gabriel."

He motioned toward his small steel-hulled freighter. "Come. I'll take you there. I got a load of supplies headed for Grenada. San Gabby's a quick stop on the way."

She had known Manny since childhood, as well as anyone could ever know him. He was the sort of person with whom you could never quite tell what was real and what he was making up on the spot. He'd been running boats up and down the Caribbean since he left the OECS Security Forces. What was in the boats he sailed around was always an open question, though no customs officials had ever found any evidence to back up their suspicions.

"So what you want in San Gabby?"

"I'm looking for Simon Brousseau." She felt a sudden stab of anxiety. "He hasn't gone diving today, has he?"

"Not so far as I know. Simon be probably resting up in San Gabriel, making the lovely ladies happy," he said.

Peta had no idea how many lovely ladies might be hiding in the small fishing village close to the drill site, nor did she care. If the choice was diving or diddling, sex was certainly the less life-threatening option for Simon.

They sailed through a seascape dotted with rock outcroppings and headed toward the Dragon's Mouth—the narrow channel separating Trinidad from the Venezuelan mainland. San Gabriel was actually a small island off the coast of the Chaguara Peninsula, the northern spit of land pointing from Trinidad toward the body of South America. It was one of a half dozen towns that made most of their living from not-so-rich Americans and Europeans who wanted to experience diving and sport fishing, but couldn't afford the big resorts and charters.

As many times as Peta had made the journey through the Dragon's Mouth by sea before, she was still taken by its jagged beauty. Distracted, wanting some escape from the endless worries about Simon and Terris that ran through her mind, at first she only half listened to what Manny was saying.

". . . So Paul Trujold, he . . . You listening to me, Peta?"

"I'm sorry, Manny. I didn't mean to be rude."

"It's all right," he said. "But you need to hear this."

Manny repeated what he had been saying. When he had finished telling her about Paul Trujold, about the real purpose of Simon's dive—to retrieve a piece of the artifact that was wedged in an underwater cave—she thought of the pendant that Arthur had given her and started to put the facts together. If there was any real basis for what Manny had told her, she could come to only one possible conclusion.

"My God, Manny. Are you sure? Because if you are, chances are Frik is responsible for Arthur's death."

"How so?"

"Arthur had a piece of the artifact. He always kept it on him. Frik could have seen it and put out a contract—"

"Yes, but you told me you saw the piece with Arthur's body."

"I did. It was covered with blood and—"

"So you say maybe the killer—"

"Missed it. Yes. It's possible, what with the police and so many people." She stopped. "God, Manny. If it's true and I don't get to Simon—"

Manny pointed at a speedboat. "That's one of Frik's boats, the one Simon's been using." He maneuvered between a small fishing boat and the powerboat tied up to the village's makeshift pier. When he was up against the dock, he asked, "Want me to stay here with you?"

"I can handle things."

Without arguing, Manny tossed her duffel and medical bag onto the wooden dock, helped her out of the boat, and blew her a kiss. She watched him reverse into the channel, and waved him onward. Turning to face whatever awaited her in the village of San Gabriel, she trekked to the top of a minor incline.

In the only bar in town, which was also its only hotel of sorts, Peta met the owner—a handsome, charming Venezuelan who introduced himself as Eduardo Blaine and kissed her hand with far too much enthusiasm and spittle for a rank stranger.

"I am a friend of your Mr. Van Alman. He called to tell me you were on your way and told me to take care of you." He held on to her hand for more than a moment too long. "I am proud to welcome you to my establishment. Your room is ready for you. It has a spectacular view."

"If I could have that back." Peta withdrew her hand. She would like to have said that Frik was far from being her friend, but instead she asked after Simon.

"He is in his room," Blaine said.

"Please tell him I wish to see him. I'll wait at the bar."

"He, um, he is—how shall I say it—not quite alone." Blaine winked blatantly, as if at a co-conspirator. "He did not wish to be disturbed."

Peta chose not to argue. "I'm told he will be going out early tomorrow morning. I must see him before then."

"If you will do me the honor of dining with me, I will promise to wake you before he leaves."

And then we arm-wrestle, Peta thought wryly. "Dinner sounds fine," she said. "But first I'd like to take a shower."

"Allow me to show you to your room." Blaine picked up her duffel.

"How many rooms do you have?"

"Four."

"In that case"—she took her duffel from him—"the key will do."

"I will bring the key to you in the bar," he said. "It is in the office. Please order what you wish, compliments of Eduardo Blaine."

Peta barely kept herself from laughing out loud. She went over to the bar, which proved not to be in Blaine's office, seated herself on a stool, and ordered and received a Carib and a pack of 555s. The pretty young barmaid in a floral dress and bare feet looked as if she was Blaine's daughter.

For some reason, the thought of the Venezuelan having a daughter intrigued her. With a mixture of amusement and guilt, she realized that she was feeling horny about the man. His Antonio Banderas looks and overly florid South American manners were not usually the sorts of things that attracted her. She remembered the sight of Arthur splattered across the bathroom at Danny's, and her guilt won out.

Deciding that this would be a good time to check on McKendry, Peta retrieved her cell phone from her handbag and dialed the hospital. She could hear a faint voice at the other end, but static on the line made it impossible to converse.

"Is there a telephone around here? I'll use a credit card." Peta lit her first 555 in three years, savored the familiar flavor, made herself the same old promise.

The girl took an old-fashioned rotary dial phone from under the counter and pushed it shyly toward Peta, who lifted the receiver.

". . . care of her." Frik's voice.

"That won't be a chore." Blaine. "She is most beautiful."

Peta covered the mouthpiece with her hand and blessed the inefficiencies of a telephone system which so consistently crossed wires that the idea of privacy was a joke. Even if the two men had heard background noises, they would take no notice of them.

"I have given you my word that I will take care of her," the Venezuelan continued.

"You do that, Mr. Blaine," Frik said. "Or I will be forced to take care of you."

As the line went dead, Peta softly replaced the receiver in its cradle.

Two possibilities raced through her mind: either Frik wanted her protected, or Frik wanted her eliminated. All she had to do was make sure that she stayed alive until she could figure out which one it was.

23

The night air was humid and still. The only thing moving in the room was Peta. She stirred, vaguely awake. From somewhere she heard voices.

She turned over, kicking off the clinging sheet. The voices kept up a steady racket, and she realized they must be coming up from the street below her window. She wished she had earplugs. Somehow she needed to get back to sleep, get some rest. God only knew what tomorrow would bring.

The voices outside weren't all that was keeping her awake, though. Since Arthur's death, Peta had sublimated any thoughts of men; none could ever take his place. When her mentor and lover had been alive, she'd had a healthy libido and often found herself aroused by some passing man's firm ass, or long fingers, or broad shoulders. Now those feelings brought only guilt.

She also considered herself pretty immune to charm, especially when she knew intellectually that it was a con. But Blaine's eyes, his ready smile, his—for lack of a better word—charisma, had burned a neat little picture in her mind. It made her squirm with competing emotions of desire and embarrassment.

She turned onto the other side.

Sleep, damn it, she thought. Stop thinking.

The unseen strangers below her window laughed as a bottle shattered.

She flipped onto her stomach, tucked her head more firmly into the pillow, and stretched out on the sagging mattress. The air was close, the voices echoing eerily. Not very patiently she waited for sleep to return. . . .

A grinding noise broke through the fog in her brain. A buzzing. Can't they stop with that racket? she thought sleepily.

She rolled over and opened her eyes. It was morning, bright morning; the type of brilliant sunlight that said dawn had passed hours ago. While her eyes adjusted, her mind identified the sound she'd been hearing: an inboard motor.

She swung her legs off the bed and rushed to the window, trying her best to ignore the rough, splintery feel of the wood floor. Pushing aside the sheer curtain, she looked out to see a boat emblazoned with the Oilstar logo moving at top speed toward the mouth of the harbor, out to the open sea. Simon's boat.

"Shit." As Peta stepped away from the window, a splinter penetrated the soft skin of her arch. On her other foot, she hopped to one of the chairs and yanked out the splinter. She grabbed her jeans from the other chair and pulled them on. The fading watery growl of the engine reminded her that with every passing second Simon moved farther out to sea and, she thought, to a dive that was likely to kill him.

Hurrying, she picked up her T-shirt from the floor. An inch-long roach tumbled out of it, another resident of this fleabag hotel having his early-morning sleep disturbed.

She was tempted to step on it, bare feet or no. After all, she thought wryly, she was paying to have the room to herself. Instead she pulled on the T-shirt without checking for any more residents, and looked around the floor for her sandals.

As she put them on she wondered why Blaine hadn't kept his promise to awaken her.

She remembered her thoughts during the evening. What the hell was wrong with her? Trust wasn't something she gave out that often—now the right pairing of eyes and smile and she acted like a lovesick lamb.

She opened her door and almost tripped over someone who lay snoring, slumped over only a few feet from her room. It was as if he had fallen asleep on guard duty, she thought. Frikkie's words echoed in her head: *Take care of her, or—*

Another roach to squash, she thought. When she had time. Right now what she had to do was catch up with Simon. For that, she'd need a boat. Diving gear.

She charged downstairs to the front desk, where a sleepy-eyed Trini woman in a simple dress stretched to its size limits looked at her as though she were crazy.

"Eduardo Blaine. Which is his room?"

The woman looked confused.

"Señor Blaine?" Peta repeated.

"Ah, sí." The woman nodded and pointed with her thumb along the hallway beside the stairs. "Room two. End of the hall on the left." She smiled conspiratorially, as if she thought Peta was going to sneak into Blaine's room and give him an early-morning quickie.

"Gracias," Peta called out as she ran down the hallway to the door marked with a gold-plated number 2 hung at a drunken angle. Banging loudly, she yelled, "Blaine? You there? Blaine, wake up!"

She stood there, waiting, the time slipping away. Simon's boat was now well out of the bay for sure, bouncing over the water.

The bolt clicked open.

"You said you'd wake me. You said that you'd be up, and wake me before Simon could leave."

Blaine—in white Jockeys, no shirt, and looking more asleep than awake—held the door open wide and backed up to let her in. He raised his left arm as if to check a watch that wasn't there.

"What time is—God, my alarm. I must have . . . Maybe Simon hasn't left—"

"I just saw his boat heading out of the harbor. Thanks for the help."

"Okay, okay! Relax. Let me get dressed. I got a boat. We'll catch him."

"He's already got close to ten minutes on us."

Blaine smiled, but the charm that had worked so well the night before had lost its appeal. "No problem, I have a very fast boat."

"Hope it works better than your alarm clock."

He grinned boyishly. Peta guarded herself against any impulse to forgive him.

"Okay, wait in the lobby. I'll get dressed and be out in a minute."

"Please hurry."

As she waited, feeling each second tick by, she thought through the possibilities. Could Blaine's boat beat Simon's? If not, what would happen if she had to dive after him? It had been a while since she had done a tech dive. Mixed gases—nitrogen, oxygen, helium. She knew it was

147

not something to rush into. Rushing could get you killed.

"Let's go," Blaine said, running out of the hotel. She followed him to the town's small wooden dock. At the last boat in the line, he stopped. "Jump in."

Peta stared. "*This* is fast?"

The boat looked like a fisherman's trawler, built for steadiness, perhaps, but surely not for speed. It did, however, have everything in it she would need for the dive, like the several pairs of tri-mix tanks which lay amid the more usual tourist dive gear.

"Don't knock my boat." Blaine untied the stern line. "Unless you want to swim after Simon."

"That might be faster."

"Just start her up," he said, running to untie the bow line. "Hit the silver button."

Peta pushed the button, and the inboard started with a substantial roar that immediately garnered her respect.

Blaine finished untying the lines and, jumping onto the deck, clambered back to the wheel. "Okay," he said. "Now hold on."

He opened the throttle and the squat boat reared up like Trigger at the end of a Lone Ranger movie. Peta flew back into her seat and tasted salty spray on her face.

"I'm impressed," she shouted over the roar.

"You should remember . . . appearances can deceive you."

Blaine turned the wheel and curled around the bigger boats, the fishing vessels taking the day off, the moored dinghies waiting for the leisure sailors to return, baked nut-brown and three sheets to the wind with multiple Caribs and Red Stripes. The boat maneuvered wonderfully, its stern sitting deep in the water while the rest of the hull nearly hydroplaned.

"That one should fit you," he said, pointing to a black wet suit. With its frayed collar and wrists it looked as though it had been through one too many dives already.

"You sure you don't have something a little more colorful? I would have preferred a stylish neon orange flare on the side."

Blaine grinned. "I'll remember that for next time. The rest of the dive gear's back there."

Peta nodded and turned to the piles of equipment. The masks, fins, and regulators looked like standard Caribbean tourist issue. Not top-of-the-line, but with the right gas mix, she'd be fine.

She moved to the rows of tanks. The first few cylinders were battered and air-filled, at least if the rubber caps over their first stages were true indications of their state. The smaller double tanks stood beside them. Tri-mix tanks—a nitrogen-helium mix and oxygen—which could be adjusted up or down based on depth or bottom time. Unfortunately, only one set of the tanks appeared to be filled.

"You only have one working set of the tri-mix back here," she yelled. "Looks like I'll be going it alone." She didn't relish the idea of diving without a buddy, especially since that was one of the reasons she was so mad at Simon.

"If only one of us can go, it should be me," Blaine called back to her. She wasn't sure if his reaction was chivalry or South American machismo, but it didn't matter to her which it was. There was no way she would hang out on the surface.

"No chance. Simon's my responsibility."

Thankfully, Blaine quit arguing. She shucked her land clothes and pulled on the wet suit. When she was suited up, she moved forward to stand beside him so that she could see where they were headed. "Is it far?"

Blaine shook his head. "About ten minutes for this boat. We should be able to see the rig as soon as we curve around that spit of land there." He pointed at a large rock outcropping that sheltered San Gabriel's harbor. "Then we head straight on. If Simon isn't down, he'll probably be able to see us."

And what then? she thought. If he saw her would that make him stop and wait?

Not Simon. He'd hurry up and dive. If she was going to stop him, she'd have to follow him down and get him to surface.

Piece of cake.

Underwater communication was so very easy, she thought sarcastically, especially with the paltry array of hand signals used by divers. A big O made with the thumb and index finger for "I'm okay." A slashing palm over the neck for "Out of air." Thumbs-up for "Let's surface." Crawling fingers for "Critter around." Or her favorite, a vertical open palm cutting the water to indicate a really *big* critter around. As in,

"Watch your butt or you'll be some prehistoric creature's breakfast."

Blaine cut the boat hard, steering around a coral reef she saw only in the boat's wake, then moved back on course for the point of the small peninsula ahead. It was obvious that he knew these waters extremely well. After a few more seconds, the boat was out far enough that Peta could see the small drilling rig and make out the shape of a boat tied up to it.

"I see his boat."

"Yes," Blaine said. He looked back at her. "One person topside. Simon must be down already."

"Shit."

The closer they got to Oilstar's exploration platform, the more ominous it looked. No one moved on the skeletal structure, and the small main cabin's windows were shattered, smashed—Peta guessed—by locals cruising by and taking potshots for their momentary amusement.

She looked at the boat they were chasing. Simon's pilot, probably some local he'd hired for the day, stood up and calmly watched their progress.

Peta checked her watch. Simon could have been down five minutes, maybe ten. Depending on depth, he was good for another fifteen or twenty minutes. Add one screwup—something to make him breathe too hard, not shift his mixture right, get snagged on a rock—and it could all go wrong fast.

She pulled on her fins and strapped a rusty old dive knife to her leg. It looked like a relic that hadn't cut anything other than stray fishing tackle since the American invasion of Grenada. Grabbing a face mask, she spat into the lens and smeared the slick liquid around before dangling the mask in the water. Funny, she thought. Who knew why spit defogged a mask?

She dug out a weight belt and slipped on twelve pounds. It was more than she'd use normally, but with 120 feet to the seabed and who knew how much deeper into the cave, she had to be sure of getting down fast and staying there.

The boat bumped. Peta bounced out of her seat.

"Sorry. Getting choppy. The sea can turn nasty quickly out here." Blaine didn't look particularly perturbed.

Peta clamped the belt tight and looked up to see him pull alongside the other boat.

"How long has he been down?" the Venezuelan shouted.

The Trini in Simon's boat shrugged, exposing the bottle of Red Stripe he'd been hiding behind his leg. "Dunno," he said sleepily in a thick accent. "Five minutes, maybe. Maybe more."

Peta stood up. It made little difference. However long he'd been down there was too long, and discussing it wouldn't make it any shorter. She double-checked her gear and assured herself she was good to go. Pulling on the buoyancy vest with the double tanks, she strapped it tightly to her back with twin wide Velcro straps. The tanks were heavy; she cinched them a little tighter, and gave the vest a shot of air. Then she pulled the mask down, popped in the regulator mouthpiece, and made a big O with her right index finger and thumb.

"Good luck!" Blaine shouted.

Without missing a beat, she sat on the edge of the boat, facing into it before she slowly tilted backward, flying head over heels into the water.

After the amusement-park fall into the water, Peta quickly oriented herself, dumped the air out of her vest, and turned facedown, away from the light and the path of her ascending bubbles. She kicked smoothly, straight toward the bottom. With the press of a button she started the timer function of her dive watch, then looked at it to make sure the seconds were ticking down.

While she was traveling to the bottom, she kept her air mix heavier on oxygen than she would have it when she entered the cave. She'd have to check depth and cut back the oxygen to something around a 15 or 16 percent mixture—quickly. If she took too long to do that, the excess oxygen would turn toxic in her bloodstream.

To get her mind off the dangers of the dive itself, she focused on how to find Brousseau. It occurred to her that the oil rig team had probably planted markers when they got to the bottom, showing the direction to the cave. A rip current could play havoc with marking poles, but if they were still there, she could follow them straight to the deep hole . . . and Simon.

The light began to fade, and with it the colors. Everything settled into a murky gloom. She took a quick glance at her depth gauge. Sixty feet. It would soon be time to turn on the headlight. She checked her time . . . passing three minutes into the dive. She was tempted to push it, kick a bit harder, but she resisted. It wasn't just a question of speed.

She knew she could swim faster than Simon. The problem was, if she did push herself, the exertion might make her breathe too fast. If she did that, the oxygen-nitrogen mix would be wrong no matter how she tried to balance it, which would make *her* the one in need of saving.

That was another danger she didn't need to focus on.

Her depth gauge was nearing one hundred feet, the edge of the recreational dive limit, when she saw something dark ahead of her.

She reminded herself that this was no rec dive.

Thinking, hoping, that the dark shape was the first outcropping of the sea floor, she turned on her light. Its pale glow caught the floating soup of "snow" in the water, making the tiny falling debris shine around her like fireflies.

Ahead of her, the shape moved, closer than she'd thought. The blackish grayness changed, and she saw her light reflected against white teeth. She thought of the hand symbol: making a fin with your hand to warn other divers.

Except there were no other divers down here. Nothing alive here at all except for her—and the shark seemed to have noticed that fact.

24

The few things Peta knew about sharks rushed into her mind, like life preservers bobbing to the surface after a wreck. The most relevant thing she remembered was that most sharks didn't want to have anything to do with mankind—or womankind. Even the supposed man-eaters, the great whites, the tigers, and worst of all a rogue hammerhead separated from its pack, dined infrequently on humans.

Eyes locked on the shadowy form of the shark as it grew larger, Peta kicked back. She knew she was sucking her air mixture too heavily. Nitrogen would start building up. That's not a good thing, she told herself, but there was this bigger problem. . . .

The shark that was coming right at her. A blue shark, she guessed, acting completely out of character.

She had two choices: stay perfectly still and hope the shark did a flyby, or do something to make it reconsider its current course. Preferring the latter, she reached down to her thigh and pulled out the rusty dive knife.

The shark was only meters away, resolute in its intent.

Peta held the knife with the handle facing away from her, blade pointing toward her. She pulled her arm close, holding the knife in tight.

There was a theory among divers that hitting a shark on the nose sharply made it back up. Especially, so the theory went, if it really didn't have you in mind for dinner. If it did, the theory was probably useless.

A meter away the shark, a gray bullet now, rocketed right at her chest, its eyes expressionless black dots.

For a moment she thought her arm was moving too slowly to catch it, but the handle miraculously hit the shark directly on its piglike nostrils. If she survived, she'd be sure to tell the experts what they could do with their shark theories.

The creature didn't stop. If anything, the handle acted like a jolt of energy. The blue shark rammed her hard, the force of it shoving her to the side and knocking her regulator from between her teeth. A giant bubble of air exploded from her mouth.

She did a sidearm recovery of her regulator, popped it in her mouth, and sucked in the mixture. When she looked up to find the shark, she saw it trailing away, as if its eyes hadn't seen her at all. A crazy undersea driver, a hit-and-run expert sailing on to his next victim.

Peta hung in the water for a moment to take stock of the damage. Her buoyancy control vest looked as if it had been shredded by the abrasive skin of the shark, but she realized that it had looked the same way when she'd put it on. Undoubtedly, the result of a zillion tourist dives. Otherwise, she was fine, and she was wasting time she didn't have.

She continued her dive down to the hole. To Simon.

Just past 120 feet, she found the bottom.

She was very close to where the drill had entered the seabed. Swimming by, she noticed that the test well itself had been sealed with concrete. The entrance to the cave couldn't be more than eighty feet away. Nitrogen narcosis would normally kick in if she lingered at this depth, but this dive was not about lingering. She had to find the cave and take an express train as deep as it went. Once there she'd have to quickly cut back her oxygen in time to prevent problems. That way at least she wouldn't go crazy with the rapture of the deep. Although, she thought, she could probably do with a little rapture about now.

Right about then, she spotted a tall marking pole left by the drilling team at the edge of an undersea rift. The markers were usually used to track where samples were taken, or places to test for underground oil. In this case, it was a pointer to Simon's destination, the underwater cavern.

She didn't like cave dives, not at normal depth, and certainly not at a tech-dive depth. Once you were inside, your options closed. You lost both light and maneuvering room. One of her best friends once did a deep underwater cave in the Yucatán. They fished him out dead the next day.

She looked at the narrow entrance. Tight, but roomy enough to swim in.

Damn you, Simon, she thought. You should have known better. You shouldn't be in there. You're too old; it's too dangerous.

Time to cut the oxygen—and fast. She reached behind and lowered the oxygen to below 20 percent, while bringing the nitrogen and helium mix up an equal amount. She took a breath. The air tasted a little metallic but otherwise fine.

Finding no further reason for delay, she kicked into the mouth of the cave. Her small light barely caught the walls, and she heard the clank as her tanks scraped the top. The cave twisted and turned, and she tried to check her depth gauge, but there was no room to reach behind and grab it.

She felt the familiar pull of a deep dive: stress, anxiety. It's okay, she thought. Calm down. Focus. No problems here. I'll just hope I have a good air cocktail going for this depth, because if it isn't good, it could be too late for me to tell. Disorientation will hit, confusion, and it'll be underwater mouse-in-a-maze time. And the maze always wins.

Stop it, Peta! Focus! she screamed inside her head.

She came to a fork in the tunnel and looked around. No Simon, no bubbles. Which way to go? One hole narrowed. No way he could have made it through that one. She looked at the other; the walls were smooth, almost polished. That seemed strange. They should have been rough, with coral fingers reaching out like the ones behind her. Instead they looked shiny. She wondered if it could be something volcanic.

She checked her watch as she swam down the strange channel. Ten minutes. That meant Simon had been down what? Fifteen or twenty minutes? He should be on his way back.

Ahead of her, the cave widened into darkness. She kicked slowly, tentatively, up to the mouth of the opening. When she was practically in the opening she became aware of a distant glow.

Using her headlamp to pick up what it could, she saw an enormous chamber, an underwater grotto. A cathedral, but unlike any she'd seen on her own dives or in pictures. It was as if someone had carved a giant, smooth bubble seventy or eighty feet below the seabed.

She shone her light on the glow—much closer now—and picked up another diver.

Simon floated near the far wall. Not moving. Suspended like a lifeless toy in a child's fish tank.

Peta stayed at the entrance to the cavern, looking at the body of the man she'd come to save. Damn it, Simon, she thought. Why didn't you let me talk you out of this?

When she knew she couldn't put it off any longer, she tilted her body and gave a few small fin kicks to sail nearer to him. His lamp pointed down, dully, at the same meaningless spot, but the reflected glow bounced onto the walls. Peta let herself look up for just a moment to see the strange markings on the smooth surface.

They were . . . she searched for a word. *Incomparable*. There was nothing she had ever seen that even came close to them. She thought of the markings she'd seen on Mayan tombs, but they were like cave drawings. These weren't primitive. They were stylized, with odd shapes that could have been metallic devices and—

She stopped. There was no time for sight-seeing. She reached out and turned Simon around. His eyes were wide open and had bulged, probably as he struggled to breathe, getting the mix wrong. She checked his tanks. They had plenty of air and looked like they were set to a good ratio of oxygen to nitrogen-helium blend. That meant it must have been his heart. It could easily have given out on him. The tension, the pressure.

Looking down, she saw that he had something clutched in his hand. A sharp chill ran through her. The material looked similar to the pendant that Arthur had given her. She reached out and tried to pry Simon's gloved hand from the object, but his fingers were locked tightly around it. For one grisly moment, she wondered whether she'd have to use her knife to pry off his fingers, but one by one they snapped back like catches on a sunken treasure chest. The object tumbled free, spinning; Peta reached out and caught it.

As her fingers closed around it, she had the same sense of the heat being drawn from her skin as she'd had when she held the piece Arthur had given her. Stranger yet was the fact that the shape looked as if her piece could fit right into it . . . whatever *it* was. And she could see places for other pieces to fit, as well.

If McKendry survived and could find Selene and her piece of the artifact, that plus Peta's and Arthur's and the one Frikkie still had could be put together to make—what?

There was no time to think about that now.

She looked to see whether Simon had carried a specimen bag and spotted a mesh bag floating empty around his dive belt. Reaching out, she slowly untied it, taking care not to expend too much energy. That could change her breathing rate and—worse—make Simon's buoyant body spin toward her.

Suddenly, she didn't want to stay in this bizarre cave for another minute. The place gave her the creeps, especially with Simon's body hanging there under the strange wall paintings. Briefly, she debated taking Simon's body with her. According to her dive watch, she had a more than adequate window of time for her return—with or without Simon. Assuming, of course, that she missed the shark on the way.

She stuck the artifact into the bag, thinking, I'm going to leave you here, Simon. I wish I could have made it here in time to stop you, to save you, but you knew the risks. My guess is that this is how you chose to die.

Her contemplation was cut short by the sensation that there was something else in the cavern, and it was coming closer.

Eduardo Blaine watched carefully while Peta's sleek form disappeared into the clear water. He followed her progress until the only sign of her that remained was the scattered trail of bubbles streaming to the surface.

When he was sure she was far enough down not to notice what happened topside, he moved to the front of the boat, peeled off his clothes, and slipped on a wet suit. He looked over at the man on the other boat watching him.

"You can go."

"No, man. Mr. Brousseau told me—"

"I'll bring him back. Don't worry. Of course, if you'd rather wait for the Obeahman to send you an invitation. . . ."

Blaine looked the man right in the eyes. The Trini blinked. He understood the message: Move or die. He quickly turned away and started his boat's engine.

Satisfied, Blaine looked back down at the telltale bubbles on the surface. Assuming the currents weren't pushing them around too much, they told him that Peta was angling away from the support leg and moving toward the center, where the test well would be.

He grabbed a weight belt and slipped on an extra three pounds of metal. He wanted to drop like a stone. If he needed to, he could shed the extra weight on the bottom.

Won't pretty Miss Peta be surprised, he thought, lifting a chest near the front of the boat to pull out his BCV, fins, and an extra pair of tanks.

In minutes, ready to dive, he sat on the railing, rolled backward, and splashed into the water.

He had no trouble finding the cave opening; it had been clearly marked by Charles and Abdul when they'd discovered it. He assumed that Peta was deep inside by now, perhaps all the way into the cavern. Soon, she and Simon would be coming back.

If Simon was still alive.

He reached over his shoulder and adjusted his air mixture, cutting back the oxygen. When he was satisfied with the new mix, he pulled his knife from its sheath and—holding it in front of him like the bill of a swordfish—started into the cave.

Having done more than enough cave diving to know what to expect, he moved smoothly through the twists and turns. He could almost anticipate the bony stone fingers that lurched out from the top and the sides. He swam sleekly, knife held in front of him, dodging the rocky outcroppings.

How long, he wondered, before he'd be in the cave, face to face with Peta and Simon? The two of them would be totally oblivious to his arrival.

Surprise, surprise.

At a fork in the cave, he chose the wider passage. No diver could make it into the narrower one. The walls of this new tunnel were smooth, looking almost preformed, man-made even. Probably created by the flow of water in and out of the main cave.

He saw the dull glow of a light ahead. Instinctively, he kicked harder.

The rocky tube widened suddenly and he shot into the cave. He could only dimly see what was happening. Simon was suspended near the far wall, which was covered by a mural that looked like something from an alien theme park.

Peta floated partially behind Simon's body.

Blaine watched as she took a specimen bag from the dead man's belt and stuffed something into it.

Good, Blaine thought. All the hard work has been done.

He kicked once, twice.

She was turning in his direction. He imagined her shock at seeing someone else in the cave, her relief when she recognized him, and finally her horror when she realized his purpose.

Horror was a bad thing. It was no fun to know that something really bad was about to happen. Better to just go quietly, unaware that—oops, you're dead. Blaine took no pleasure in the horror. Work like this was meant to be done well, but not necessarily savored.

He came at her hard, pushing Simon's body ahead of himself like a battering ram. The panic was rising in her face, and he could see her gulping air as she hit the wall. Not good, he thought. You must breathe evenly when you're diving this deep.

He noticed that his own breathing mixture felt thin and that he was gasping a bit from too much exertion. Unavoidable under the circumstances, he thought. He would check it later.

Keeping Peta pressed to the wall with Simon's lifeless body, he moved his knife in a broad, sweeping arc and expertly cut the main hose from her regulator. Immediately the air mixture rocketed out. He shifted his grip to her BC to steady her as he cut her secondary hose.

She kicked at him. That was another downside of the subject of the work being aware of what was happening. Nothing alive *wants* to die.

Fortunately the water and the dead weight between them made her slow, inaccurate. It was too late for her as the twin jets of free air shot from her tanks and wedged her tighter between the dead body and the wall.

Blaine sheathed his knife, scooped up the specimen bag, and kicked his way back to the cave opening. He held the bag tightly in his hand, the prize for Frikkie.

A nice prize, with the added bonus that the witnesses would never see the surface again.

Death wouldn't come all that quickly for Peta, but it would come. It was sad, really. She was a beautiful woman with a lot of fire.

He would have liked to have bedded her at least once.

25

Blaine moved slowly to the surface, taking his time. He didn't let himself dwell on Peta's struggle below. It wouldn't have been pretty, but—by now—it was over. Time to be forgotten. She was quite beautiful, he thought again, and quite brave. Altogether rather remarkable.

Pity how things turned out sometimes.

At fifteen feet from the surface he slowed to a stop. Breathing a trimix made rest stops absolutely necessary to ensure that no bubbles brewed in his bloodstream as he changed pressure. It was always good to vent some internal gases at low depth. Like a race-car driver making a pit stop. If life had been different, that's what he would have done: raced cars at high speed. He certainly had the balls for it.

Looking down, he saw a shape moving through the water. It circled coyly under him. His watch indicated that he had been at fifteen feet for only a minute—he should stay at this depth for another two minutes at least.

Beneath him, the shark described another circle, spiraling up his way.

Wouldn't that be ironic? he thought. Get the artifact, kill Peta, and have a shark rip me to pieces.

He looked up at the hull of his boat. Enough of a rest stop, he thought, kicking toward it.

In moments, he broke the surface. The water had turned choppy and he could feel a breeze building up from the southeast. Little whitecaps slapped him one way and the other as he treaded water. He swam to the edge of the boat and latched on. Removing his vest and tanks in the water, he climbed on board and pulled up his gear behind him. In short order, with his wet suit unzipped to the waist, he had the engine going and had cast off from the rig.

He stuffed the specimen bag into his shorts. This was one prize he would keep very close to himself. He toweled the water from his hair, sat on the edge, and looked down, hoping to see the shark. Keep coming up for me, he thought, and I'll put a damn bullet in your primeval head.

For a split second, he believed he could see it in the deep water below him, but then it faded and he guessed it had given up the chase.

He tossed away the towel, then eased back the throttle, prepared for a nice, leisurely cruise back to the shore. The boat belly-whapped on the choppy water, sending a cool spray shooting back at him. Feeling relaxed and satisfied, he brought out a silver metal box from under the foredeck hold, popped open the latches, and removed his sat phone. After turning it on, he said, "Frikkie."

The phone dialed automatically. He could hear the whirring ring: once, twice. Come on, he thought. You have to be there. This is what you've been waiting for.

"Yes?"

"I got it."

"Good. Correct that. *Great*. Take care with it."

Blaine smiled. "It's as safe as my family jewels, Frik. I tell you, though, it is a strange-looking thing. I do hope it was worth that beautiful woman's life."

"Wait! What did you just say?"

"Peta. I thought it might be tidier if she didn't surface to ask questions. Seemed like a nice place to leave someone buried. She and Simon kind of disap—"

"Go! The hell! Back! Now!"

"What?"

Even as Blaine spoke, he started cutting the wheel of the boat, turning around. It rocked as its own wake hit it from behind, and for a moment the propellers cut at air. Then he gunned the throttle.

"Are you going back?"

"On my way. Now tell me—"

"You idiot. Did I tell you to kill her?"

"No, Frikkie, but it seemed like a . . . how you say . . . no-brainer. Why would you—"

"Because she still has a piece of the artifact, you fool!"

The Venezuelan let that sink in. This was not good. People rarely screwed up on Frikkie more than once. They didn't live that long.

"You'd better hope to God she's still alive down there, Blaine. And if she isn't, you'd be better off not coming up again yourself."

He didn't respond. He could only think that it had been a long time since he'd left her in the cave. The best chance that she was alive was if she was somehow able to breathe the free-flowing gases from her tanks. Slim possibility of that, but a possibility nonetheless.

"Are you at the rig yet?"

"In thirty seconds, Frikkie. I'll go down. I'll see."

"She'd better be alive, Blaine. You hear me?"

"I hear you."

Blaine shut off the call and, one hand holding the wheel, grabbed his fins and suited up again.

Peta saw the precious mixture gushing out of the cut hoses like streams of water from the mouth of a crazed snake.

If something like this happened during a rec dive, she could just hold the free-flowing hose up to her mouth and breathe while she ascended. This deep, though, that wouldn't work. With the air shooting out so fast, there was no way it would last long enough for her to get out of the cave, even if she *could* sip the air like that.

Her second option was drowning. Already, she was feeling a little glow in her chest, the beginning of that amazing reflex that would eventually demand that she open her mouth and breathe, no matter what was touching her lips. She would suck in the water, putting an end to that crazed demand.

In minutes she'd be dead.

Then she realized that the answer was right in front of her: Simon. His tanks were intact and still had plenty of air in them. If she could hold her breath a little longer, she might be able to get to them.

Trying to avoid looking at the bulging eyes and the rubbery, puffed-out lips, she reached for the regulator. You're saving my life, Simon, she thought as she took a breath. For a moment she wondered if it had been a regulator failure that had killed him, but the mechanism worked fine. She took a few even breaths before she slid off her own BC vest and tanks, and watched them float to the top of the cave. With Simon's mouthpiece locked between her teeth, she reached around him and undid the buckle and the Velcro of his BC. As she pulled it open, she tried to slide it down, but his arms wouldn't cooperate.

Take your time, she told herself. You have to be patient. Don't expend too much energy.

As gently as she could, she pushed his right arm out of the vest. It wasn't easy. The arm felt stiff, too long for the armhole. She had to wedge Simon's body against the wall and use all her strength to force it through.

With one arm out, the other became much simpler.

Once she had the tanks free, she turned away from her friend's body and ended up facing the wall mural. Something in the shapes drew her attention, as if there were a secret there that she would understand if she just stared at it long enough. Was that shape a head? No, not a head. More like something from a microbiology class—as if the mural were some grotesque enlargement of a slide.

Several sharp beeps drew her attention away from the images. She looked around, afraid that someone else might be attacking, and realized that the sound was coming from Simon's dive watch.

Time to get out of here, she thought. She had to let the regulator slip from her mouth as she slid her arms into Simon's considerably larger vest. Putting the mechanism back in her mouth, she took another slow, steady breath. She had to stay calm, not breathe too fast.

It occurred to her that she wasn't entirely sure what she'd find when she did escape this cave. Would Blaine be waiting in his boat to see if she made it out? What about Simon's pilot? What would she do if there was no boat up there waiting for her?

None of those questions had answers now. She had to keep her focus. The first task was to get out of this cavern and back to the surface.

She looked ahead to the cave opening, then around at the other walls, their surfaces as smooth as glass. What this place was, she had no idea. She did know that if she stayed here much longer looking for the answer, she wouldn't live to tell anyone.

She took one last look around the domelike cave. About to turn away, she spotted something she hadn't noticed earlier: a hole, low to the ground on the other side of the cave. Another way out, perhaps. A good thing, given that she didn't know what Blaine might have left for her on the path they'd used to come in.

Swimming over to the second passage, she got her head down low to shoot her light inside. The dim light didn't reveal much. She hesitated for a moment, and went in.

This channel was much narrower, barely large enough for her body and tanks. The walls were even smoother than in the first cavern, glassine and iridescent, silky to the touch.

Half a dozen feet in, the tube opened into a small chamber, a circular passageway with three other thin tubes shooting off in different directions. The chamber was big enough for her to kneel and look around.

On the wall behind her, she saw what looked like a shape. While she watched, it seemed to move—a dark blue-black shimmer. Tiny plankton floating in the water gave the shape a hazy, blurry outline, and she guessed that the apparent motion was a result of the light reflecting on the strange surface, like the inside of the shell of an oyster. The image of an oyster reminded her of the strangest aspect of this cavern: there should have been fish and crustaceans making this nice deep-water pocket home, but she saw nothing alive. Nothing at all.

She heard a series of high-pitched beeps. Her own dive watch this time. She looked at the maze of other channels ahead leading to other chambers, other secrets. They might lead to another way out, but she didn't have time for errors. She would have to leave the way she'd come in.

Swimming as quickly as she could without straining, she passed through the big cavern and into the channel. Not until she had exited the hole into open water did she pause to check her watch and her gauges. She was doing fine. There was plenty of time for a safe ascent if nothing else went wrong.

Following one of the giant Erector-set legs of the platform, she ascended slowly. As she looked up, she noticed something moving on the surface. When the object came to a stop, she managed to focus on it until she made out the shape of a boat. It looked like Blaine's boat, but why would he have come back?

After another few feet of ascent, she saw the churning foamy bloom of a diver entering the water. She realized that not only was Blaine back, but he was coming down to make sure she was dead. What other reason could there be?

She reached down instinctively for her knife, but this wasn't the place to fight.

She checked her compass. Tired as she was, the best thing would have been to go straight up, but with a killer coming down to the scene of the crime, that option was blocked. So instead, she started kicking, turning her ascent into a long angle, heading west. If she could make it to one of the other legs before Blaine noticed her, she could use it as cover.

With luck, he would swim by and never know she was around.

Hanging twenty feet below the surface to rest and let her blood gases even out, she wondered if there might be another reason why he had come back.

Not that it mattered. She was just glad he had been courteous enough to bring her a fast boat. Any other concern would have to be left for later, when there was time to think about what had happened and why this artifact was worth the lives of so many people.

Arthur, Keene, Simon, Paul Trujold, all dead. It's a miracle that McKendry and I aren't also among the deceased, she thought as, with a few gentle kicks, she propelled herself to the surface.

26

Blaine rolled into the water and started a quick plummet back to the cave opening. He didn't take the time to consult a tech dive table, but he was sure that two quick ups and downs at such depth had to be bad.

Besides, this was probably a pointless dive. Unless he could find the object Frik wanted so badly—on Simon, or Peta, or still wedged somewhere in the underwater cavern—the dive would only confirm that Peta was dead. And that Simon was dead. After overstepping his authority so badly, he was sure to join the dead soon himself, if the dive didn't kill him first.

This must be the way an American death row prisoner feels, he thought, hoping against hope for the governor's eleventh-hour pardon.

His stomach in knots, he approached the cave opening.

A school of annoying yellowfins hovered there, as if they were thinking about going inside to nibble on something tasty. They dispersed like seeds blown from an aquatic dandelion as Blaine approached, only to reform into a loose school a dozen feet away.

Ready to enter, he adjusted his air mixture. If he kept the oxygen as lean as possible, he might avoid getting bent. One of his tanks scraped along a rocky outcrop with a noise far worse than fingernails on a chalkboard.

He kicked onward, passing into the channel where the walls became smooth and finally widened as he neared the main cavern. As he reached that opening, diver's intuition told him that something was wrong.

He flashed on the shark.

Had it beat the yellowfins in here? he wondered. Was that why the fish had hesitated? If so, the shark wouldn't take too kindly to being disturbed while dining.

Entering the cavern, he realized that it was not the shark that had given him pause. It was Simon, who, freed from the weight of his BC vest, bobbed near the top of the cavern above the crazed squiggles.

She was a clever girl, that Peta, using Simon's equipment to save herself. Frikkie would be happy—overjoyed, even—when he heard that she was alive and that he would have a shot at getting the other piece of the artifact.

That might even get Frik off his back, Blaine thought. He turned slowly and kicked his way out of the cave. Sooner or later he would think about whether it was necessary to deal with the fact that Peta knew he had tried to kill her. Not yet. Not unless she was somewhere up there waiting for him. She was a tough cookie, quite capable, he suspected, of exacting her own justice.

When he had ascended far enough to see clearly where the leg of the oil rig broke through the waterline, now only forty feet above him, he discovered her payback. She was not waiting on the surface to kill him after all. Instead, she had taken his boat and left him with no transportation back to shore. It would be one hell of a surface swim back to San Gabriel.

Resting at fifteen feet for another safety stop, he considered his options.

He could get lucky and flag down a passing fishing boat. That was unlikely, though. The few boats that passed the rig would be piloted by superstitious Trinis who would think he was the Obeahman.

Another option was to pop enough air into his BC to ride the choppy wake of the sea, turn on his back, and kick his way to shore. That would take three hours, maybe more. He would be baked crisp by the sun and easy bait for any passing sharks, but it was not impossible.

Whatever option he attempted to exercise, the real problem was that he would get very thirsty with the hot sun bearing down on him. What was that cliché line from "The Rime of the Ancient Mariner" that they had taught him in English class back home in Venezuela? Water, water, every where . . .

Like hooking a billfish, his mind latched onto the answer. The rig would have an emergency radio. He could simply climb out of the water and call Frikkie. He almost laughed into his regulator. She was not so clever after all, little Miss Peta.

His watch told him that it was time to get to the surface. Once there, he shed his tanks, fins, and BCV, and dragged them to the rig's docking platform.

On the long climb, he thought he could see his boat heading north through the Dragon's Mouth. It looked like Peta had decided to go all the way home to Grenada, rather than take a chance of running into Frik in Port of Spain.

Reaching the main deck of the rig, he was happy to discover that while vandals had thrown rocks and fired guns at the windows, they had lacked the courage to board the platform for robbery. The emergency radio was intact, and he soon contacted Oilstar's main dispatcher, who agreed to send a helicopter for him.

Having done that, he called Frik to let him know that Peta was fine. Then, satisfied that he had handled the crisis as well as he could, he reached into his shorts, pulled out the specimen bag, and examined the bizarre object that Frik apparently considered to be worth the life of Simon Brousseau and Abdul, and heaven knew how many others.

The boat rode the choppy sea giddily, a child's toy bouncing in a giant bathtub. Peta glanced over her shoulder at the rock spires piercing the water behind her.

As soon as she'd passed through the Dragon's Mouth and moved away from the sheltering effects of Trinidad, the sea had turned rough. She had ridden tramp freighters between Grenada and its southern neighbor many times as a girl, and she recalled how rough the journey could be, even in those relatively large boats. The passage would last more than three hours, even in Blaine's fast little craft. If she spent the time focused on the ups and downs of the sea, she would soon be leaning over the rail like some land-loving tourist on her first voyage.

To take her mind off of the bumpy ride, she tried to understand what she had just been through and to guess at what made the pieces of that weirdly shaped object so precious that people had to be killed.

She thought of the artifact she had hidden away in the bank vault. It was a match to the one she believed was the reason Arthur had been blown up, and to the one Simon had died to recover. All of the pieces had come from that undersea cavern with its Daliesque wall mural.

What the hell was that place? What made the artifact important enough to Frikkie that he would send his supposed friends to their deaths so that he could get the pieces?

Why? What did he know?

All Manny had been able to tell her was that Paul had said it would change the nature of energy production around the world. Perhaps it could put not just Frikkie but all of OPEC out of business, changing the balance of power around the world practically overnight.

Was that important enough to have her killed?

Obviously, Frik thought so. She had to remember that: he wanted her dead. When he found out she had survived, he'd try again. Which also meant she would have to be prepared to kill to protect herself.

The sunlight disappeared. Looking up, she saw a lone gray cloud, but when she looked east, she saw a dark line following the first, like an army arrayed behind a single scout. How long, she wondered, before the whole battalion reached her? Open ocean in a tiny boat was not a good place to be with a storm coming on.

Behind her, the island of Trinidad was just a memory. If she headed for Tobago, she'd be steering straight into the oncoming storm, but Grenada was a long way away.

A childhood recollection bubbled into her brain. She had been six, spending a week with her grandparents in Carriacou. Her grandfather decided to take her fishing in his little Gouyave sloop, a tiny single-masted sailboat hand-built in Grenada's famed fishing village.

The day started out sunny and bright. They sailed easily out of Tyrrel Bay and around the southern tip of the island, heading west into the deeper waters on the Atlantic side. As they cruised along, she trailed her fingers in the beautiful blue water. It had felt like magic to her.

Passing the big rock called Saline Island, her grandfather told her to check the gear and bait the hooks on the two fishing rods he'd brought along—a big one for him, a small one for her. She remembered it because it was the first time he had let her ready the lines. From the bucket of small silver fish called jacks she pulled one out, and hooked it just ahead of its dorsal fin, then repeated the process with the other pole.

After her grandfather had brought down the sail, the boat rocked in the current. They cast their lines and, as if God had been smiling on them, were soon catching fish. She remembered that she hadn't wanted to stop, not even after they had a half dozen in the boat.

"This be plenty," her grandfather said, chuckling.

She had been so fascinated by the process of casting and reeling and pulling the fish into the boat that she hadn't noticed how much the little craft had begun to rock. What she recalled most clearly was the feeling when the sun had vanished. It wasn't like the times when the thin skittering clouds would cut the glare. That time the sun had disappeared and she'd felt the chill of a strong wind on her neck.

"We done with fishing now, little one," her grandfather had said. She remembered as if the image had been burned into her mind: the way his face looked; the twinkle gone, the fun vanished. "We been too long at sea and Mother getting mad."

Standing at the wheel of Blaine's boat, she could remember with her whole body the feel of that little sloop as the growing waves tossed it around.

Her grandfather had struggled with the sail, having to keep it partly furled in the strong wind that had arrived with the clouds. She had wanted to say "Can we go home, Grandpa?" but she sat silently. He obviously wished to get home too.

When the first drop of rain hit her arm, she thought that she had never seen such a large drop of water. It was soon followed by another and another.

As their tiny craft rounded Mushroom Island and her grandfather eased them into a turn toward Southwest Point, they were hit by one large wave that nearly knocked her into the sea. His large hands grabbed her and shoved her into the growing puddle at the bottom of the boat.

She remembered that he'd smiled again. "We be home soon." His eyes narrowed as another wave broke over the railing, drenching both of their faces. "You not gotta swim for it. You know everything gonna be fine, Peta."

She had nodded, though she hadn't known that at all.

"Grandpa—I'm scared."

The little boat had passed Southwest Point and the rocking eased a little. Her grandfather hugged the coastline to stay in the lee of the island. "I know, little one," he'd said, leaning forward. "But I tell you, when you not alone, you not ever be afraid, okay?"

In that moment, it hadn't mattered that the sun was gone, or that their faces were wet with the streaming rainwater, or that the ocean wanted to come into the boat. They were together, and there was nothing to be afraid of.

Alone in Blaine's boat, Peta looked to the east and saw the line of rain approaching. A bright silver flash in the sky ahead of her heralded the arrival of an airplane at Point Saline Airport.

Today, she would stay ahead of the storm.

She would make it back to St. George's and watch the storm from the safety of her own home.

The image of the strange mural on the wall of the cavern rose in her mind and she knew there was a much bigger storm brewing than the little squall that was blowing in from the Atlantic.

Who am I kidding? she thought.

Her grandfather had been dead for over twenty years and she still missed him; would always miss him, the way she would always miss her father and Arthur.

No matter how much she missed them, though, they were gone and they weren't coming back. She was alone now. And she was afraid.

27

Joshua Keene sat up gingerly, as if his body might be rigged to explode. Slowly, he captured a few memories. He recalled flashes: fighting the terrorists onboard the *Yucatán;* seeing Terris McKendry shot in the chest two, maybe three times, impacts that knocked the big man backward, as if missiles had been launched into his body's core. He saw battered bicycles, heard them clattering to the oil tanker's deck, felt as much as heard the bamboo *snap* of a terrorist's neck under his own grip.

After that, the explosion, fire, his body flung backward as if he had been kicked in the chest by Bruce Lee. He remembered the night and the smoke and the long, long fall to the dark water that cushioned him about as softly as a concrete parking lot. He recalled the water closing over his head, a vision of sharks, and then . . . nothing.

He tried to focus his eyes to see where he was, but all he could see was the foggy image of a beautiful tanned woman with a haze of red-brown hair that looked like a halo.

An angel, he thought. I'm dead. And passed back into semiconsciousness.

The next time he awoke, his vision was clear. The same woman stood beside him. "I'm Selene Trujold," she said. She poured a finger of scotch into a white enamel cup and inhaled its aroma. "Here. Drink this and then we'll talk."

He took the cup from her, remembering the brief glimpse he had caught of her before all hell broke loose. "How long have I been out? Hours? Days?"

"You've been here for a couple of days. I had you fished out of the water after the explosion on the tanker."

"Why?"

"There were helicopters coming, a lot of chaos. I couldn't be sure you weren't one of us."

"You could have tossed me back to the sharks when you found out that I wasn't."

"You're right. I could have done that. I still can, if you don't prove useful to us."

She *is* a piece of work, Keene thought, remembering his assessment of her when he'd first spotted her on the *Yucatán*. "I had a friend with me," he said. "He was fighting one of your people. Somebody shot him—one of your goons."

"None of us are goons, Mr. Rip Van Winkle or whoever you are." Her tone, acrid at first, softened. "But I *am* sorry about your friend." To Keene's surprise, she sounded sincere. He sipped at the scotch, then drained the glass. The whiskey burned in his chest.

"More?" She took the cup from him.

"Not yet. I want to keep my head clear."

She smiled. "That'll be a switch. You haven't been conscious, not to mention compos mentis, since we hauled you into the Zodiac and cruised away from the tanker."

"Did you achieve your objective?"

"We thought so—at the time. I expected a much larger explosion, but I'll accept any victory. If nothing else, I'm sure we called some attention to Oilstar's activities."

"And your own," Keene said.

She shrugged. "For better or for worse." She poured some of the scotch into the same cup for herself. "Scotch and coffee, two of the greatest amenities of Venezuelan civilization." She looked contemplatively into the honey brown liquid and raised the cup. "Even out here in the jungle, I wouldn't do without them."

Antagonism crawled down Keene's spine. He looked at her angrily, started to say something, and passed out. He woke up with a pounding head and a throbbing body hinting at more wounds than he wanted to know about. His skin felt oily with perspiration, but he could not determine whether the sweat was from jungle humidity or a severe fever.

He'd been having the most bizarre dreams he'd ever remembered.

First he was making love to a woman with velvet skin, short cinnamon hair, a coffee-with-too-much-milk complexion, large intent eyes, a small nose, and a delicate chin. In the midst of their lovemaking, she ripped off her face as if it were a mask and he was catapulted into fiery nightmares filled with terrible visions that pounded inside his skull.

He pressed his fingertips to his chest and found bandages and pain. He touched the patchwork of injuries, pressing down hard because the pain reminded him that he was still alive. His mind was full of questions. Where was he?

He heard jungle crickets, the belching music of small frogs and of trickling water, the crackle and whisper of dried leaves woven into a fragrant roof over his head.

"You awake now?"

Keene turned his head and groaned as even the small movement set a series of pains in motion.

Selene sat on the ground, her back against the inner wall of the hut. She gave him an odd smile, an expression that surprised him more than the amazing fact of finding himself alive. He tried to talk, but his voice came out in a squeak that embarrassed him. "What . . . happened?"

"You've been dried, fed, and nursed back to life. Now it's time for some payback."

"Payback?"

She laughed. "Nothing too strenuous, I promise you. First you tell me who you are."

"Joshua Keene."

"I assume that since you and your friend were on the *Yucatán,* you work for Frik Van Alman. Is that correct?"

"Not precisely."

"Then what, precisely, were you doing on the tanker?"

Keene hesitated, confused by his pain and wondering how the beautiful woman questioning him could be the enemy. "It's complicated. Terris and I are . . . were in a group with Frik. He asked us to look for you," he said at last.

"What sort of group? Why would you just blindly follow Frik's orders?"

Keene felt the fuzz returning to his brain. He tried to shake it off. "It's called the Daredevils Club. It's like a brotherhood of adventurers. Frik asked for our help, and we saw the opportunity for some action.

He wanted something he said your father stole from him and sent to you."

"Frikkie Van Alman is a sorry excuse for a human being. I know the things Van Alman says about Green Impact. He's a liar. A killer. A megalomaniac." Her whole demeanor hardened. "My father is dead. Van Alman killed him because he knew too much about Oilstar's operations and their intent."

"I had nothing to do with that. Neither did Terris, and he's dead too."

Selene turned to walk back to a small camp stove where she was heating some water. The tail of her shirt rode up and he saw smooth skin.

"You need to listen, Joshua. Green Impact is not a bunch of wild dogs trying to cause senseless destruction. Not my people, and not me. We're doing this to stop Frik from destroying our future."

"Are you sure you're not as deluded as he is?" Joshua's throat was dry, his voice hoarse. She moved toward the doorway. "I've got some things to take care of." She tucked her shirt back into her khaki shorts. "We'll talk more when I get back."

Yet one more time, Keene drifted off into a restless sleep. He awoke in pain and filled with sadness, but less confused. This time he knew where he was and what he was doing there, though there were still plenty of gaps in the past . . . what was it? A week? Two? He had heard about temporary trauma-induced amnesia and knew that it wasn't likely to last. The memories would return in bits and pieces, like misrouted mail.

He struggled off the mildewed canvas cot where he'd been lying and made it outside onto a small verandah. Sitting down on one of two handmade chairs, he surveyed his surroundings.

The verandah overlooked a tiny tributary in the lush labyrinth of the Orinoco Delta. He could see some of the remaining members of Green Impact gathering food, preparing supplies, practicing skills. One man, probably a guard who had remained awake through the previous night's shift, slept in a mesh hammock. Tall trees filled with colorful tropical birds flanked the stream. Dwellings clustered together in what appeared to be an encampment, raised on poles above the marshy ground and constructed of thin stripped logs with roofs thatched with heavy dried palm fronds.

"I'm glad to see you up," Selene said, appearing from behind and taking the chair next to him. She was holding the same white enamel mug, only this time he could smell coffee.

"Here." She handed him the cup. "It's strong."

Keene took it from her and placed it on a rickety little table that separated the chairs. "Do you know for sure that Terris McKendry is dead?"

"There were many casualties that night," Selene said, looking away. "Five of my people, the skeleton crew on the tanker, and, yes, I suppose your friend, too."

Her expression serious, she reached into her shirt pocket and pulled out a strangely shaped object. She tapped it on the table with a dull-sounding click.

"That's what Frik's so hot to have? That's the reason Terris died?" Keene could hear the rising fury in his own voice.

"Yes. It may not look like much, but this one piece could change the world. Frik doesn't understand much about it, but he wants to possess it badly enough that when my father tried to keep it from him, Frik killed him."

"How do you know?" Keene asked her. "We were told it was a lab accident."

"Right! Funny that it happened the day after he and Frik had a confrontation about this very thing. Frik shouted at him, threatened him." She held up the odd fragment, turning it so that the jungle light was reflected in skewed patterns. "My father wrote me a letter explaining where this thing came from. He was so frightened of what Frik would do that he separated the pieces of the artifact, sent this one to me for safekeeping, and sent another to himself. I'm not sure what happened to the rest. I think Arthur Marryshow might have another one."

"Arthur's dead too. Killed in an explosion on New Year's Eve not long after your father died."

Selene looked astonished, then even angrier. "See what I mean?"

Keene contemplated his own doubts. Arthur Marryshow and Paul Trujold, dead within days of each other. Both men concerned about Frik Van Alman's peculiar artifact. He didn't believe in coincidences. "What else do you know about . . . that?" He pointed at the fragment.

"All I know is that it was dredged up by Oilstar's test drilling rig, the one just off the coast of Trinidad," she said. "According to my father, the composition is like nothing ever found before, nothing that any human made."

"Are we talking little green men here?" Joshua allowed himself a small smile.

"You tell me." Selene thrust the fragment at him. "My father believed it has amazing properties. He was sure that when all the pieces were back together, this artifact—*device,* whatever you want to call it—could be the key to an energy source that would make filthy petroleum companies as obsolete as woodcutters from the Middle Ages."

"Frik runs an oil company. Why would he want it so badly?"

"Because he wants to make sure nobody else gets it."

"Now *that* sounds like Frik."

The coffee tasted bitter in Keene's mouth. He added even more sugar than the Venezuelan norm. He didn't like Frik; never had. The Afrikaner was pushy and self-centered, with an abrasive personality. But a cold-blooded killer . . . ? "So what do we do now?" he asked Selene.

"*We?*"

Keene thought of what Frikkie Van Alman had told them—the lies and the innuendos. If Selene was telling him the truth, then Frik already had plenty of blood on his hands, and he didn't seem worried in the least about consequences. "Yes," he said. "We."

"Well, to begin with, the *Valhalla* is an abomination," Selene said.

He pictured the huge structure of the rig's production platform. The first time he had seen the monolith, it had looked to him like an elephantine skyscraper of concrete and steel, bristling with tall derricks, piping, and tubes, belching flames and smoke. Little had he known that the pair of bright pilot flares burning at the edge of the extended derricks would become a funeral pyre for his friend Terris McKendry.

Selene looked at him, her eyes bright and intense. "Even before I found out from my father what that bastard was trying to do, I knew that it was screwing up the ecosystem here in the Serpent's Mouth—spilled oil and solvents, natural leakage, 'acceptable losses' of toxic chemicals and lubricants. It raises the temperature of the water, killing some fish, attracting others, messing with the entire balance."

She leaned closer to him. "And the sharks. The population has increased three- or fourfold. That's not natural."

The mention of sharks brought a new flood of memories, beginning with his game, a stunt, preparation for the confrontation to come later that night. He envisioned four concrete legs thrust downward all the way to the sea bottom, where a honeycomb of holding tanks were filled with the fresh crude oil, and remembered his fears during the swim from the tanker over to the production platform.

Green Impact had proven far more deadly than any aquatic predator.

"What do you think will happen as the drilling continues?" Keene asked.

"I can only guess," Selene said, "Who can say for sure what sort of global chaos might follow? Oilstar is producing from one of the boreholes now, draining out a lot of crude oil, but other crews are still exploring. Frikkie wants to find the rest of that artifact. He needs to see if there's anything else down below at the Dragon's Mouth site. There have to be checks and balances."

"And Green Impact is one of those checks?" Anger and uncertainty replaced Keene's usual good humor.

"Yes we are." Selene got up and motioned him to follow. "Come on. Let me show you around."

At Green Impact's hideout in the jungle, the group had its supply cache, canned food and propane gas tanks brought in by flatboat, and what remained of its stockpile of weapons.

Automatically, his mind started cataloging the remnants and planning what would be needed to make a real attack against Oilstar. By Keene's estimates, there was barely enough ammunition left after the assault on the *Yucatán* to defend the compound if it was discovered. It would take months to pull together enough explosives and ammunition to have a real chance at another assault, even if Frikkie did little to improve security on the rig.

Selene explained to him that they traded with the Warao Indians, who went to trading posts and small villages on the larger waterways to surreptitiously pick up items the ecocrusaders needed. No one noticed the Indians, who came and went as they pleased, like jungle shadows, but the trading post owners would certainly pay attention to a group of white strangers. Once or twice, Selene explained, she and her friends could pass themselves off as German bird-watchers or Canadian ecotourists, but as time went by, suspicions would grow. They would have to move on.

Three days later, Selene took Keene out in one of Green Impact's small motorized boats. As they moved through narrow caños into broader streams, following the tributaries of a diffused Orinoco to the sea, they passed half-naked Warao fishermen standing at the riverbanks, in search of birds or fish or eggs, the day's catch. Keene looked at some of the dark-skinned Indio children who hid beside their bare-breasted mothers. He smiled at them, but they didn't wave back.

When they reached the end of the jungle and the open waters of the Gulf of Paria, Selene brought the boat to a halt, letting the outboard putter into a low purr as if catching its breath. Keene looked up to watch a flock of scarlet ibises take wing from the muddy shallows.

"Amazing, aren't they?"

Keene nodded, watching the ibises fly off to find other feeding grounds, like matadors waving their capes in the humid air.

Selene turned the boat around and headed back upriver, winding in the direction of the Green Impact encampment. As they approached, she shut off the Zodiac's motor and drifted, turning into a small caño, brushing past reeds. She startled a cluster of small yellow frogs, which plopped and splashed into the brownish water.

"This isn't the way back," Keene said.

She smiled at him. "You have a good memory. This is a special side trip just for you and me."

She took the black rubber raft as far as the little stream would allow, then beached it in the mud. When she climbed out, the soft ground squished under her boots. "We're just a stone's throw from the camp. This is my retreat. No one else knows about it."

She reached back to take Joshua's hand. After he climbed out of the boat, she didn't release it, but led him through the grasses to a little dry patch, a hummock raised above the water level and filled with flowers and sweet grasses. Small birds fluttered and twittered, as if incensed at the human intrusion into what appeared to be a perfect, cozy meadow in the middle of the Orinoco Delta.

Selene took his other hand. Keene found himself helpless, as if his grip had turned to water. Her faded, loose shirt hung partially open. She raised his hand and slid it between the opening in her shirt, cupping it against her left breast. Keene tried to reclaim his hand. She pressed it tighter and he felt her nipple stiffen.

"Don't pull away," Selene said. "Feel my skin, feel my heart pumping, the blood beneath my flesh. I'm *real*, Joshua Keene, just as everything I have told you is real."

"Why me?" he asked.

"I'm not sure," she said. "Maybe it's just that I've been in the jungle for too long."

"What about the men in your group?"

"I'm their leader," she said. "It's tough enough for them to obey a woman without any other . . . complications."

"I've wanted you since the moment I saw you," Keene said. "Even when I thought you were the enemy."

She took his face in her hands and kissed him, gently at first, then with increasing passion. "I have wanted you too, Joshua Keene," she said. "I could love you, I think."

They undressed each other slowly, taking turns, one article at a time. Then they made love in the soft grass under the open tropical sky, laughing as the bugs flew around and the grass tickled and scratched their naked skin.

Keene's body still felt tired and a little shaky, but enough of his wounds had healed. He lay beside Selene, watching the glow of the sun as it filtered through the overhanging branches, slipping toward afternoon and the western horizon. He wanted to stay this way, without cares, ignoring the future, but he could not remain in an endless present. He knew he had other obligations to face, and decisions to make.

Looking up into the knitted tree branches that formed a canopy overhead, feeling Selene warm beside him but not looking into her captivating eyes, Joshua said, "I meant it."

She propped herself up on one elbow, looking at him, but he continued to stare upward. She stroked his chest. "What was it you meant?"

He sat up and faced her in the rapidly diminishing light. "I'll help you shut down the *Valhalla* platform."

28

Paul Trujold, Arthur, Joshua Keene. Dead of unnatural causes. And now Simon. All but Trujold members of the Daredevils Club.

Something smells rotten, McKendry thought for the umpteenth time. But what . . . besides his own body, which could use some heavy bathing after weeks of hospital sponge baths? Chances were, boredom had led to his feeling that something was awry. He had little else to do but follow rehab instructions and concoct plots where there probably were none.

After Peta's initial hands-on care and during the subsequent weeks of his recovery, he had grown tired of hearing about the "miracle of his survival." Being transferred to rehab was a welcome change, until he found out that he would be staying there through Easter. Fed up with the time-consuming process of recuperation, he became obsessive about obeying instructions. He did whatever he was told to do, and then did it again for good measure, figuring that he had no choice if he wanted to get back on his feet and pick up where he and Keene had left off.

"They tell me you'll be well enough to leave soon," Frik said, entering the room without knocking. "If that's true, you're well enough to answer a few questions."

As boss of Oilstar, Frik had made several perfunctory visits to the hospital. Each time, within five minutes, he was there and gone. McKendry had no illusions about this being a simple courtesy call to wish him better or to express his continued grief at the loss of Joshua Keene.

Seeing Frik, he felt more than his usual annoyance at the man's lack of sensitivity. He had recovered from gunshot wounds before, more often than he wanted to count. He could deal with the residual pain using salves or painkillers, even this time when the flash burns from the explosion were an added annoyance. But nothing seemed able to drive away the ache of his friend's death. A few genuine words of condolence from Frik might have gone a long way.

Taking McKendry's silence to mean assent, Frik said, "I've been wanting to ask if you got any information about the artifact."

McKendry held his anger in check. "I was a little too busy to ask Ms. Trujold about her jewelry."

"Of course." Frik's paternal smile and pat on the shoulder were almost more than McKendry could tolerate. "I tend to get focused on my own goals sometimes. As I've said before, I'm very sorry about Joshua. I think the choice of his replacement for the club should be at your discretion."

McKendry clenched his hands under his thin blanket. "At this moment, I don't really care about the Daredevils Club, Frik. What I want is to feel Selene Trujold's throat inside my grip." He hesitated, but only briefly. "You know, you wouldn't need to worry so much about Green Impact terrorists if you had anybody aboard your tankers or your production platform who gave a damn about security. Joshua and I swam over from the *Yucatán*. We climbed aboard the *Valhalla* platform, ran around for over an hour, and swam back. He even scrambled to the top of the highest derrick. Not a soul saw us. Everybody was busy partying and ignoring standard procedures."

Frik gave a shrug. "This is South America. What can you do?"

"You can be professional, damn it!" McKendry said. "Put me in charge of security on that rig. I need an excuse to stay around and find Selene anyway."

Frik grinned as if he couldn't have been more pleased. Apparently, getting McKendry to work on the rig was precisely the motivation behind his visit. "You've got the job," he said, "starting as soon as you're ready. Complete carte blanche. Do what you need to do, with one proviso. When you find her, I want that artifact."

A few days later, McKendry stood on the broad deck of the *Valhalla* production platform in dark blue jeans so new that they were not yet stained with enough oil and grease for him to fit in with the rig crew.

This high off the water, he had a commanding view of the lowlands all around, the broad channel of the Serpent's Mouth with the island of Trinidad to the east and the wide and uncharted swamps of the Delta Amacuro on the Venezuelan mainland to the west.

Standing there, washed by humid breezes that reminded him he was alive, he grieved for Joshua Keene. The medicines he was taking were doing wonders for his residual physical pain, but they did nothing to soften the grief.

He kept remembering the flash of fire.

The explosion on the tanker deck seemed to be tattooed onto his retinas, so that when he shut his eyes he saw the silhouette of Keene's body, black against the flame front, flying into the night. Again and again, he felt the bullets strike his rib cage, like railroad spikes driven in with a sledgehammer. Barely conscious, he'd sensed the *Yucatán* moving on like a lost, lumbering juggernaut through shark-infested water.

Even as he was sure that he was dying, he'd prayed that his friend was still alive.

Almost in self-defense, McKendry turned his thoughts from Keene to his new job. The crew had accepted his presence as security chief, following strict orders from Frik Van Alman. They were clearly intimidated by his size, his brooding nature, and the fact that he had survived what should have been mortal wounds. As far as they were concerned, he was a hero for having prevented a real disaster on the tanker. They approached him with equal measures of admiration and fear.

That was well and good. But what he really required from them was respect, and obedience to a new work ethic.

As Oilstar's newly appointed—self-appointed, really—security chief, McKendry was nothing if not serious about his work. He spoke with all of the levels of management, twenty-five people at a time. Though he hated to talk in public, he gave lecture after lecture.

It took him two days, ten talks, until he had spoken to every single person aboard the *Valhalla*. As they met in the mess hall—where cooks were busy preparing spaghetti and fried fish, big pots of black beans, fried bananas, and heavily spiced rice—he saw their admiration turn to resentment with each of his pronouncements. Seeing the resistance, he called in reinforcements from the mainland, twenty private security troops who helped him go through the crew's personal lockers one at a time, rounding up shopping carts full of rum, scotch, whiskey. The galley even kept a stock of Carib, a flagrant breach of regulations.

During a ceremony reminiscent of a funeral at sea, McKendry made the crew stand and watch as he opened the bottles and poured the alcohol over the side, down into the sea. The quantity of liquor was certainly enough to be detectable even in the warm tropical water; he wondered if sharks could get drunk.

All personnel were required to have valid passports. Even prescription drugs had to be documented with the rig medical staff. Smoking was forbidden anywhere outside the living quarters and the coffee shop, and the workers squawked about not being able to carry lighters outside into the rig machinery and gas-separation towers. He had to crack a few heads together just to enforce commonsense housekeeping procedures. Even then, he was forced to send a boatload of twenty-three disgruntled and intractable rig workers back home with minimal severance pay and no future prospect for a paycheck from Oilstar.

After that, when he looked the remaining crew members in the eyes, he saw a change in their former laughing, carefree attitude. He had their attention, for now. As for what would happen after he achieved his goal and left them to their own devices, that was a different matter. If Frikkie Van Alman didn't keep watch, they could revert, and Oilstar could go down the tubes.

Frankly, McKendry didn't care. He was neither their father nor their baby-sitter.

Having lived in Venezuela, he was familiar with the general mañana approach. It had driven him nuts then, and it did so now, even though he understood its origins. Venezuela was one of the prime movers in the formation of OPEC in 1960, and though oil prices had dipped in the 1980s—he could remember the resultant economic and political turmoil—the nation still lived with too much spending money and too little personal productivity, not to speak of enduring and overthrowing a succession of dictators. He figured that Frik's tolerance for the Venezuelan attitude was possible only because so much of his workforce was Trinidadian.

Not that they were so eager to lift that bale or tote that barge either.

The sooner he could get on with his real reason for being here, the better, he thought, as he raised a pair of binoculars and examined the topography around him: marshy islands, drunkenly balanced trees laden with greenery, the labyrinth of caños, the low swamps.

Scattered, disorganized villages dotted the seashore where the Orinoco petered out into the gulf. Looking at the landscape, he saw endless hiding places for the ecoterrorists. Grim and angry, standing alone under the whistling girders of the north derrick, the one Joshua had foolishly climbed, McKendry swore anew that he would find Selene Trujold and her murderous companions—with or without the law and the Venezuelan military, with or without the help of Oilstar.

For him, tracking down Green Impact had become personal.

To help speed the recovery from his injuries, McKendry used the exercise facilities onboard the *Valhalla* platform, a health club that could have commanded high prices in the States. Most of the time, he felt as if it were his private domain. The potbellied rig workers never seemed interested in using their off-duty hours to exercise. They didn't bother to keep themselves in shape, and instead grew thick in the gut and spent their downtime smoking cigarettes, playing card games, and watching videotapes which, to his amusement, included a complete library of his former boss, the Spanish action star Rodolfo.

McKendry didn't need to build his muscles, just keep them from atrophying; the recuperation-forced lethargy had already done enough damage. In less than a month, he was up to fifty push-ups and half an hour on the exercise bike at its highest tension setting. Satisfied, he put himself on a maintenance program and gave himself until May 31— Joshua Keene's birthday—to complete the details of his security job and begin the second part of his mission: finding Selene and recovering the piece of Frik's coveted artifact.

He would keep his word to himself and to Frik, even though, to the Oilstar exec, losing Keene seemed to be nothing more than "the cost of doing business."

What he needed, McKendry thought, was a plan, preferably one that was proactive rather than defensive. Instead of waiting for Green Impact to rally its forces, to pull together the survivors of its terrorist team and find another way to strike against Oilstar, he would take the initiative.

First, he would find out where Selene and her terrorists had gone to ground. The Orinoco jungles were wide and complex, but they were not impenetrable. He had no doubt that he could track her down, given time, and a little help from the Daredevils Club.

Those who were left.

Those he could trust.

He eliminated Peta, to whom he already owed a debt of gratitude, and Frik, whom he neither liked nor trusted. That left Ray Arno. Last New Year's Eve, when Frik had challenged all members of the Daredevils Club to take on this joint mission, the stuntman and explosives expert had offered his assistance. Now McKendry needed him to put together a team to find Selene Trujold's encampment and strike Green Impact.

On the last day of May, McKendry put through his call to Las Vegas.

A day and a half later the thump, thump of chopper blades heralded Ray's arrival. McKendry looked up at the dark bumblebee shape of the helicopter flying in from Port of Spain, and climbed to the top of the helipad, using the ladders and steep metal stairs instead of the elevator.

The helicopter circled around, wavering as it hovered in the air, and settled askew on the painted circles of the landing pad. As the chopper's rotors gradually slowed, the passenger door popped open and Ray Arno climbed out, all energy and muscles. McKendry came forward to meet him, extending a large hand whose grip was matched by Ray's.

"Thank you for coming." Terris had to shout to be heard over the throbbing vibration of the helicopter

"No problem, Terr." The stuntman looked him up and down. "You look awful, if you don't mind my saying so."

"I lost a lot of weight and—"

"And your best friend. I was really sorry to hear about Josh."

McKendry nodded his thanks and led Ray to the lift. They took it down past convoluted pipes, exhaust torches, and fractionating tubes, where the production rig could perform preliminary refining of the petroleum they brought up.

"Tell me about this," Ray said.

"The crude oil is piped out to tankers like the *Yucatán* and taken to Venezuela's major refineries on the northern coast at Puerto La Cruz and other places."

"And Frik gets richer every minute."

"Not just Frik. Venezuela's oil boom began in the 1920s. The surge of unexpected money rocked the South American economy. Even with the extraordinary tax breaks and tariff exclusions granted to business developers from the States, Venezuelans suddenly found themselves the most affluent people on the entire continent."

"Tough job if you can get it," Ray said. "Bet it took them no time to pick up European and North American vices."

The two men climbed past teams of workers wearing gloves and helmets, boots, and colorful jumpsuits smeared with crude oil. The *Valhalla* rig workers stood around talking, halfheartedly monitoring the production equipment. They glanced at their tough new security chief as he passed, then went back to their tasks with greater fervor.

When the two men reached the habitation decks, a large module that seemed to be halfway between a military barracks and a run-down resort, McKendry went on talking.

"If you help me finish this up," he said, "it'll be a story you can tell for ten New Year's Eves in a row. It'll finish up what Frik asked us to do and—"

"If you want my help, Terris, you have it, but all I need is a story for one year. Not that I mean to go out of action anytime soon."

They walked through a pool hall, with its billiards tables and pinball machines and garish video games. There was also a small bowling alley, a Laundromat, even a movie theater—amenities that Oilstar used, along with large pay, to tempt crews into remaining offshore for months at a time. McKendry was pleased to see that no one was sitting around killing time during duty hours.

"Some joint," Ray said, stopping to look back at the path they had taken. "Maybe my next Strip hotel should be an oil rig. Listen, I really could use a drink. A cup of coffee will do."

McKendry led him to a table in the extensive cafeteria where chefs were working with large hot pans, filling and preparing a lunch of spiced rice, black beans, chicken, fish, sliced mangoes, papayas, and bananas.

Ray had heard some news about the attempted hijacking of the *Yucatán* and the potential disaster that had been averted. Over a large pot of coffee, McKendry gave him the full details. He described Green Impact's agenda, talked about Selene Trujold, and detailed how it had all resulted in his own near fatal shooting, and the death of Joshua Keene.

"Selene escaped," he said. "Green Impact must have their camp out in the delta jungles. I think we'll be able to find them." He scowled. "I want to disable those bastards for what they did to Joshua."

Ray perked up. "We can also get the piece of the artifact from Selene."

"True enough," McKendry said. "But that's not my primary objective."

"Explain that to Frik," Ray said.

"I don't think I owe Frik an explanation for anything."

"Okay, okay. God you're jumpy." Ray took a sip of coffee. "So what's the plan?"

"Joshua and I made the acquaintance of the Venezuelan minister of security, a Señor Juan Ortega de la Vega Bruzual. We had a nice chat with him in Caracas. He wants to keep himself out of the news, especially with all the recent political turmoil, but Señor Bruzual would be very happy to bag these terrorists, put their heads on stakes as it were, and show them off to the world news media. He thinks it would demonstrate that the country is getting back on its feet after all the attempted coups and the economic disasters."

Ray Arno pursed his lips. "Is he going to help?"

"Off the record, yes. We talked again after I called you." Not an easy task without Joshua's language skills, he thought. "He told me he'd provide a handful of mercenaries to join any attack squadron we put together. He said he'll supply us with whatever we need. Weapons, matériel—"

"Good enough. But I want no killing except in self-defense. We could use two or three men who know the territory and speak the language. I want as few people as possible on the team, people I can trust and train." He ran his fingers through his curly hair. McKendry wondered why he hadn't noticed the gray before. "I think we should also track down Manny Sheppard. That old buzzard knows this end of the Caribbean like the back of his hand. He's probably been up and down the Orinoco Delta, in and out of those tiny streams, more often than you've had a beer."

McKendry grunted his assent. Manny's name had popped up more than once in Arthur's New Year's tales, and in Ray's, too. "Does he know his way around this kind of an operation?"

"Manny was in OECS security. He's trained with the U.S. Special Forces. I'd say he could help out."

"Sounds like he'll be a major asset. The next question is, do you know where to find him?"

"I know he doesn't carry a phone or have a listed number. I'll start by contacting Peta and go from there. Better yet, I'll take a quick trip to Grenada." Ray smiled. "Fortunately, I have friends in high and low places. Given time, I can find anybody."

29

Peta had returned to Grenada with a lot of thinking to do. Most of it was unpleasant at worst and difficult at best, so she was perfectly happy to find ready-made excuses to avoid it.

She got her wish. Independence Day festivities, just over, had increased her patient load. The newly arrived medical students, unruly as the ones before them, demanded far more than their fair share of attention. Not only did she have to help them in the classroom, but she was constantly needed to reassure angry landlords who wanted to kill the kids or sue their parents, whichever turned out to be simplest.

Her life developed a tedious rhythm. She worked. She slept. She ate. Now and then she had dinner with an old friend, but knowing she was not good company, she soon gave up on that. She had heard nothing from Manny and assumed that he was off-island on one of the mysterious trips which often kept him away for months at a time.

Now, suddenly, somehow, it was nearing the end of May.

Carnival wasn't until August, the students had settled down, and fewer tourists than usual demanded her time. She even found herself with a whole weekend to spend sitting on her balcony. The postcard perfection of St. George's and the Carenage provided her with a backdrop for a too-long-delayed replay of the happenings in her life since December.

Mostly, her mind was not so much filled with questions, but rather with answers she was loath to accept. For one thing, she was sure now that Frikkie—who had not so much as called with a trumped-up apology for the events at San Gabriel—didn't care if the rest of the Daredevils were killed. In fact, though she had no proof, she suspected that he had been instrumental in killing Arthur.

Worse yet, thinking back to that night in New York almost five months ago, she remembered that Ray had gone to the restrooms a little while before Arthur. Ray was a demolitions expert. It would have been easy for him to rig a bomb in the toilet, wait for Arthur to enter, and then detonate it by remote control.

That would place Ray Arno squarely in cahoots with Frik.

But why?

What she needed was someone to talk to about all of this, someone she could trust completely.

With Arthur dead, that left only Manny. She would have called his home to see if he was back in town, but he eschewed telephones and refused to have one in his house. His message center was Aboo's, a bar owned by his father.

Since she was tired of her own company and her circular thoughts, around sundown on Sunday she left her house to find him.

Accompanied by the sound of church bells, she walked past the Parliament building and through the marketplace, abandoned this late in the day to island dogs and stray humans picking through the wilted leftovers of Saturday's traffic. Rather than struggle over the hill on Young Street, she cut through Sendall Tunnel to the Carenage. Grenadian drivers weren't known for their caution, and the narrow hundred-year-old passage under the large hill provided little room for error. She walked at a brisk pace, hugging the stone wall. Then, safely through, she slowed to stroll along the Carenage, enjoying the sounds and smells of the compact waterfront.

When she passed the new Cable and Wireless building, she crossed the street to Aboo's Bar.

The small, run-down blue shack doubled as St. George's Grand Central Station for a certain class of people. Though Peta had chosen never to ask Manny about it or to explore it herself, rumor had it that there was a dark room behind the bar which had served—still served—as the meeting place for everyone from murderers and ministers to government officials and their underage mistresses.

The bar itself was small and utilitarian. Manny was behind the counter, relieving his father of Sunday-evening duty. He grinned broadly when she entered and instantly pulled out two cold bottles of Carib from the ice chest, one for each of them.

"Looking good." He kissed her on one cheek, then the other, and handed her a bottle.

Peta smiled. "I'm glad to see you too."

"You come all this way for a beer or—"

"I need to talk to you." Peta drank deeply, hot after her long trek.

"So talk." Manny waved at the empty bar. "Crowd won't hit till after church."

Peta settled herself on a worn barstool and lit a cigarette. Manny took it from her. "You gotta stop," he said, inhaling deeply. Peta nodded and lit another.

"You're hopeless," Manny said.

"Probably." She flicked into a piece of misshapen aluminum that passed as an ashtray. "There's so much . . . I'm not sure where to begin."

"The last time I saw you, you were headed up the hill in San Gabriel," Manny said.

"Right. I was off to save Simon."

"Did you?"

Peta shook her head. Like someone who had lost her place in a good novel and found it again, Peta was off and running. She told him about finding Simon and about the attempt on her life. "Blaine got the artifact. If the sharks didn't get him, I assume he made it to the exploration platform and, eventually, back to Frik," she said.

"So you think Frikkie has it now?" Manny asked.

"Absolutely." She crushed her cigarette, reached for another, and thought better of it. Twirling the pack around like a top, she filled in Manny on her convictions about Frik and her suspicions about Ray.

Manny put his hand over hers to stop the nervous mannerism. "I can't believe Ray would do anything to hurt Arthur, so let's talk about Frik," he said. "Correct me if I'm wrong here. You're saying Frikkie has two pieces of the artifact, one that he had in the first place and the one Simon died to retrieve. The same one Blaine took from you. And you're saying that you think Arthur died because of the piece *he* had—which the police took to their evidence lockup. Have you tried to retrieve that one?"

"Yes. I've called NYPD countless times. They're not ready to let go

195

of it. The good part is that they've assured me they won't release it to anyone else."

In San Gabriel, Peta had told Manny that she had a piece of the artifact, yet neither one of them added the obvious: if Frik knew she had it—and if her theories were correct—he wouldn't hesitate to kill her for it when he was good and ready to do so. Now, Manny verbalized his fears for her safety. "We know he's unscrupulous," he added, after a short pause.

"Believe me, I've thought about that a lot," Peta said. "I think that I'm safe, for the moment."

"Why?"

"Because it suits his purposes. We talked before about the possibility that Frik was the person who had Arthur killed to get at the artifact. We know for a fact that the killer didn't get it. My guess is that Frik called NYPD, said he was Arthur's closest friend, and asked them if they had it."

"In which case," Manny said, "they would have told him that they had guaranteed to hand it over to you when they're done with the case."

"Yes, so his best bet is to make nice to me and try to regain my confidence so that he can talk me into giving him both my stone and Arthur's."

"I have to think about this." Manny stared through the open doorway, as if simply looking at the sea would provide answers. "Oh shi-yit," he said. "Trouble approaches from all sides."

Peta followed his line of vision. Out on the horizon, she saw the masts of the *Assegai*.

"Maybe he's come to apologize." Manny's voice was heavy with sarcasm.

"Apologize for what?" Ray asked, filling the doorway with his muscular form.

"Here's the other trouble I saw," Manny said.

"I got here yesterday. Didn't your father tell you?" Ray shook Manny's hand and hugged Peta. She froze, not knowing whether to shrink from his touch or hug him back, the way she had always done. He looked at her strangely, but said nothing.

"My father didn't say a word." Manny handed Ray a beer and Peta a second. "Better get a refund on your bribe. How much was it?"

"Twenty dollars."

"American?"

Ray nodded. "He said he hadn't seen you for weeks. I asked the other people in here too. A couple of leathery old men and that layabout fisherman whose wife always comes in looking for him."

Manny laughed. "How much did you tip *them*?"

"Not much." Ray set down his beer among the many circular rings on the single Formica tabletop in the corner of the bar. "Feels like home," he said, cooling himself under the slow-moving ceiling fan.

"To what do we owe this visit?" Peta asked.

"I've been with Terris and—" He stopped short, clearly reluctant to continue whatever it was he had to say in front of Peta. "Look, this is confidential."

"Don't worry about it. The last thing I need is your little-boy games." Peta slid off the stool.

"I'm sorry," Ray said. "Arthur's dead, but you're not yet officially a member of the club. That doesn't mean you don't have my respect."

"No problem. I'm leaving."

"Stay," Manny said. "I'm not a member of the club either. Whatever I can hear, you can hear."

Peta was torn between her first instinct, which was to tell Ray to stick it, and her need to find out what part—if any—he had played in Arthur's death.

"If you have doctor-type things to do, I can call you later," Ray said hesitantly. "You're in my database."

"Bad idea," Manny said. "You know as well as we do what a problem it is keeping things confidential when dealing with our telephone system."

Peta knew that Ray couldn't argue with him, not after being privy to many an argument with Grenadian officials about the fact that line tapping was legal on the island. Any attempt at privacy here was more of a challenge than all of the death-defying feats Ray had accomplished in his lifetime.

Judging by the look on the American's face, he was making a tough decision. "I've been on the *Valhalla* with Terris," he said finally. "Took a short island hop from the rig to Trinidad, then a flight here." He looked around, as if searching for eavesdroppers, then lowered his voice and looked at Manny. "We need your help."

Without wasting words, he filled them in on McKendry's plan to find Selene. Even before he was finished, Manny had admitted that he knew where to find the camp and agreed to participate on the condition that killing was minimized.

"I'm coming too," Peta said.

"No—"

"Yes. I'm going to do what Arthur would have done. First of all, it'll save time if I fly you to Trinidad. Second, you may need a doctor—"

"No—"

"Don't argue with her," Manny said. "It's both of us, or neither. I'll sail down so we have my boat. I can leave in the morning."

"I'll clear things with my locum tonight," Peta added. She thought for a moment. "Frik will probably call me on the pretext of seeing if I'm all right after the incident in the cavern."

She was about to ask what she should say to him when, right on cue, her cell phone jangled.

"Yes."

"Frik here. I'm sailing in. I want to apologize to you for the debacle in San Gabriel. Will you have dinner with me?"

"I'm busy," she said.

"Tomorrow?"

"No. I'm flying out in the morning."

There was silence at the other end. "I really need to see you," Frik said at last.

"It'll have to wait."

"I won't be here again until Carnival."

August will be too late to feel me out, too late to find out what I know, Peta thought. Nevertheless, deciding she needed some insurance should he become persistent, she said a cursory farewell to Frik and a warm one to Manny. To Ray she said merely, "Be at the airport at noon."

Exiting Aboo's, she made her way past the awnings of the tourist shops toward the coal pot where an old woman was roasting corn on a makeshift grill over glowing coals. She bought several ears, wrapped them in one of the sheets of newspaper piled next to the fire, and flagged down one of the few taxis that roamed the Carenage on a Sunday evening.

With darkness descending and the sound of a lone steel drum in her ears, she directed the driver to take her home. She called the airport to tell them to have her plane ready for departure at noon. Then she ate her corn, bathed, and packed a small overnight bag. Before midnight, she was fast asleep.

The next morning, carrying nothing but a tote and her medical bag, she drove her Honda to the bank. She took her pendant out of her safe-deposit box, pocketed it, and headed toward Morne Rouge and her Rasta friend, Ralphie Levine. He was the only person on the island who could be trusted to do what she needed to have done: replicate the piece in her pendant and swap the two, putting his fake in the bezel while he held on to the original.

Everything went so smoothly that Peta was at the airport thirty minutes early. She made one last check on her plane and headed upstairs to the coffee shop. Ray was already there, eating a lunch of chicken roti. He pulled a small bone out of his mouth.

"Have some," he said, pushing the roti toward her. "It's good."

"I know it is." Though she never tired of the lightly curried chicken, cut into small pieces and wrapped, bones and all, in a thin East Indian flatbread, she scooted the dish back at him. "I don't eat before I fly."

"What's wrong, Peta? Have I done something to upset you?" Ray looked genuinely distressed.

"I don't know, Ray. Have you?"

"I would never do anything to hurt you. Surely you know that."

Ray took her hand. His touch was warm and reassuring. "I do know that." She smiled at him and retrieved her hand. "Now let's get out of here."

It wasn't until the two of them stepped onto the tarmac that she saw Frik. He was dressed in long pants, wore shoes, and carried a briefcase— formal attire for him. His eye remained partially closed; his hand was wrapped in pressure bandages in a continuing attempt to minimize scarring from the deep burns he'd suffered.

"I know where you're going and what you're going to do," he said. "McKendry told me all about it. I'm coming along."

"Not a chance," Peta said quietly. "It's my plane and you're not getting on it."

He blocked her path. "*You're* telling *me* what to do?"

"Yup. Now get out of my way."

Frik didn't move.

"You heard the lady, Van Alman," Ray said.

"Even if we wanted you on board, you're in no shape to come," Peta added.

Frik stood his ground. Peta and Ray walked around him and headed for the plane. He followed them. Peta slowed down almost imperceptibly. When he was so close that she could feel his breath on her neck, she stopped in her tracks and turned around, forcing him to step aside.

"What part of 'no' do you not understand?"

Frik stared at her, eyes filled with hatred. Waving his bandaged hand perilously close to her face, he said, "You'll regret this, bitch. One hand—no hands—I'm twice as good as any woman."

30

In early June, standing at the head of Oilstar's La Brea dock, McKendry looked over his assault team. Except for the fact that Manny Sheppard had been missing for two days and that they still had no specifics about the whereabouts of the ecoterrorists, they were as ready as they would ever be.

The three men Bruzual had sent slouched together against one of the pilings, smoking Peta's cigarettes and polishing their weapons. The one called José drew his knife against a stone to sharpen the edge. As he spun it, McKendry saw the initials J.R. etched into the pommel.

"You're his buddies. Where the devil is Sheppard?" McKendry looked at Peta and Ray accusingly.

"Triple A to the rescue," Manny said, appearing out of nowhere. With a self-satisfied grin, he handed McKendry a grease-stained scrap of paper with a sketch on it.

According to Manny, he had glided up to the shoreline of the jungle in his small outboard boat and asked an elderly Warao fisherman for information about Green Impact. Normally, the indigenous jungle Indians would not take part in any outsider activity, and they certainly wouldn't have betrayed Selene Trujold, so Manny had expected no answer. But the old man had caught a large and frightening catfish that day—surely an omen, since the Warao considered catfish to be magical creatures. He had given Manny all the details the team could possibly want, including a sketch of the camp itself.

"So when do we leave?" José sheathed his knife and rested his hand on the butt of his pistol.

"When we've all memorized the sketch," Ray answered. He looked none too happy with the man's apparent bloodlust. "Meanwhile, let's go over what we know."

"Again?" Another of Bruzual's men, Diego.

"Yes," Ray said. "Again. Peta?"

"As far as we know, Selene's group lost several members during the raid on the *Yucatán*. They probably have between ten and twenty members left, hiding in the jungle, planning more attacks against Oilstar. Some Warao Indians are also likely to be in the camp, but they're workers, not converts to the cause—paid with trinkets and supplies. It's unlikely that they're motivated by political convictions or personal loyalty."

"We figure the Indians will disappear as soon as they see trouble," McKendry added.

"You're right," Manny said. "They're too smart to stick around waiting to be shot or"—he looked at José—"knifed."

Ray nodded. "I'm going to say this one more time. No violence except in self-defense. We're there to disable the camp and find Frik's piece of jewelry."

"And Selene," McKendry said. "I hope I can keep my hands off her neck long enough to hand her over to Bruzual for trial."

Peta looked at him with a worried expression, but Ray, who knew him better, just grinned.

As day became night, with Manny at the helm of the fiberglass boat supplied by Bruzual, they left Trinidad and headed toward the shores of the Orinoco Delta. The stars, bright during the team's journey across the gulf, were soon obscured by the jungle. Only a few pinpricks of light were visible as they entered one of the narrow channels between overhanging mangrove and palm trees. No one spoke, not even when they reached the first of the *palafitos,* sturdy handmade huts that stood on pilings at the water's edge.

In the lowlands of eastern Venezuela, the slick whisper of water in the caños was like a wet tongue moving through the grasses, thick weeds, and leaf-heavy branches. The night songs of crickets and frogs in the dense underbrush made a din that masked the sounds of the quiet movement of the oars. The fiberglass boat prowled like a piranha through the narrow rivulets. Now, the low strumming of a guitar was added to the nocturnal orchestra as Manny guided the boat up beside Green Impact's black Zodiac rafts.

The terrorists, falsely secure in their isolation, had not thought to have anyone keep watch.

With Manny leading the way, the assault team slipped through crackling weeds to the sturdy *palafito* poles. He used worn bumps and notches as if they were a ladder to scramble up the nearest pole to the floor above. McKendry and the three men provided by Venezuelan security minister Bruzual stayed close behind, with Peta and Ray in the rear.

McKendry heard a rustle of palm fronds, small monkeys or rodents scampering across the thatched hut roofs. Through the leaves of a fern he was using as cover, he saw the intense white lights of Coleman lanterns set on tables and attracting swarms of jungle insects. The air smelled of hot oil, fried fish and bananas, and bitter tobacco smoke.

As he climbed the pole behind Manny, McKendry could see a long-legged man through the door opening that led into the next hut over. The stranger's bare feet were propped up on a windowsill and he was strumming a guitar. It was the young minstrel he and Keene had met in the delta cantina what seemed like forever ago.

Other than that, the compound was quiet. McKendry wondered briefly what had happened to the musician's girlfriend. Perhaps, he thought, she's already in bed, somewhere out of sight. He knew that in the jungle, people bedded down once darkness fell, and rose with the dawn. He and his team planned to take advantage of the routine and the darkness.

Manny and McKendry stepped into the first palafito and looked around. It was empty, probably a simple storage hut or one of the dwellings used by a recently killed member of Green Impact. The log floor creaked underfoot.

McKendry motioned for José to slip across to the next dwelling, where the guitarist was making enough noise to muffle their stealthy approach. The mercenary moved like a shadow into the hut and behind the guitar player. There was a flash of metal, a jangling chord, and the guitar fell silent, leaving the jungle with only the insects and amphibians to provide music. Bruzual's man eased the guitar player back in his chair as he died.

"No," Ray said, his voice low and angry.

José looked up at him through the window and made an apologetic gesture, as if he'd had no choice but to do what he had done.

"Thank God," a Green Impact member grumbled from the next hut, unaware of why the music had stopped but evidently pleased. "Now we can finally get some sleep."

Peta stifled a gasp and moved forward as if to help the guitar player. Ray stopped her and signaled José to come back. They watched until the guitarist stopped twitching and simply bled onto the uneven floor.

Ray faced the Venezuelan. "Now, get your ass back and disable every last one of their boats," he whispered angrily. "And remember. If anyone else dies, so will you."

As a scowling José crept through the mud toward the wider caños, Ray motioned for Terris and Manny to move clockwise around the compound while he and Peta and the other two mercenaries headed counterclockwise.

McKendry thought for a moment that Rodolfo would have believed this was exciting. He would have wanted to come along—and he would either have been killed, or have gone back to huddle in the boat, making up stories he would tell later to the women in silvery miniskirts who clung to him in Caracas's discos and nightclubs.

"Let's get moving," he whispered to Manny. "Or we'll end up like that poor son of a bitch in there."

31

Taking a roundabout route, Ray Arno circled the outer perimeter of the encampment, with Peta and the mercenaries forming a ragged line, twenty paces between each of them. As he moved through the mud and underbrush, ignoring the insects and the wetness, he reminded himself that he had been on movie sets that had made him more miserable than this.

Following naturally was the thought that those jobs had never been as important as this. It wasn't hyperbole to say that the fate of the world could depend on their success. And that success depended on this assault team.

Manny and McKendry were good men. Peta was a trooper. The men provided by the Venezuelan minister of security were what gave him pause.

He had worked with mercenaries before, more than once. The whole point of using them was that they did what they were paid to do. Problems arose only if they were serving two masters, in which case they would do what they had been told to do by the highest bidder.

According to the plan, José should have incapacitated the guitarist, tied him up so they could question him to see if he knew where Selene was. Not kill him. There was nothing Ray could do about it now, but there would be plenty he could do when it was time to make the final payment to José.

Frowning, he looked at the encampment, mentally ticking off at least a dozen safety violations that some OSHA representative on a movie lot would have written up. Here, it might even be an advantage. He knew from Manny's rough map of the camp where the terrorists kept most of their supplies. What wasn't on the map was where Green Impact kept its munitions. Food was in sealed lockers, some of which were suspended from trees, though the monkeys could still get at them. The rest of the cases and cans remained in the individual huts.

Two large propane tanks provided fuel for grills in what passed for the camp's mess. He was surprised to note as he circled the building that the tanks also ran a heater and water pump attached to a shower at the back of the mess.

He was examining the tanks when Diego, one of the Venezuelan mercenaries, found the weapons cache in a small, partially camouflaged hut apart from the main encampment. After making whispered calls and gestures, to which Ray, Peta, and the third Venezuelan soon responded, the mercenary used a long knife to pry open the first storage locker.

Both of Bruzual's other men dropped their old rifles and hauled out assault rifles and boxes of ammunition, making far too much clatter in their excitement. Ray cautioned them to be quiet, but the mercenaries seemed unduly greedy. He wondered if they would simply snatch the contraband rifles, which they could sell at a handsome profit on the black market, and flee with them.

Most of all, Ray was concerned with keeping the resources out of the hands of Green Impact.

He reached a decision. Glancing first at the luminous dial on his wristwatch, he nodded to himself and rapidly opened the rest of the cases. With a shoestring attachment of wires and connected detonators, he rigged up three armed grenades, stuffed them in among packages of C-4 and Semtex, and played out the cord behind himself.

The Venezuelans looked at him, scowling with disappointment as they saw what he meant to do. Clearly, they would have preferred to confiscate the explosives, not destroy them. Ray held the detonator string in the fingers of one hand and urgently waved them away with the other.

One of the Green Impact men rustled through the bushes, calling out, "Hey, what's going on?" The voice held annoyance and curiosity, but not suspicion. Not yet.

Ray yanked the string, pulling the grenade detonator pins. The Green Impact guard, finally doing his duty, switched on a big flashlight and shone it around the jungle. The beam of light, splashing like melted butter across the branches, struck a scrambling Ray and his partners.

"Hey! I see you!" the Green Impact man called out.

As if on cue, the grenades exploded. Thatch smoldered and burst into flame. Green Impact members started screaming.

"I see you too," Ray muttered as the shock wave bowled him over into the muddy ground.

32

By the time the grenades exploded, Manny and McKendry had reached the third hut. They saw two blond men on separate cots scrambling awake, shouting, looking at each other. In an instant, both of them had grabbed pistols from beneath their beds and lurched up, swinging the weapons to point at the door.

McKendry was determined to make an arrest, as if to prove to himself that he was in control. He even shot the first round, hitting one of the terrorists squarely in the right shoulder. The crack of his weapon fire sounded loud but was rapidly overwhelmed by the racket in the encampment.

The second blond man pulled up his own pistol as Manny charged forward and threw a pillow at the man's arm. The terrorist's shot was wild; the bullet splintered one of the wooden poles beside Manny. Even though there was no longer any need for silence, Manny chose to pull a sap from his belt. He pushed the terrorist's gun arm away and swung the sand-filled pouch hard into the man's skull. His head snapped back and he collapsed onto the bed he had only partially gotten up from.

McKendry bent over the first downed terrorist, pleased to see he was still alive and conscious, though barely.

"Selene Trujold. Where is she?"

The man coughed and bled. His eyes sharpened with awareness enough to gasp, "Fuck you!"

McKendry stood up, his face grim. "Bleed to death, then."

Outside he could hear more weapon fire accompanying the crackling flames from the explosion. He didn't mind that Ray had blown up the explosives depot, leaving Green Impact without its stockpile. Now was the time for open action.

The flames from the explosion lit up the area, casting witches' shadows and creating more uncertainty than illumination. He could see that the fire had spread to the central mess hall.

A moment later, the propane tanks exploded in a cough of feathery blue fire that bowled over two of the Green Impact terrorists and splintered the trees within fifteen feet into kindling.

At ground level, Ray and Peta and the two mercenaries were rounding up some of the Green Impact terrorists; a few others hid in the underbrush and opened fire.

McKendry didn't care about them. He was interested in only one person, and he was determined to get her—for Keene, and for himself. He could save her a lot of trouble if she capitulated. A whole lot.

Pushing his way to the open deck of the palafitos that overlooked the calm caños, McKendry shoved aside a small table where two unwashed coffee cups sat.

Below, he saw someone climbing into a boat. He could not tell for sure in the darkness, but his every instinct told him that it was Selene Trujold. Without calling for others to join her, she slid out into the waterway, moving with spare motions.

In a blaze of anger at José for disobeying instructions, McKendry raised his rifle, sighting in. He would deal with the Venezuelan later. The lazy slug was probably curled up in the bottom of one of the boats he'd been sent to disable. Meanwhile, he could not let the woman get away, not after what she had done to Joshua.

An expert marksman, he aimed, centering the crosshairs on Selene's head as she entered a shaft of starlight. Through his sight, he watched her head turn to the right, toward the fringe of the jungle. She raised her arm, and he could see the pistol in her hand.

Allowing himself no distractions, he focused on her temple and squeezed the trigger—

"No!"

Manny Sheppard slapped the barrel of McKendry's rifle aside as the gun went off. Looking downstream, he saw Selene drop, facedown, into the bottom of the boat, which was drifting slowly downriver.

He turned to glare at Manny.

"We need her alive, remember," Manny said. His voice was very quiet. "She has to tell us where Frik's artifact is."

McKendry remembered that Manny had been a friend of her father's, and that he had known Selene since she was a little girl. He remembered, too, that he was not a killer. Not like this. Shooting someone—man or woman—in the back in cold blood.

He looked back at the boat, which continued to drift. As he watched it, he saw a bloodied hand emerge from the inside and grasp the edge.

He shoved past Manny Sheppard. Ignoring the ladder, he leapt from the hut to the floor of the jungle and wove his way through the underbrush. He knocked branches away and splashed through shallow rivulets.

His headlong rush came to an abrupt halt when he tripped over José's still-warm body. The Venezuelan had taken a bullet straight through the forehead. His knife, small protection against a pistol no matter how accurately thrown, was nowhere to be seen.

Helluva marksman, McKendry thought, remembering Selene's raised arm. He stood still and stared into the impenetrable darkness, in the direction her boat had taken.

Behind him in the camp, a few scattered shots rang out before the gunfire ceased completely.

By dawn, after searching through the caños and the islands in the vicinity of the camp, Manny found the bloodstained boat. It was still drifting downstream, but there was no sign of Selene Trujold, or her piece of the artifact.

33

For three months after his idyllic afternoon with Selene, Joshua had worked with the members of Green Impact to scrounge weapons, ammunition, and explosives. He and Selene went over and over the plans of the *Valhalla* until they both knew them by heart. Finally, the day after his birthday, he took off with a Warao guide to see if he could get more information and supplies in Pedernales.

It was his first trip out of the jungle since the night on the *Yucatán*.

They took a boat for some twenty winding miles from the jungles to Pedernales, where he had been told he could safely gather additional information and equipment for the operation against the *Valhalla* platform.

The town lay at the tip of Punta Tolete, where a confluence of delta streams emptied into the gulf. While apparently the closest thing to a town within reasonable distance, it was really not much more than a supply stop. Any hope he had of finding more than basic survival necessities was crushed upon his arrival.

The hub of civilization in the Delta Amacuro, the settlement had grown from nothing half a century ago, when oil exploitation on the adjacent Isla Cotorra had brought the petroleum business to the continent's edge. Enough traffic and business and people came to the area to set up a town and create a booming local economy.

By the mid-1970s, however, the oil fields had been played out, and the operating firm had abandoned the wells and pulled up stakes, leaving the locals to fend for themselves. The town's economy crashed, most of the transplanted people departed, and only empty, dilapidated buildings remained. In recent years, speculators had reopened the operations, squeezing hard until crude oil began to flow yet again.

Pedernales was reborn, but it remained a sickly child at best.

Since the locals had not seen Keene in the area before, he was able to move around without fear of being recognized or asked inconvenient questions. For all the villagers knew, he was another one of the yuppie ecotourists who came to the delta, traveling by motorboat up the caños to look at the birds and the wildlife before returning to their expensive homes and fancy restaurants to talk about their "dangerous jungle ordeal."

Except for a side trip to Isla Cotorra, Keene spent his time in Pedernales bartering for necessary supplies and trying to gain the confidence of the locals. He did not come close to finding what he wanted, but he did discover that he would have to make do with whatever resources Green Impact could scrounge. On the South American coast, he would have no access to the truly high-tech materials he preferred.

He was not particularly perturbed.

Sometimes it was less efficient—and less satisfying—to rely on fancy gizmos. The *Mission: Impossible* routine, he thought, didn't work nearly as well in practice as it did in concept.

After almost a week away from the encampment, and Selene, Keene grew anxious to get back.

"Time to say good-bye to the big city," he told his guide. Though sure that his sarcasm was lost on the man, Keene offered to buy him a meal and a drink in a seedy seaside cantina that appeared to be the center of the town's entertainment. They started out at the bar, where, with a great stroke of luck, Keene found several disgruntled oil workers who had been fired from the *Valhalla* rig.

Without the prospect of continuing paychecks, the rig workers were perfectly happy to talk with a man who would buy them as many cervezas *más frías* as they wished to imbibe.

Keene's Spanish was good enough that he quickly put them at ease. He discovered that, after the *Yucatán* incident, Oilstar had hired one bastard of a new security chief who had overhauled all the rig procedures, cracked down on booze and drugs and cigarettes, and enforced discipline with no exceptions. A veritable military commander.

Sipping his beer, Keene nodded sympathetically. His commiseration was genuine. From what he had seen while sneaking aboard the *Valhalla* with Terris, the previous procedures had been laughably lax, but he wouldn't have gotten along well with such rigid rules himself.

By the time the evening was over, the men had told Keene more than he had hoped to discover, and an overall plan gelled in his mind. Given a few lucky breaks and a lot of determination, he was quite convinced, he could succeed in his plan to force Frik to sit up and take notice. He had never trusted Frikkie Van Alman, and now he understood why. The Oilstar man had much to answer for. Not that Selene was an angel. She was an expert manipulator with plenty of blood and blame on her own hands, but Paul Trujold's daughter was just a minor player compared with Frik.

Leaving at dawn in their inflatable boat, Keene rode back through the caños with his guide, a silent man who spoke enough Spanish to be understood, but chose not to speak much at all. Keene talked for his own benefit, but soon gave up expecting a response from the Indian. Painfully aware of how much he missed McKendry, he made himself as comfortable as possible and began the kind of mental gyrations that had proven useful in the past.

He had acquired some supplies, though not enough, and a few luxuries, including a well-wrapped package of chocolates that the trade-post owner had sold him for an exorbitant amount of money. Chocolate was common in Venezuela, but these were imported from Belgium. Why anybody would want to do such a thing baffled Keene, but what did he care as long as they earned him extra Brownie points from Selene.

She gave him a sense of purpose, which he needed more than ever. Since the fateful night on the oil tanker, he had felt lost and empty without his partner and best friend. Life had seemed to be one continuous string of adventures when they were together.

Not, he thought, that what he was doing now was dull.

The whole truth was that he was the sort of man who needed to have a driving goal, even if it drove him over a cliff. Still, if not for the ministrations of Selene Trujold, he would have been unlikely to pick this particular obsession.

He thought back to the night on the *Yucatán*. Again, in his mind's eye, he watched McKendry get shot twice and catapult backward off his bicycle onto the equipment-strewn deck . . . before he himself was hurled overboard in the grenade explosion.

He sought to find something amusing in the image of himself hitting the water, but without McKendry as his audience and straight man, nothing seemed funny. Perhaps someday his cocky good humor would return. It sure had gone AWOL since his recovery and time in the jungle.

Around lunchtime, lulled by the boat's movement and the early-June heat, Keene dozed off. When he awoke, in the midafternoon, he noticed a succession of Indians looking out at them from the sides of the water. Without signaling to his Warao guide, they hauled up fishing baskets and nets and disappeared into the jungle.

"Why are they so skittish?" he asked, hoping for an answer.

His guide pointed at the sky ahead.

Tendrils of smoke stained the fluffy low thunderheads brewing deeper over the delta jungle.

A hot dread and certainty told Keene that the source of the smoke was the Green Impact camp. "Faster!" he yelled to the Indian, who urged the outboard motor to a quicker pace. But the guide was cautious as he looked around, apparently searching for assassins in the underbrush.

As the boat came up against the narrow streams that led to the palafitos, the Indian slipped over the side and sprinted barefoot into the jungle away from the camp. He didn't wait to be paid, didn't help to unload supplies, didn't even glance at Keene's stricken face.

Setting aside his personal fear, Keene raced toward the camp. What he saw pumped him full of adrenaline. Carnage, bloodstains, and a handful of bodies left lying in and around the ruins of the huts. Some of the wet green trees were smoldering, but most of the wood and thatch huts in the encampment had burned themselves out, leaving mounds of white ash and charcoal poles. The dry palm fronds and lashed twig walls must have gone up like tinder.

He stumbled around in a daze, calling out Selene's name. The compound's weapons cache was in splinters. A crater sat where the lockers full of explosives had been detonated. He found seven corpses. Two looked like Venezuelans, mercenaries he guessed from their nondescript fatigues, which lacked the insignia of any legal or military organization. The remaining bodies were Green Impact members, five of the twelve robust men and one woman he had left behind.

There was no sign of the others. This was no jungle raid by robbers intent on grabbing supplies for a black-market sale; this was a planned operation, well executed, with no intent other than to wipe out Green Impact.

Desperately he rechecked the dead, searching for the woman to whom he had become so attached. She was not among the recognizable bodies. There was no skeleton in the charred shell of the palafito the two of them had shared.

Praying that she had gotten away, knowing that to be as much a fantasy as hoping Terris McKendry was still alive, Keene vomited on the ground. Trembling, he sat up and spat at the unknown perpetrators of this new crime. There is one place, he thought. One infinitely small possibility.

He jumped back into the small boat and motored it as quickly as it would go. In the ever-narrowing caños, he repeatedly got caught up in mud banks and overhanging bushes. Relentlessly, he pushed on toward the place where he and Selene had made love that day, the little meadow surrounded by tall grass and trees.

This is my retreat, she'd said. If she'd made it out of the camp, it was where she would have gone.

Keene found the sheltered jungle clearing, and in it he found Selene. She was propped against a mound of dry grasses. Scarlet and yellow birds fluttered around, but she didn't move as he approached.

"Selene!"

He thought he saw her shoulders twitch.

Reaching her side, he knelt down in the damp earth. He took her hand and stroked her cheek. Her skin was gray and clammy, her lips dry. He kissed them, but it did nothing to awaken her. She made small sounds, and he heard a rattle within her chest and throat. Blood was congealing on her shirt and abdomen and on the ground around her. The blood was leaking from beneath her hands, which were clutched under her right breast.

Beside her, he found a blade: Venezuelan military issue, with the initials J.R. scratched into the rubber grip.

Keene had enough experience with battlefield injuries that he didn't try to think about how to save her; not here, far from even so much as a well-stocked first-aid kit. He felt tears moisten his cheeks.

"Can you hear me, Selene?"

She seemed to know he was there beside her. Without opening her eyes, she roused herself enough to lift her left hand, stretching it toward him. In her fingers, she gripped the artifact.

Keene could not have cared less about the mysterious piece of technology that had been scraped up by Oilstar's test drill in the Dragon's Mouth. As far as he was concerned, it was the cause of all of the death around him. McKendry, the members of Green Impact, and now Selene.

She pushed harder. "Take it," she said, and he did. "Up to you now," she whispered. "Oilstar's fault. Stop—"

Then she did stop: breathing and living.

Keene felt the sharp edges of the object in his left hand, felt the temperature of his palm drop as it sucked the heat from his skin. He wanted to fling the damned piece of junk into the steamy jungle, where it would sink into a caño or be overgrown with weeds. But to Selene it had been worth dying for . . . and Frikkie seemed to believe it was worth the price of murder.

With his right hand, Keene picked up the knife that had killed the woman he had begun to love. "Rest in peace, Selene," he said, testing its weight in his hand. "I promise I'll take care of Oilstar."

34

On her way to The Traffic Light, Peta's pager buzzed.

She ignored it at first.

The restaurant where she'd been headed was so named because the owners had imported and erected what had, until recently, been the only traffic light on the island. The traffic light didn't work, nor was it meant to do so. It was a curiosity, intended for no other purpose than to direct people to stop and sample the food. Of course, the truth was that the place was already so popular with the locals that they had all the customers they could handle.

After months of eating only because it was mealtime, finally, tonight, Peta had been looking forward to stopping in at The Traffic Light and eating Maggie's oildown. She had never been good at making the Grenadian national stew of breadfruit cooked in coconut milk with salted meat and vegetables, mostly callaloo, and lots of seasoning, but she loved to eat it. Especially now, in early August, when lobster season was in full swing and Maggie could be persuaded to throw in the occasional tail.

That was the way Arthur had liked it best too.

The two of them had shared oildown at The Traffic Light once a month. The meal was followed by a monthly evening of poetry. Since Maggie would not accept payment from either of them, they submitted to the poetry in exchange for the meal. Arthur didn't mind. In fact, he occasionally read some of his own scribbles to an enthusiastic audience. Peta only half listened, dreaming on a full stomach about Captain Bligh enduring a mutiny because he had used essential water for his breadfruit saplings instead of giving it to his crew.

The pager buzzed again insistently.

Peta pulled to the side of the road and checked the number. It was her service. Everyone's service, really, since it was the only halfway efficient one on the island.

Hoping it was something that could be taken care of over the phone, she grabbed the cell phone from her purse and called in.

"One of your patients called. A girl. Patty Grant. She says a man's been knifed in her house. Something to do with Carnival. Says the house is in the bushes and hard to find, so she'll send her brother out to the road to flag you down."

Though she didn't recognize the name, Peta made a note of the address, apparently a shanty in the rain forest, on the road to the Grand Étang, the island's dormant volcano.

She sighed heavily. So much for oildown.

The whole island was only twenty by twelve miles. As the crow flies, the house was probably no more than six or eight miles away, but it would take her the better part of an hour to get there. The road through the rain-forested mountain was far and away the best on the island. The problem was getting to it. Most of the secondary roads barely deserved the name. They were often unpaved, and those that were had more potholes than pavement. They wound like coiled vipers through the countryside, almost as if to make up for the fact that there were no poisonous snakes on the island.

Hungry, she reached into her pocket for a protein bar and settled into the driving, marveling as she always did at the spectacular landscape and the variety of fruit there. The rain forest around her contained an astonishing mixture of trees: breadfruit and banana, cinnamon and nutmeg—the island's most famous spice—clove, coconut palm, mango, cocoa, apple, soursop, cashew, avocado, plum. And more. Papaya. Orange. The list of edibles was endless.

For those whose taste ran to meat, there were all manner of animals, some of them unique to the region. The forest hid the armadillo or tatoo, the manicou or opossum, not to speak of the Mona monkey—an island delicacy.

Through her open window, Peta could feel the increasing humidity and hear the song of exotic night birds. For too long, she had claimed to be too busy to climb the trails. Too busy trying not to think.

She passed a house where several young men and women were partially dressed in brightly colored satins. Carnival dancers preparing for the next day's parade.

Carnival season in Grenada was joyous for some, anathema to others. There was dancing in the streets and strange business afoot as gangs of young locals, faces painted with tar, created equal parts of music and mayhem. They wore masks and devil costumes soaked in a combination of charcoal and engine oil and jumped out at you, pulling you close to dance with them and leaving you smeared with greasy black residue.

As a child, she had been terrified of them. They represented both the devil and the priesthood, warning in both personas of hell and damnation, yet promising redemption, too, to those who did not thwart them. As an adult, she avoided them where possible and wore old clothes throughout Carnival in case she ran into them anyway.

The Jab Jab Molassi.

Another all-male club, she thought, recalling Arthur's tales of his years among them.

It took her a minute to remember the last time she had participated in the parade, or any of the revelry of Grenada's late-summer festival. She had told herself that she didn't have time for that, either. In truth, neither the activities nor the hedonism held any appeal, but at this time of year, they were hard to avoid. As July became August, the people of Grenada geared up for the days of revelry as if they were readying for war.

Beginning with the Rainbow Festival in St. Andrew's, during the first weekend in August, big tents mushroomed around the island for the steel-band and calypso competitions. Because the calypsos were, in the main, politically based, the lyrics inevitably spawned more fights than were usual on the island and, under cover of Carnival's loose attitude, more assaults on tourist.

This year however, there were fewer political songs, and many more that stretched the moral boundaries of the island. Watching the frenzy mount and the competition grow ever fiercer, Peta could not but wonder how many—or how few—Grenadians remembered that Carnival was supposed to be about Lent. It had been easier to remember when it coincided with the Lenten season. Once the influx of summer tourists induced a change to August, none but the most religious among the revelers gave much thought to its origins.

She chuckled somewhat wryly at herself.

For the first time since she could remember, her Catholic roots were showing. As an intelligent being and as a doctor, she had an intense awareness of life's transience, but she'd never concerned herself with what lay at the end of her tunnel.

Not so these days.

These days she thought a lot about her own mortality.

Doubtless, this was related to Arthur's death. This would be her first Carnival without him. Wherever he was, that was where she wanted to go. Not right away, of course, but ultimately. When it was her time.

Meanwhile, the annual celebration had to be endured.

In the gloom of dusk among the trees of the mountain, a light flashed ahead of her. Glancing at the odometer, she realized that she was nearing the location of her house call. She had been averaging no more than fifteen miles an hour. Even had she not recalled the location on her own, she was hardly likely to have missed the figure waving a flashlight at the side of the road.

She stopped the car and stuck her head out of the open window.

The messenger directed the flashlight's beam into her eyes. She covered them with one hand and, with the other, opened the car door.

"How's the patient?"

"Patient be dead."

The stranger, a masked male youth judging by the width of his shoulders, stepped into Peta's line of vision. He was quickly joined by a group, seven or eight strong, of Jab Jab Molassi.

In the distance, she heard drumbeats, punctuated every now and again by the bleating of a goat. At the Grand Étang Lake, Mama Glo, the goddess of the river, was worshiped, especially during Saraka, the period of honoring the dead and appeasing evil spirits. Animals were sacrificed. The days of feasting and singing and dancing attracted Shango worshipers, who believed that the African god of thunder and thunderbolts punished troublemakers and rewarded his worshipers.

Heart pounding, Peta reached for her cell phone—and realized that she had left it inside the car. She felt for her belt and pushed the button on the left of her beeper. It went off with resounding clarity in the night darkness.

A Jab Jab laughed and closed in on her. He removed the pager from her belt and tossed it into the trees.

"We have maldjo," he said, in a mixture of patois and English. "We have the evil eye."

"Maldjo," his buddies chanted. They were close enough that she could hear their breathing. Feel it. The smell of the cheap rum they'd been drinking mixed with the stench of tar and engine oil smeared across their bodies.

One of them tousled her hair from behind.

"You want my money?" Peta reached into her pocket, ready to give them whatever she had on her.

They laughed, quietly, and pressed closer.

One of them smacked his lips, as if anticipating a tasty morsel. "This one's delicious. I gon' eat *her* a-w-e-l up."

Another stuck his head through the open car window. "Hey. Look-a what I found." He slid his body into the car and emerged with her medical bag. "Must be good stuff in here, me t'ink."

A hand tugged at her blouse, another at her skirt. She pulled away, into the arms of a third, who kissed her resoundingly on the mouth. What an idiot she was coming out here alone, at night, during Carnival. She was heavily outnumbered. They were young and they were strong and, judging by the alcohol on the breath of the one who had kissed her, they were considerably more than a couple of sheets to the wind. If they decided to rape her, which seemed inevitable, there was nothing she could do. If she shouted, who would hear her?

Still, it couldn't hurt to scream. Maybe kick a few gonads.

"You want to use your maldjo on me?" She turned to face the one who had kissed her. Immediately she heard what she expected, the sound of one of the Jab Jab coming at her from behind.

Using all of the knowledge Ray had taught her, she kicked backward. Her foot found substance and one of the boys screamed and doubled over.

"You wan' it rough, bitch?" another youth said as he grabbed her by the hair.

She pummeled him with both fists and screamed at the top of her lungs.

A Moke rounded the corner and came to a screeching halt in front of them. Her would-be molesters froze in the vehicle's headlights as, crossbow in hand, Frikkie Van Alman jumped out of the driver's seat of his low four-wheel-drive jeep.

Immediately, the Jab Jab Molassi scattered, shouting, "Sorry, man . . . mistake, man . . . sorry, man," as they vanished into the surrounding forest.

Peta took in a deep breath. "Great white hunter rescues damsel in distress," she said, trying to slow her rapidly beating heart.

"I am delighted to be of service," Frik said. "Perhaps you will allow this to make up in some small measure for the recent unpleasantness between us."

His casual air, combined with the apparent miracle of his timely arrival, told her instinctively that the whole thing had been a setup. Asshole, she thought. Fucking immature asshole.

She feigned more trouble catching her breath while she got her emotions under control. He might be an immature asshole, but he was also dangerous and armed. "Are you talking about Simon, or about your performance at the airport?" Or Blaine, she thought.

"Both." He lowered the crossbow. "I've apologized to you about the incident at San Gabriel. I'm afraid Mr. Blaine got overzealous. He won't be causing a problem for any women for a while, I assure you. As for my little, um, tantrum at the airport. Blame that on my male ego. Whatever the reason, I'm over it."

"Am I supposed to say thank you for that, too?"

Frik made a weak attempt at a chortle. Then, never one for subtleties, he offered her the protection of his boat through the rest of Carnival.

Setup or no, Peta remained concerned for her own safety. For the moment, she decided, it was best to pretend friendship. She had little doubt that the same ego that Frik had blamed for the incident on the tarmac would persuade him that she was genuinely fooled by his attempt at charm.

She followed him back through town to the marina, recently renamed Blue Lagoon, where the *Assegai* was moored. The gate man let them in. They parked near the all-but-deserted bar and made their way down the narrow walkway to the boat.

As always, the dogs, Sheba and Maverick, greeted their master energetically. He settled them down, then ushered Peta on board. She accepted a drink from his ample stock and they exchanged a few pleas-antries as they seated themselves at the big wooden table that stood on the afterdeck. The image of Arthur falling asleep on this very table the night they'd saved him from the Communists, seventeen years earlier, entered her mind.

Drink in hand, Frik's tone went from solicitous to confidential. "I know what you think, Peta. You think that I had something to do with Arthur's death."

He waited for her to say something. Keep waiting, you bastard, she thought.

"You couldn't be further from the truth, you know. Arthur was my dearest friend. I would never have done anything to harm him and I will always miss him. Come, I have something to show you."

He took her into the ship's saloon and showed her the pieces he had of the artifact. They were resting in some sort of wire frame. She rec-ognized the oddly shimmering surface of the pieces and marveled at how perfectly the piece she recognized from the undersea cavern, the one Blaine had taken from her, fit into what had to be the one Paul had left Frik. Intuitively, she could see where the little cups and nodules on her piece would fit, and how Arthur's, stuck in NYPD's Midtown North evidence lockup, would link neatly to all three.

"It may surprise—even shock you—to find out that I know you have a piece of the artifact," Frik said. "I saw it around your neck during the newscast, that god-awful night in New York."

What is your game, Frik? Peta thought. Why are you taking me into your confidence? "What do you want me to say about that?" she asked, mostly to buy herself time.

"I don't want you to say anything. I want you to give your fragment to me . . . for the good of humanity."

Frik held out his hand. She stared at it. He had delayed this long to make his demand; why make it now? Why not wait until New Year's Eve?

Clearly, the answer was that he had trusted her then and did not trust her now. She could think of at least two obvious reasons for that, one at the bottom of the sea and one up on the mountain.

"I don't have it on me," she said, and fingered her neck as if to demonstrate that the pendant was not there.

"Bring it here tomorrow. I'm having my usual carnival party after the parade. It wouldn't be complete without your presence anyway."

The last thing I need, Peta thought, is one of Frik's drunken parties. Then again, if she didn't accept, the little mob scene on the Grand Étang road was likely to be repeated, sans the arrival of the white knight.

Humoring him, praying that Ralphie had the replica ready for her, she smiled congenially. "I could use a few laughs. I'll bring it with me tomorrow night."

35

Feeling for all the world like one of Siegfried and Roy's caged white tigers, Ray paced around his Las Vegas penthouse. Even after a year of living in the apartment, its triangular shape, like that of the hotel beneath it, made him vaguely uncomfortable.

He stalked through what he thought of as the great room, with its sixty-foot-long wall of tempered, tinted glass, its twelve-foot ceiling and comfortable groupings of chairs and sofas.

Trying to clear his mind, he took in the view.

The windows and sliding door at one end faced west across his private helipad to Palace Station Casino and the mountain ranges beyond it. He could just make out the bloodred rock formations of Red Rock Canyon at the corner. The main wall of windows faced southeast, giving him a perfect view of Circus Circus and the rest of the Strip, with the Sahara across the street at the easternmost corner. If he stepped right up to the glass, he knew, he'd be able to look down at the head of the fifty-foot-tall lizard that appeared to be crashing out of the hotel's outer wall. The latest battle between his stuntmen-performers and the animatronic beast should just have finished. Inside the casino, the creature's tail would have stopped its periodic waving just below the ceiling.

He prowled down the back hall past the guest rooms, and ended up on the balcony off his own bedroom. From that vantage point, he could look northeast at Stratosphere Tower and downtown, and he could see the glow of the spinning neon Daredevil Casino sign on the nose of a replica of a space shuttle that jutted at a steep angle out of the side of his hotel's tenth floor, with the tail and cargo doors angled away from the building. It looked as if the building were the shuttle's external fuel tank and the craft was separating on its way toward the stars. The sides of the shuttle had dozens of viewing ports; the nose cone was glass, allowing tourists to get a one-of-a-kind picture of themselves suspended against the Las Vegas skyline. In what would have been the cargo bay, Ray's high rollers could enjoy a five-star meal served in a multitiered restaurant. Each table was set against the cargo doors, which were made of specially tinted glass, creating the perfect setup for patrons to see the Stratosphere and the lights of downtown.

All very impressive, Ray thought, yet nothing in the spectacle of his hotel, or Las Vegas itself, held his attention. The Daredevil Casino was already showing a huge profit, enough for him to seriously contemplate buying land to build the Rig, an idea that had stayed with him since his visit to the *Valhalla;* yet he felt edgy. Restive.

What he really needed to cure his restlessness was a new stunt job.

No, he thought. The way he felt was only partially due to his lack of a film job in the offing. More likely it was a symptom of withdrawal after the jungle battle against Green Impact. He had long since admitted to himself that he was a risk addict, and this sitting around was making him itch for the rush of adrenaline he'd felt as the bullets flew and explosives roared through the Delta Amacuro swamps.

Perhaps, he thought, he should coin a syndrome for what ailed him: danger deprivation syndrome. DDS. Sounded painful and impressive.

He passed through the dining room, where he could see northwest over his hotel's thrill rides, and reentered the great room from the corner.

Walking through the apartment's main room, past the recessed security screens that allowed him to watch the action downstairs, he opened the door that led to his private lab, a windowless, environmentally stabilized room in the middle of his penthouse. It always amazed him how cramped the lab felt, though he knew it to be as big as his bedroom, which comfortably fit a California king-sized bed, a separate sitting area for very private conversations, and an anteroom for his morning workout equipment.

His lab, on the other hand, was crammed with storage cabinets along the wall on both sides of the door. In the middle of the room stood a giant table covered with metal frames and cables and bits of equipment he hadn't put away. To his right, a Peg-Board took up half of the wall, with tools and safety equipment hanging from seemingly random hooks. Below that, more storage cabinets held larger pieces of equipment and supplies. The left-hand side of the room held his desk and file cabinets. Several dry-erase whiteboards hung above them, filled with reminders about appointments and notes about Frikkie's strange artifact. The left half of the back wall was taken up by a giant screen.

Ray sat down at his desk, tapped a key to wake up his computer, and swiveled around to stare at the computer model on the wall screen. It was a three-dimensional image of what the artifact would look like when put together. After Frikkie had sent him the surface dimensions and other characteristics of the piece Simon had died finding, Ray had updated the model. Now it looked a lot like a strange geode, roughly spherical but with odd bumps and depressions. The figure-eight section from the original assembly Paul Trujold had discovered stuck partway out on one end. He thought irreverently that it looked like Mr. Potato Head with only his nose attached.

The telephone rang, startling him out of deep contemplation. He leaned back in his chair and automatically picked up the receiver, without twisting to look at the caller ID. There were fewer than a dozen people to whom he had given this number anyway, and several of them were dead, so they no longer counted.

On the phone, dogs barked in the background. He recognized them as Sheba and Maverick.

"Yeah, Frik."

"We have to be subtle. I'm calling from Grenada. I'm here for Carnival."

"When you're king of the universe, the first thing you can do is change the Grenadian phone system." Ray was only half joking.

"Peta just left," Frik said, apparently unconcerned by Ray's biting comment. "I told her that I saw the piece of the artifact around her neck during the newscast in New York. She's bringing it to me tomorrow."

Ray was silent for a little too long. What on earth could have induced Peta to agree to that? he wondered.

"Are you there?"

"I'm here."

"You sound surprised. I was sure you knew that she had one." Frik sounded hugely pleased with himself. "McKendry is still on the job searching for Selene to get the pieces Paul sent to her."

"That leaves Arthur's," Ray said without thinking.

It was Frikkie's turn to be surprised. "What do you mean, Arthur's? I didn't know that he had a piece. How do you know? Why didn't you tell me before?"

Shit, Ray thought. He'd been so surprised by Frikkie's knowledge of Peta's piece that he'd assumed the Afrikaner would also know about Arthur's. He said as much over the phone. "I guess it's true what they say about assumptions."

Ray glanced across at his door, as if he'd momentarily forgotten that he was alone in the penthouse. Swiveling all the way around, he unlocked the top drawer of his desk and took out an odd-shaped blue-green object.

"Damn it! I must have that piece, Ray."

"The NYPD has it, Frik. No way to get it out."

"I'll pull strings. You'd be amazed at what a large enough donation to the Policemen's Fund can buy. They'll be glad to help me."

As Ray turned the piece over and over in his hands, it reflected the light from the wall screen. Playing with it as if it were a worry stone, he watched as it seemed to warp the light such that its own image, and not the rest of the model, was visible like an afterimage on the irregular surface.

"I tried that," he said. "Remember, I have a lot of friends in that precinct. I've done more than my share of filming there. They won't release it to anyone other than Peta. She signed a priori for Arthur's effects."

Peta would feel safe as long as Frik thought she was the only one with access to Arthur's fragment, Ray thought. He needed her to be fearless.

"Peta said something about going to New York on her birthday as a kind of statement. Since she's being so cooperative, why not ask her to retrieve the piece from the precinct and bring it along to Vegas at New Year's?"

The Afrikaner's frustration seemed audible, even before he said, "I can't wait that long."

"What's so almighty urgent?" Ray was aware of the rush he was getting from the conversation and happy to discard his recent ennui. "She'll bring Arthur's fragment here on New Year's Eve. You'll be lucky to have Selene's piece by then anyway."

"I suppose you're right," Frik said, though to Ray he didn't sound entirely convinced. "By the way, have you been able to work anything out with your computer models?"

"Not that I could say over an unsecured line if I had, but no. I know its shape, and I know the reactions from Paul's notes. Other than that, it's a complete mystery."

"Well keep working on it, would you." If possible, Frikkie's voice seemed to hold more frustration than before. "As for the other matter, I suppose you're right. I can wait for New Year's Eve to get the other pieces. I want the whole Daredevils Club there when we put this together and find out what it really does."

I bet, Ray thought, but all he said was "Good-bye." He hung up the phone and held Arthur's piece between thumb and forefinger. Angling it, he tried to line up the fragment with the image on the wall screen. As the images merged in his vision, he felt his head swim, and a wave of nausea overcame him.

Centering the piece on his desk, he stared at it, shook his head as if to clear it, and closed his eyes. After counting to five, he reopened them and refocused on the object.

Nothing had changed; his nausea and the illusion of the artifact's curious reflection of itself remained.

36

Not much outside of restaurants and bars stayed open on the island on Carnival Monday. The occasional minibus driver picked up a load of passengers, the police and fire stations stayed on alert, and the clinic opened its doors, which was fine with Peta. She had no urge whatsoever to participate in Carnival, particularly after her experience with the Jab Jab Molassi. She had no interest in watching the parade or in following it to Grenada National Stadium for the calypso finals and the crowning of the king and queen of the Carnival.

It was well into the afternoon before she finished seeing her patients, which was perfect because Ralphie was rarely around before then. His routine was absolute unless he was ill or off-island. He disappeared after his morning sea bath, and appeared again on Morne Rouge Beach in the late afternoon with his knapsack. Settling himself against the fence in front of the house nearest to Gem Holiday Beach Resort, he carved black coral, smoked the occasional joint, and engaged in brief conversations with passers-by. Mostly, he kept to himself.

Always, she knew where to find him.

She had brought her party clothes from home, figuring she would use the bathroom at her clinic to dress. If it weren't for carnival, she'd have gone home, then down to the Carenage and hailed a water taxi to take her to Ralphie at Morne Rouge Bay and back to Blue Lagoon Marina. Today, however, was not the day to do that—not with all the drunks and tourists jockeying for space on the Carenage.

At about four-thirty, she made her last patient notes and dressed—

or more precisely, undressed—to kill, in a miniskirted black T-strap dress.

Praying that Ralphie would have her replica ready, she threw a pair of silver stiletto-heeled sandals onto the front seat of the car and, barefoot, drove her Honda down the hill to Gem. He was not yet at his post, so she stopped in for a brief hello with the hotel manager, a woman whose string of children Peta had delivered, picked up a Coke at the beach bar, and walked onto the sand. She could smell the aroma of fresh seafood cooking in the perpetual pot that was kept going by the beach folk. One of them, still dripping from his dive, cracked open a sea urchin and offered it to her. She could not resist the treat. He wouldn't take any money, so she tossed him a couple of cigarettes.

Attracted to the sight of the giveaway, a jailbird con artist whom she knew only as Coconut asked for a smoke. She tossed him one.

He grinned and stuck it between his lips before motioning with his hands as if he were striking a match.

"Seen Ralphie?" she asked, pulling a disposable lighter from her purse.

Coconut shook his head. "Not for a few days. Maybe he go off-island."

Peta pointed at the small pile of green coconuts at his feet. He pulled his machete from the sand, picked up one of the nuts, a little smaller than an American football, and began the ritual he would have to complete before she could ask him any more questions. Twirling the coconut in his left hand, he expertly swung the machete across the end, trimming away the green husk and exposing the soft interior shell. With a final whack he lopped off the end and handed it to her.

She exchanged it for the lighter and drank down the liquid inside the coconut, relishing its cool sweetness. When she'd finished, she handed it back to Coconut, who chopped it open and returned the two halves, along with a shaving from the husk. Using the shaving like a spoon, she scooped out the white, gelatinous insides that off-islanders never saw in the old, dried-out nuts they bought at the supermarket.

"Ralphie has to be around somewhere," she said, throwing the empty shells into the nearby tin drum that passed as a trash can.

Coconut grinned. "I find him for you—cost you a pack of smokes."

Peta sat down on one of Gem's beach chairs. "Sure." She brushed away a family of no-see-ums that were settling on her arm in anticipation of sundown. "Why not."

She adjusted the chair, lay back, and fell asleep. The steel-drum sounds of the New Dimensions, a local reggae and soca group, awakened her an hour later. Their music came from the *Rhum Runner,* a tourist-filled catamaran making a stop on its daily sunset round. Two old ladies sat under a palm tree near the cat, trading baskets of T-shirts. A third had thrown a row of brightly colored towels over the fence. She sat in front of them braiding a tourist's hair with the help of her granddaughter, a pretty girl of no more than nine.

"Ralphie come soon." Coconut plopped himself down on the sand next to her and held out one hand for payment. "I find him wa-a-y down Grand Anse."

"I don't see him," Peta said.

"He come along slow."

"Why should I believe you?" Peta asked, amusing herself.

Coconut lifted his machete and grinned. She took a small purse out of her pocket and counted out $1.30 Grenadian, enough for a pack of 555s at the supermarket up the road or a half pack at the bar.

"I'm thirsty for beer," Coconut said.

Peta shook her head. "Don't push your luck."

He shrugged congenially, as if he had expected no different. "You be at Fantazia tonight for Calypso Night?" he asked, pointing at the building attached to the back of Gem's beachside restaurant, Sur La Mer.

"Maybe," Peta said, though she had absolutely no intention of partying there or anywhere else, with the exception of her obligatory appearance on the *Assegai.*

"Good enough." He took off for the bar just as Ralphie strode into view. "See," he called out. "I told you."

"Hey, Ralphie."

"Hey, Miss Peta."

"You finished the job I gave you?"

"I finished it." He moved off toward the fence. She stood up and followed him. He settled himself on the sand, took out a piece of coral and a small knife, and began to carve. She sat down next to him and waited in companionable silence, knowing he would give her what she wanted in his own time and not before.

After half an hour or so, he dug into his bag and pulled out the replica, set in the original gold bezel, and the loose real fragment. She took them from him and examined them closely.

There was no way to tell visually which one was the duplicate and which the real thing.

The only way she knew the difference was by feel. The original fragment seemed to draw the heat from her hand, making it tingle like pins and needles. The other felt like any piece of carved coral.

"Amazing job, Ralphie. I don't know how to thank you. You just might have saved my life."

"Then I have all the thanks I need," he said gravely, and refused all offers of payment.

"I have one more favor to ask." She held out the original toward him. "I don't want to have this with me tonight. Will you hold it for me until tomorrow?"

He nodded and took it from her.

"Aren't you curious about this?" Peta asked.

"I'm curious about how the universe works," he answered.

Peta smiled at him. He was really something, her friend Ralphie. He could have followed in his family's political footsteps. He could have lived like a rich man. Instead, he carved coral and sought the secrets of the universe. She thought about Frik, about how his search for the same secrets was motivated by a desire for self-aggrandizement.

She leaned over and kissed Ralphie on the cheek. "If for some reason I don't come back and get it from you, find Manny Sheppard and give it to him."

"You go to come back," he said, as if he knew.

As Peta neared Blue Lagoon, she heard again the sounds of the New Dimensions. They were doing well for themselves, she thought, wondering if Frik had also hired Bosco, as he usually did. She had known Grenada's one-man band all of her life, and enjoyed seeing him. He was an event unto himself, playing bass and keyboard, percussion and drums, doing his own arrangements, and playing pan and singing. Cute and fun, he was much in demand.

She parked her car outside the marina so that, if necessary, she could leave in a hurry, and footed it the rest of the way. The area was alive with music and people. Rum punch was being poured liberally and everyone was having a high old time, drinking, toking, dancing to the lively steel drums of the local musicians who had apparently forgone their usual gig at the Grenada Grand Beach Resort to oblige Frik.

She waved at the musicians and made her way through the crowd. Hiking up her miniskirt, stilettos dangling from her hand, she climbed onto the *Assegai*. The wooden table had been removed from the deck to make room for a spotlit dance floor.

As one song ended and another began, a circle of partygoers gathered around Peta. Some of them began to dance. She slipped into her sandals and moved to the irresistible rhythm of her favorite local calypso, Marsha MacDonald's "Going Under."

"Go, girl," someone yelled. Someone else turned the spotlight on her. Frik.

She had noticed him among those who preferred to watch. Now she saw that his gaze was riveted on the pendant she was wearing around her neck.

At the end of the song, the musicians closed their set.

Frik moved toward her, took her arm, and guided her down into the cabin, where a huge black form lay growling.

"Quiet, Sheba!"

The dog sent out one more test growl, objecting to the invasion of her territory, then stopped.

Peta followed the Afrikaner through the boat's small galley and forward to his private study. The cozy wood-paneled cabin curved with the prow of the *Assegai* until it formed a point. Cushioned benches lined both walls, broken only on the starboard side by a locked cabinet which she knew contained an entertainment center and his communications equipment. Where the curving walls brought the benches together, a low trapezoidal wooden cabinet served as a display table. Standing in the middle of it was the small wire frame which held the two pieces of the artifact that Frikkie had so far recovered.

"Thank you, again, for coming," he said. "And for bringing the piece." Safely out of sight of the revelers, he reached out toward the pendant.

"Not so fast," Peta said, enjoying the look on his face as she backed away. Smiling, she asked him to give her the privilege of placing the fragment into the model herself. "Just a whim," she said. "Humor me."

A trifle impatiently, Frik agreed.

Heart pounding, praying that Ralphie's work was as perfect as she thought it was, she removed the pendant from around her neck, pushed the fragment out of its bezel and into the space he indicated.

It slid in and—*Thank you, Ralphie*—connected perfectly with the real pieces of the artifact.

"That just leaves Selene's fragment," Frik said. "And the one that's in New York with Arthur's effects."

"I'm curious," Peta said, trying to sound casual. "How did you know about that one?"

"Ray told me just recently," Frik said. "Is that a problem? It *is* mine, you know."

"A problem? N-no. I don't suppose it is." She had never been completely sure that Frik knew about the piece in New York or, if he did know, just how he had learned about it. Her suspicions about the Daredevil stuntman returned tenfold.

"Ray says the piece is in New York, with Arthur's effects. I'd like to go and get it," Frik went on, his voice carefully benign.

Damn it, Peta thought. How was she going to get out of this one? "It can be released only to me, personally."

"So I understand. Why don't you let me fly you there. We can—"

Peta held up her hand. "I have a practice. I have students at the medical school coming in this week to begin the new semester and I need to prepare. There's no way I can leave Grenada right now."

"But—"

"Don't pressure me, Frik. I'm not one of your flunkies." Her anger finally overrode her caution, adding heat to her words. "I give you my word I'll retrieve the piece in time for the New Year's Eve meeting in Vegas. That'll have to be good enough."

37

On the night of the August new moon, Terris McKendry stood on the *Valhalla* platform and wondered if he would ever again be able to trust a night of such darkness. To him it seemed that the world was holding its breath, waiting to unleash some hidden terror. His uneasiness had returned each month since the night on the *Yucatán* when he and Joshua had first encountered Green Impact—the night that had cost Keene his life and made him into a cold-blooded murderer who would shoot a woman in the back.

Restless, he walked the metal decks at the wellhead level, high as a skyscraper above the placid water. Level after level, he climbed from one yellow-painted staircase to another, pacing, working off his nervous energy as he stared out into the night.

His heavy boots rang loudly in his ears, even against the hiss and thrum of the ever-working mechanisms of the production platform. The rig was a constant drone of machinery, effluents hissing through pipes, waste-gas flames crackling at the long ends of boom derricks.

McKendry gripped the warm metal railings and peered a hundred feet down to the water. *Valhalla* produced too much background noise, too much light and sound. It cast a bubble of restless civilization around them, like a campfire driving off predators in the wilderness.

Pacing around to the western corner of the platform, he saw the two exhaust flares extended like spitting dragons into the darkness, bleeding off belches of unwanted gases from the simmering oil well deep under the waters. On the opposite side, the living quarters rested under the helideck. At this time of night most of the workers would be off shift, playing billiards, watching action movies, cheating each other at cards. Separate from the habitation modules, the shack of the radio room was lit; undoubtedly Hercules, the Trinidadian man on duty, was chatting with radio pen pals from across the world.

As his uneasiness built, he strode to one of the phones that allowed communication between the distant parts of the rig and punched in the code for the small coffee room where his security men often took a break. "Gonzales. Get everyone outside. No more breaks this shift. Do your rounds every fifteen minutes tonight, not every half hour. I want all of you to keep an eye out."

"What's wrong, sir?" Gonzales said.

"Just do it. There's nothing wrong with being on your toes." McKendry made sure his men did their jobs, but never bothered to get cordial with any of them. He couldn't imagine why the guards would rather sit in a confined room on plastic chairs drinking sour coffee instead of walking around the rig decks in the warm night and stretching their legs. In the Tropics he had found that some men just plain took pride in their laziness.

On the other end of the line, Gonzales grumbled to the others in the coffee shop, "It's the dark of the moon. Makes him paranoid."

McKendry scowled and said in a gruff voice, "You can complain to Mr. Van Alman if you don't like my orders. I'm sure he'll be happy to let you find another job." Angrily, he hung up. Maybe he was being overcautious, but it only took one mistake, as the captain of the *Yucatán* had discovered.

He walked to the edge of the platform and again scanned the vast stretch of water between the rig and the invisible mainland of Venezuela.

Why did he really care what happened to the *Valhalla*? Because he'd promised Frikkie that he'd protect the rig? It wasn't as if Frik was much of a friend. After the assault on the Green Impact camp, the billionaire had been concerned only with the recovery of his mysterious artifact. The dead mercenaries on his side and the half dozen dead terrorists on the other didn't matter to the man. All he cared about was that somehow Selene Trujold had gotten away, even though she had been shot.

After what the terrorists did to Joshua, McKendry thought, it matters to me.

Drifting across the water like a black fly on a dark lily pad, Joshua Keene closed the distance to the *Valhalla* platform. He moved without lights, circling his motorized inflatable raft to the Trinidad side of the rig so that he could come in opposite the additional glow of the exhaust flares at the ends of their extended booms.

As he turned the Zodiac toward the rig, he cut the motor. In the ensuing silence he could hear the industrial buzz, even from a distance of more than a mile.

Entering the rich, warm waters around the *Valhalla,* he trailed streamers of potent shark repellent. Though sharks rarely attacked inflatable rafts, he wanted to avoid any commotion at all.

It took a long time for him to paddle the raft up to the elephantine concrete legs that held the huge production rig high above the calm water, but he didn't dare use the puttering outboard. If all went well, he would be calling enough attention to himself in a little while. He tied up to the emergency ladder built onto the closest concrete strut, the same one he and Terris had used the night his friend died. Before climbing out of the Zodiac, he secured all of his weapons around his legs, chest, and back, fastening packages of compact explosives, his igniters, and grenades. He even had the knife that had killed Selene: the most appropriate weapon to use while destroying Oilstar, he thought.

In his pocket he could feel the weirdly curved edges of the strange but unknowably precious piece of the artifact. He kept it to remind himself that Selene had died for it.

Though it made his own movement more difficult, he wrapped a dull black rain cloak around his shoulders, which would keep him all but invisible in the shadows.

Rung after rung, he began to climb; it was eighty feet from the water to the lowest deck of the production platform. It would have been so much easier to use one of the lift platforms, he thought, but he knew the clanking and ratcheting noise would be sure to draw investigation by one of the rig's newly inspired security guards. Now that he had heard so much about the draconian new security chief Oilstar had hired, he expected he'd have to be much more cautious than on his first visit.

Keene reached the first deck, opened the small access gate, and pulled himself up onto the platform. Though he'd thought he had recovered from his wounds, he felt exhausted from the climb, especially with the extra weight he was carrying. Not for the first time, he wished that some of the other members of Selene's team had escaped Oilstar's assault on the jungle base. He would have liked some help in this operation, commandos willing to sacrifice their lives.

Wishing and hoping, though, weren't going to change the fact that those who hadn't died had been captured and turned over to the Venezuelan government, which made them as good as dead, anyway. Joshua knew he was all alone, with only his anger, his need for revenge, and a half-baked plan.

On a rig like this, however, one person could cause a lot of damage.

There were enough explosives strapped to his body to create a substantial disaster. Given good placement and a lucky break, he would be able to rig the explosives and get away from the *Valhalla* before his fireworks display turned the rig into a seaborne version of *The Towering Inferno*. He was determined to accomplish his goal at all costs, but this was no deliberate suicide mission. A lot had happened in the last few months that he needed to mull over. Selene Trujold's death, the loss of Terris McKendry, Frikkie's betrayal.

After shucking his dark rain cloak so that it would not hinder his movements, Keene stole across the metal decks. He moved toward the cluster of fractionation pipes. Ahead of him he could see the closed-down electrical and mechanical workshops, the crew change rooms, circuitry lockers, and mudrooms that surrounded the smelly drill floor around the main wellhead. He looked up and saw business offices; they looked like tiny cubicles on a spaceship.

During the two months it had taken him to gather the explosives he needed, Joshua had studied as much as he could about production rigs and their numerous vulnerabilities. He ignored the optimistic and reassuring press releases from Oilstar and other major petroleum companies, instead paying particular attention to the infamous *Piper Alpha* disaster of July 1988 in the North Sea just off Aberdeen, Scotland.

A smoldering fire in one of the modules had built up until it set off a small explosion in an adjacent chamber, which had then triggered another explosion, tearing apart half of the giant oil platform. Rig workers had been trapped in the habitation module as fire and smoke spread. Emergency sprinkler systems had failed. Radiomen had called "Mayday" repeatedly until finally they had to abandon the communications offices as the fire and smoke advanced.

Some crewmen had been stranded by the advancing flame front while they raced to lifeboat stations; others were trapped high above the turbulent and cold North Sea. Given no choice, some men had leaped sixty-eight feet from one of the decks into the water. A handful of desperate, doomed workers had even jumped from the heliport, faced with either being burned to death in the advancing fire or dying as they plunged from skyscraper height to the sea. Several crewmen had climbed down knotted ropes or hoses to reach sea level as explosion after explosion rocked *Piper Alpha*.

Rescue crews had raced in boats and helicopters from nearby drilling platforms, but the fire was so bad that few of them could even approach the burning rig to fish survivors out of the water. The debris from one explosion killed half the crew on an approaching rescue craft.

In all, 165 people had died on *Piper Alpha,* making it one of the worst disasters in oil-drilling history.

Keene tried to imagine seeing the same inferno on the *Valhalla.* In front of the vision in his mind he saw Selene's face, heard her last words as she died beside him in the clearing near the Green Impact encampment. The fires grew brighter in his imagination.

Yes, he thought, that would just about do it.

38

Oilstar's security squads grudgingly did what their boss had ordered, but McKendry noticed without surprise that they walked their routes together, sticking to the brightly lit decks, chatting with late-shift crewmen—in other words, going out of their way to avoid anywhere that trouble might occur.

The big man patrolled the darker ways himself, slipping through the claustrophobic and tangled pipe forests and chemical-storage areas, letting a sixth sense prickle his skin.

He felt uneasy.

Looking up into the dark and moonless sky, he was positive this uneasiness wasn't his imagination.

Of course, he had been just as positive month after month, ever since the night Joshua Keene had died.

His doubts ended when he reached the fourth deck and stopped, feeling electricity go up his spine. Someone—perhaps a survivor from Green Impact—was here on the *Valhalla* platform.

His flashlight beam revealed no movement in the dark corners; not that he expected any. No professional would have waited around. Then he discovered that one of the access hatches leading up from the support legs and the distant water was open. It was near the central wellhead and the shut-down mechanical shops. When he examined it more closely, he saw that one of the naked yellow lightbulbs had been smashed. Crumpled in the shadows, he found a lightweight black cloak—the kind he himself would have chosen for camouflage.

Whoever had been here, or was still here, apparently thought that security on board was as lax as it had been in the past.

He directed the beam of the flashlight all the way down to the water. Though the beam diffused, he saw something dark tied up to the ladder attached to the wide concrete leg. Running to the nearest lift platform, he descended to water level, where he studied the unobtrusive black boat tied to a ladder rung. The single rubber raft could have carried only a few of the terrorists, but even a small group could cause extreme damage to the rig if they knew what they were doing.

McKendry took out a knife and, with a quick motion, slashed the rope holding the Zodiac in place. He shoved with his foot so that the raft drifted into the water.

Whoever had come to his rig wouldn't get away now. He'd have them cornered on the *Valhalla* platform, where he could deal with them in his own way.

Creeping across the decks and ducking the rig's still laughable security, Keene found a set of lockers that contained Oilstar work clothes. Diligent practices on the rig had been increased, and he thought he saw more guards on patrol, but they didn't appear to be doing a better job than before. They talked loudly and walked in packs, making it easy for him to elude them.

From one of the lockers, he pulled on a greasy, thick jumpsuit that had the hand-lettered name Virata written on the left breast in bold strokes with a black Magic Marker. The jumpsuit smelled like grease and piss, but he'd endured worse. He found a hard hat adorned with crudely placed racing decals and snugged it against his hair.

Walking away from the lockers he was less stealthy, and instead walked as if he belonged on the rig. The explosive packs strapped to his chest and legs, as well as the packages he carried in one hand, made him look bulky and cumbersome, but if all went well, he wouldn't have them for long.

Outside the mechanical rooms and shop offices, he found the central pipes and controls for the fire-suppression systems and alarms. He was relieved to see that the safety valves were split into two systems, one of which went toward the habitation quarters to protect the crew complement. An independent set dealt with the production facility, the pipes and chambers and machinery of the production rig itself.

He shut down, then permanently disabled the alarms, sprinklers, and safety systems in the production portions of *Valhalla*. Once the explosives went off, the alarms and sprinklers would activate inside the habitation module, getting the snoozing off-duty teams out of bed. That would give the crew members a chance to get away, but nothing would stop the flames in the production area. These sleepy South American crewmen certainly wouldn't try to save the rig. They'd rush to the lifeboats, which would drop like padded sledgehammers into the water far below.

Keene supposed that kept him from being a cold-blooded murderer; now he qualified as just a warm-blooded one.

He worked for ten minutes setting up his explosives against a thirty-foot-high distillation tank connected to three systems that led to the heavy-gases storage chambers and out to the flame boom. His examination of design blueprints of the *Valhalla* had showed that even his token amount of explosives would ignite this one tank. Once it blew, it would set off the second, which would set off the third, and so on like red-hot dominoes until nothing was left of the oil rig's production facilities.

Given a huge supply of Oilstar funding, Van Alman might be able to repair and eventually restart production on the *Valhalla*. But the cost to him in damage to public relations would be insurmountable.

Keene twisted the last wire onto the timer. He still had a few small grenades clipped to his belt, just in case he needed a little help getting away. If he got out of here and climbed down to his inflatable boat in time, he could roar off in the Zodiac with the outboard cranked full. With the rig blazing behind him, he could make his way back to the Venezuelan mainland and eventually return to North America.

This year he'd have one hell of a story to tell the remaining members of the Daredevils Club on New Year's Eve. He would take great pleasure in rubbing Frik's nose in it. First he had to finish his job and get off the rig alive, though.

He stood up. Before he could turn, there was a click as the hammer of a pistol was drawn back.

"Don't move."

Keene froze. Thoughts raced through his mind. He hadn't even heard footsteps.

The background white noise of the drilling rig showered like snow around him. He rested a hand on one of the small grenades at his waist, cradling it. He could easily yank the pin out, toss it next to the other explosives. The grenade would blow up before the security guard behind him could stop it. The only problem was that he would be gunned down in an instant, or the explosion would take him with it.

He considered trying to bluff his way out, holding on to the grenade as long as possible. If he could redirect the guard's attention, maybe he could toss the grenade far enough so that he could get away as the explosions rippled through the rig. In the meantime, he would have to dodge bullets, too. It was a near-zero chance of survival.

But near-zero isn't zero.

"Turn around very slowly and show me your hands," the security guard said.

Something in the voice tickled the back of Keene's memory, but he tried to ignore it and stay focused on the mission. He turned, keeping his eyes fixed on the explosives and his hand covering the grenade. Maybe he could fool the guard, act like a regular Joe.

He started to set a smile on his face and looked up to make eye contact with the stranger. When he did, he saw the impossible: Terris McKendry, very much alive, aiming a pistol at his chest.

Keene blinked. McKendry's face looked like an astonished child's as his jaw fell open. "What the hell?"

Stupefied, Keene almost dropped the grenade. The motion startled McKendry, who jerked the pistol.

Involuntarily, Keene ducked. "You're dead," he muttered.

McKendry looked at his friend as if that were the stupidest thing he had ever heard, but he clamped his lips shut. Keene knew that the same words had been about to come from the other man's mouth.

"I watched you die," the bigger man said. "Blown overboard. They never found your body. The sharks got it."

"I saw the bullets hit. I saw you thrown off the bicycle."

For a moment the two men held their weapons, facing each other. Keene kept his hand on the grenade; McKendry's pistol was still targeted at his partner. Finally Joshua laughed out loud, the braying chuckle that had always annoyed his friend.

"What are you doing here?" McKendry lowered his weapon a fraction of an inch.

Keene tucked the grenade in his jumpsuit pocket. "What are *you* doing here, Terris? Helping out those bastards at Oilstar?" He raised his hands to indicate the totality of the *Valhalla* platform. "Don't you know what Frik did?"

"Why are you doing the dirty work of those Green Impact scum, Josh? Selene Trujold has the blood of dozens on her hands. Probably more. You saw yourself what she did to the crew on the tanker."

"Yes," Keene said, uneasy. "But I also saw what an Oilstar assassination squad did to her and all the other members of her team; slaughtered most of them and sent the rest off to rot in some Venezuelan jail."

McKendry turned gray. "You were there?"

"I was off in Pedernales getting supplies. When I came back, I found the camp destroyed. Selene died in my arms." He gritted his teeth. "Damn it, Terris! I loved her."

"She would have killed you eventually. Maybe I saved your ass."

"Maybe you don't know what you're talking about."

"She was a killer, Joshua. A mad dog, willing to murder innocent people to make her point. I had to shoot her." McKendry sounded as if he were working as hard to convince himself as he was to convince Keene.

"You're full of shit, Terris," Keene said. "She wasn't shot, she was stabbed."

"What do you mean she was stabbed?"

"I mean she was stabbed. With this." He pulled the knife from his waist and held it pommel-out to his partner. The etched initials J.R. caught the light.

"Where did you get that?"

Keene couldn't figure out his partner's reaction. "I picked it up from the pool of Selene's blood that she dropped it in. Terris, what is your problem?"

The big man's pallor had improved. He shook his head and stood up straight, as if a large weight had been removed from his shoulders.

Keene knew better than to push the subject. He sheathed the knife and said, "Did you ever stop to wonder about the real reason Frik wanted this artifact?" He grabbed Selene's fragment out of his pocket and held it up. At times, he had wanted to wipe the surfaces clean, to remove the discolorations, but instead he had let the bloodstains dry on it. Selene's blood.

McKendry stared at the object. Keene dangled it like a carrot in front of his friend's eyes. "Yes, I got it, Terris. I also found out why Frik really wants it."

He rapidly summarized what he had learned: Paul Trujold's discovery of the artifact's true power, and the real purpose behind Frikkie's Daredevil scheme—knowledge that had cost Selene's father his life.

Keene watched McKendry absorb the information, run it through his logic filters. He knew McKendry's process, knew his partner would come to the same conclusions he himself had reached.

Finally, in a lowered voice, McKendry said, "If it were anybody else telling me this, I wouldn't even listen."

"But it is me, Terris. Damn it, it's the truth."

McKendry gestured with the pistol, not in a threatening manner, just as the most obvious means to point. "I think you'd better disassemble those explosives. You won't be needing them now."

Keene hesitated, feeling his heart turn to lead in his chest. "I promised Selene," he said. "With her dying breath she asked me to shut down Oilstar, to get even with them. I can't ignore that."

"And I gave my word to protect this platform. It may not be worth what I thought it was, but I won't let you destroy the *Valhalla*." He paused. "There's got to be some other way."

The two men held their ground, each waiting for the other to speak or offer a suggestion. After a minute, Keene said, "Crap. Maybe I don't have to blow up the *Valhalla* to be true to my promise."

A short time later, the two men stood side by side at the edge of the heliport deck, high above the water. McKendry's on-duty security men had encountered them and waved at their chief. They had not bothered to question the identity of the man wearing Virata's work overalls. McKendry growled under his breath; Keene snickered at their incompetence.

The smaller man held the odd artifact that had been excavated from deep beneath the sea. He stared at it for the last time.

"I sure wish I understood what this is," he said. "But I know it's not worth all the grief it's caused." He held it high, dangling it more than a hundred feet over the waters of the Gulf of Paria, and thought of his promise to Selene. Frik Van Alman would be more upset about not regaining the artifact than he would ever have been about losing the oil rig.

He smiled at the thought of his revenge, muttered something under his breath, and let go.

As the artifact droped from his fingers, it reflected the lights of the rig oddly, as if the perspective were wrong. The optical illusion made it appear to hang in the air.

McKendry's big hand reached out in a flash and grabbed the object before it could fall to the water.

"No. That wouldn't finish it, Joshua." Keene glared at his friend, feeling betrayed, but McKendry continued. "Frik would find it. Somehow."

"That's ridiculous. He couldn't know—"

"Anything is possible. He could have a camera on us right at this moment."

Keene didn't answer. McKendry grinned. "I've reduced you to silence. That's a change. Listen to me, would you? Getting rid of this would not make Frik stop what he's doing. You said yourself this thing could make internal combustion engines a distant memory. That would destroy Oilstar, destroy Frikkie."

"What if he comes after it before then?"

"He won't," McKendry said.

"Why not?"

"Because he trusts us to be good soldiers and do as we were told. On New Year's Eve, you and I will go to Las Vegas and make Frik answer for himself. We'll see to it that this discovery gets put to good use for the whole world, not just for one greedy son of a bitch."

Keene sighed and stared out at the water and the nearby coast of Trinidad. The sky was lightening, shifting from indigo to blues and grays and pinks as the first rays of the sun refracted through the gathering clouds. Red sky at morning, he thought. A storm was on the way.

"You always did hate loose ends," he said, turning to face his friend.

McKendry didn't so much as crack a smile. "And you always did talk too much."

39

No matter how hard she tried, Peta was unable to find closure on Arthur's death. Time, purportedly the ultimate healer, passed, but the void he had left in her life kept growing.

After Carnival and the arrival of a new round of students at the medical school, the only distraction she allowed herself was watching news reports of the American elections on television. She found the debates entertaining. The rumpus in Florida kept her laughing, as had the Monica debacle. While morality on the island was purported to be of great significance to its populace, and in particular to those in government, the truth was that Grenadian politicians made Clinton's high jinks look like a good day at Sunday school.

The difference was that here the personal lives of government officials were conducted behind closed doors. Talk at the Watering Hole never lacked its dose of rumors, whispers, and gossip, but it was laced with rum, not with legal action.

With New Year's Eve only ten days away, Peta went to see her travel agent, whose office on the Carenage always seemed to be run with less efficiency than its well-decorated interior might have indicated.

Her travel plan was simple—provided she could get the airline schedule to cooperate: fly to San Juan and connect to New York, if need be via Miami. She had no wish to stay over in New York. All she wanted was time to go to the precinct, collect Arthur's fragment, and be at Danny's on Forty-sixth Street at five o'clock on New Year's Eve. Sentiment drove her to be there on her birthday—their birthday—even though she would be there alone. That and the distant hope that by being there, by keeping their date, she could finally find some degree of closure.

The way she figured it, she could have a car pick her up at Danny's at seven—in time to get her to the airport for a nine o'clock flight to Vegas. Traffic to the airport would be light on New Year's Eve. The flight would get her to her destination by eleven, Vegas time.

Having taken care of her business at the travel agency, she went next door and upstairs to the Nutmeg for a peanut punch and a roti. Sitting at a table next to the open area overlooking the fishing boats and ferries, she made a few notes, reminders of the things she had to do before leaving: go to the bank for money; collect the real artifact from Ralphie; call Ray to let him know that she was coming to the meeting via New York and give him her arrival time in Vegas; and call the maitre d' at Danny's to tell him to reserve a quiet corner table for her for five o'clock. The restaurant wouldn't be crowded yet at that hour, and even if it was, George would find a way to get her a table.

She thought about what to take along and decided that one small roll-on suitcase, her medical bag, and a handbag would be more than enough to hold the necessities. It wasn't as if she were planning to do the town—New York or Las Vegas. Besides, as Arthur had so often told her, she could always buy what she needed at the other end.

She wondered irreverently, without the usual accompanying stab of pain, if the same principle held true for the journeys to heaven and hell. Maybe, she thought, she was beginning to heal after all.

That evening, Peta made the necessary arrangements with her associate and put in a call to Danny's. George was delighted to hear from her.

"Let me look at the reservation book," he said. "Yes. Here it is. I thought I hadn't erased it. Five o'clock. Dinner. Dr. Whyte and—"

He stopped abruptly. She thanked him and quickly hung up. Next, she called Ray in Las Vegas.

"I have a dinner reservation at Danny's at five o'clock. I called George. He said they hadn't erased the booking Arthur made before . . ."

"I was there when he made that reservation," Ray reminded her, as if she could have forgotten. "You're not even staying over for one night?" He sounded almost irritated with her.

"Is that a problem?"

"I suppose not," Ray said. "You're cutting it awfully close. I just hope there are no flight delays."

"If there are, you can wait to start the meeting."

"New Year's Eve waits for no man."

"Fine. I'm not a man anyway, in case you hadn't noticed."

Ray chuckled. "One more thing. The Strip is closed on New Year's Eve. It'll be shut down by the time you get here. I'll have one of my limos picks you up. The driver will know how to circumvent the barriers. Better yet, I'll arrange for a helicopter out of McCarran and a pilot. Easy enough to land on my helipad and that'll take care of any time crunch."

"Great idea," Peta said, "But you should recall that I won't need a pilot. Just have your driver there to get me to the chopper and make sure all of the authorizations have been cleared."

For the sake of comfort rather than status, Peta had made reservations in first class; for the sake of a show of authority once she got to the police station, she wore a suit—or more accurately, Liz Claiborne wool crepe separates she'd picked up at Saks during her last visit to Manhattan. The black calf-length wrap skirt and fitted fingertip-length black jacket were very New York. A white crew-neck cashmere sweater, opaque black tights, and a pair of black leather knee-high boots completed the look. Hair up in a bun; the real fragment, back in its bezel and hidden beneath her sweater in case some turn of fate brought Frik to the airport; this year's white gold button earrings; and she was good to go. Normally, she would have carried a coat, but since she was only going to be there for a matter of hours, and her jacket would do fine for Vegas, she simply threw a shawl and a pair of warm gloves into her suitcase.

She felt hot and overdressed until she boarded the plane, but she was quickly grateful for having worn a jacket. As usual, Grenada's airport air-conditioning was on slowdown, but the plane was freezing. She hated using the blanket and pillow the airline provided, so she rolled up her jacket as a pillow, snuggled under her shawl, which she pulled out of her bag before throwing it into the overhead compartment, and dozed off.

San Juan's airport was hotter than Grenada's and more crowded. With a lot of hours to kill between flights, she hailed a cab and went to the closest beach hotel. Once there, she changed into the swimsuit she'd shoved into her handbag and grabbed a chaise under an umbrella. Even in the middle of winter, it was hot and humid. They were so damn lucky in Grenada, she thought. Eighty-four degrees, day in, day out, and always an ocean breeze coming off the Atlantic side of the island.

Later, she walked along the beach and watched the sunset. She stayed out there for a while in semidarkness, then walked back and ordered herself a drink. Her flight was due to leave at two in the morning. She glanced at her watch. It was one minute past midnight.

"Happy birthday, Peta," she said. She looked up at the stars. "Happy birthday, my love."

After switching planes in Miami and catching a restless nap during the last leg of the flight to New York, she swore off red-eyes forever. Thanks to delays in the air over JFK, the plane circled for what seemed to be years before it landed. She occupied herself by applying some makeup, putting her jacket back on, and wrapping the shawl around her shoulders in preparation for a New York December day.

By the time the aircraft taxied up to the arrival gate, Peta was ready to scream. There were a dozen people ahead of her in the cordoned-off taxi line. She waited impatiently for the pompous uniformed airport official to whistle her up a cab. When he did, she waved away the suggestion that she share it with someone else in line.

The traffic into Manhattan seemed endless. The cabbie's chattiness, in the past a source of amusement, got on her nerves. By the time he pulled up in front of the Midtown North police station, she felt so guilty about her attitude, she overtipped.

Inside the precinct house, she took out her wallet and retrieved the receipt they'd given her. It was dated December 31, 1999, and signed by Sergeant John Lewis.

Trailing her suitcase behind her, she moved up to the counter. "I'd like to see Sergeant Lewis."

"So would I, lady. We could use him around here."

"Where is he?"

"Retired." The policeman sighed heavily and turned away, but not before Peta got a look at the name on his badge. Patrick O'Shaunessy.

"Detective O'Shaunessy."

He turned back to her. "I'm flattered, ma'am, but it's sergeant. Sergeant O'Shaunessy."

As best she could, Peta stemmed her rising unease. "Well, Sergeant," she said, "I've come to collect, um, my friend's personal effects which were impounded as evidence almost a year ago. I hope you can help me."

He took the receipt from her and examined it closely. "Excuse me a moment, please. I'll be right back. Why don't you take a seat over there." He indicated a slatted bench against the wall.

Peta watched the hands on the large clock over the desk. When he had been gone for twenty minutes, she began to panic. Something was wrong. Very wrong.

"Miss? Dr. Whyte. I'm Captain Richards. Could I see you in here, please."

Breathing a sigh of relief, Peta stood up and followed the plainclothes officer into a small office. The captain, a man not much beyond middle age, pointed at a chair and she sat down.

"I'm sorry, Dr. Whyte. I'm afraid there's been some kind of clerical error." He waved the receipt. "There is absolutely no record of this case."

40

"What are you saying?" Peta stared at the police detective in disbelief.

"I have no other way of saying it. There is absolutely no record of this case."

"That's crazy!" She realized that she was shouting, but made no effort to lower her voice. "I know the case was closed, but you'd think *somebody* around here would remember a bombing and death on New Year's Eve. Damn it, it was only a year ago—"

"Look, lady, calm down." He walked to the door, which she had left slightly ajar, and closed it. Returning to his desk, he sat on the edge facing her. "I'm sorry about this. Really I am. But there's nothing I can do."

Peta sat back and stared at him. Feeling utterly defeated, she took out the pack of cigarettes she'd bought in Miami, peeled off the cellophane wrapping, and took one out. A thousand disconnected thoughts seemed to be chasing each other around her head.

"You can't—ah, the hell with it."

He took a lighter out of his pocket and lit her cigarette. Still leaning forward, he whispered, "I'm going to tell you something, but if you repeat it, I'll deny I said a word." She started to interrupt him, but he held up his hand. "Listen carefully, 'cause I'm only going to say this once. Early last August, some NSA suits came in here and took away a bunch of records. They erased everything about them in our computers and told me that as far as I was concerned, that explosion that killed the doc . . . it never happened."

"Why—?"

"Hey, the Feds come in here waving writs around, you don't ask questions."

She nodded, though her mind was more confused than before. "So why are you telling me?"

The captain leaned back onto the desk and said, "Doc Marryshow, he saved my life way back when I was a rookie. I was burned real bad, y'know. He lived a couple of blocks from here. Used to pop in to see how I was. He was real interested in police work too. Always asking me questions . . ."

A few minutes later, Peta stood outside the precinct house. She had never felt more confused and angry. Sheltering herself against the old brick wall of the building, she pulled out her cell phone. Grateful that it was a multisystem unit and that she didn't have to search for a public phone, she dialed Ray's private number.

As she listened to it ring, she wondered what exactly it was that she was going to tell him—and why. There wasn't anything either of them could do at this stage.

She disconnected the phone.

Screw Frik. Screw the Daredevils, all of them. She really didn't give a damn about any of them.

All she cared about was going to Danny's to keep her promise to Arthur, and to herself. She pulled her gloves out of her handbag and put them on, wrapped her shawl around her neck and over her head like a hood, and dragged her case the eight city blocks from the Midtown North precinct station to Danny's.

George spotted her as she entered the small foyer. He ran toward her, put his arms around her, and held her, gently, as if she were fragile and might break.

He took the suitcase from her and led her inside. At the far end of the bar, the piano player recognized Peta. Smiling broadly, he switched gears into "Happy Birthday to You," played a few bars of "Hot, Hot, Hot," then segued, as he had done so many times before, into a lively rendition of "Dollar Wine."

I should have told George to tell him to cut that out, she thought, forcing herself to look across at the piano. Sitting there, his back to her, was a café au lait man about the same size and build as Arthur.

Where are you when I need you, David Copperfield? There is no magic and this was a terrible idea, she thought.

The man turned around to face her.

"You son of a bitch! How could you!" she yelled as adrenaline powered by a mix of untrammeled fury and profound joy propelled her across the room. She rushed at him, punched him full out, and knocked him backward onto the piano. "One whole year, you let me believe you were dead."

For a few moments, Arthur let her rant. Then she felt his arms around her. He held her so close she could hardly breathe. When the tears came, he kissed them away.

When they stopped, he led her to the corner table marked *Reserved*.

"Would you give me a chance to apologize? To explain," he said, holding her hand across the white linen tablecloth.

"Do I have a choice?"

"I had to do it," Arthur said. "Ray helped me. We faked the whole thing."

Peta's mind flashed back to the bloody fragments on the men's-room floor. "If it wasn't you—"

"I assure you it wasn't." Arthur accompanied his weak attempt at humor with a kiss on her hand. "When I went out there, I opened a door near the bathrooms for Ray to bring in a body he'd 'borrowed' from the morgue's John Doe slab. We'd figured any male would do, given that he was about to be blown to bits."

"So you locked the corpse, with explosive attached, into the bathroom, and slipped out the rear door?"

"Right."

"But why, Arthur? And where have you been all this time?"

A part of their conversation a year ago struggled into Peta's consciousness. *There's new trouble brewing in the Middle East, big trouble. After the meeting, I'm going to Israel. I'll be teaching medics about frontline emergency burn treatment.*

There had been trouble all right, and it wasn't over yet. "It was the Israel thing, wasn't it?" she said.

He nodded. "That was part of it. But also, there was no other way I could properly investigate Frik. He's dangerous, Peta. It's not just the artifact. I still have to find proof, but I can tell you that he has his hands in a lot of other dirty business."

"Seems to be a proliferation of that around here," Peta said.

"Of what?"

"Dirty business. My guess is, it's reached epidemic proportions." She told him about her experience that afternoon with New York's finest. "They knew it was a setup, didn't they? The police."

"Yes. But not until the people I work for squashed the investigation."

"How long have you—?"

"Been back? Long enough to have my contacts retrieve my piece of the artifact."

She pulled her hand away from him. "Why didn't you get in touch with me? I've been through hell—"

"Orders. There's still too much going on. My silence is part of the deal. I've already said too much."

"Will they ever let you tell me?"

"I'm working on it. That's all I can say—for now."

"I can be trusted to keep my mouth shut. You know that."

"That's not the point."

She looked him straight in the eye. In a monotone which held no vestige of emotion she said, "Tell me, Arthur. What *is* the point."

He leaned forward so far that his face was almost touching hers. "The point, my darling Peta, is that once I tell you . . . if I tell you . . . you'll be as involved as I am."

Give it up, girl, she thought. At least for now. Leave the recriminations alone and delight in the gift of his presence. "Have you seen Ray?" she asked, making an enormous effort to appear normal.

"I was with him when you called to tell him you were coming to Danny's. I booked a seat here right away, and another back to Vegas on the flight with you. The plan now is to test the whole artifact's capabilities at the meeting, where we can keep Frik under wraps." He glanced at her neck. "I heard about the stunt he pulled in Grenada. And that you had to give him your pendant."

"Sadly, yes."

Saying nothing about the switch she had made with the pendant, Peta raised her glass. You want closemouthed. I'll give you closemouthed. "Happy birthday, Arthur Marryshow," she said. "Happy birthday to us."

41

"Josh." Ray Arno shook Keene's hand as he stepped off the private elevator into his penthouse. McKendry followed on Keene's heels. "Terr. I tell you, I could hardly believe it when I heard the message on my machine, saying that you'd both be here. Good to see you both alive."

"Good to be seen," McKendry said.

Ray had to work to maintain his smile. Both men seemed to have aged a decade in the past year. McKendry, especially, must have shed another ten pounds since Ray had last seen him. Both men carried grim, haunted looks, as if they'd been through hell and had not quite made it all the way back.

Ray offered drinks and showed them around the penthouse. When he'd given them the inside tour, he hit a switch that automatically drew all of the curtains, revealing picture windows which overlooked the panorama below.

"Behold. My own private playground," he said, pointing out the various hotels along the strip. Naming the mountains. Taking what was almost an owner's pride in Red Rock Canyon and snowcapped Mount Charleston.

The visitors took in all the grandeur without much reaction. Keene's usual ebullience was conspicuously absent. He had moved to a window and stood gazing out at the glittering panorama.

"Is Van Alman coming?" he said finally.

The tight voice and the use of the last name instead of "Frik" were not lost on Ray.

"He's due any minute."

"Lots of good people are dead because of his little treasure hunt."

"And because of us," McKendry said. "We've been over all this, Josh—"

"I know, I know, but I detest him and his goddamn device. If he'd let it be . . ." He took a deep breath and turned from the window. "We got our piece, didn't we? Like good little errand boys we went and found it, and we're here to deliver it. But at what cost? If it had been up to me I'd have tossed it into the Cayman Trench and told Frik to go dive for it himself."

The Cayman Trench . . . hundreds of miles long, five miles deep. Ray shook his head. No one would ever have found it there.

"Why didn't you?" he asked.

"Because I needed to know that the past year wasn't for nothing. And because I promised someone that if this device could be put to good use, I'd see to it that it was. I also promised that if it was going to be used for wrong, I'd prevent it. By any means necessary. Otherwise this is the last place I want to be."

"I'm glad you came," Ray said softly, sensing Keene's pain. He'd never imagined the man could be this bitter. "We're dwindling in number."

McKendry shook his head. "Yeah, I keep trying to figure out what's happening. Arthur last year. Now Simon's gone. This goes on, there won't be anyone left."

"Fine with me," Keene said.

Ray stared at him. "You're kidding, right?"

"Not a bit. I picked up a new perspective on a lot of things in the past year . . . what's important, what's not. And you know what's last on the list? This idiotic club. How'd I ever get involved with such a bunch of arrested adolescents?" Keene made a disgusted sound. "What could I have been thinking?"

"Let me remind you. You were thinking, Life's too short to play it safe," said a new voice.

They all turned. Frikkie stood in the doorway, a shiny titanium briefcase dangling from his good hand.

"Well, well," Keene muttered. "If it isn't Mr. Teen America himself."

Frik either didn't hear the remark or chose to ignore it. "And you were thinking you didn't want to miss what could be an historic mo-

264

ment. Truly a *defining* moment in history. For all we know, A.D. may come to mean 'anno device' instead of anno Domini."

Ray saw Keene set his jaw and knew what he was thinking: no one could mix grandiosity and arrogance like Fredrick Van Alman and, yes, sometimes you wanted to punch out his lights. But Keene only dropped into a chair and swiveled it toward the window; he went back to staring silently at the bedizened desert, effectively removing himself from the room.

"What's with him?" Frik said.

"Better you don't ask," McKendry replied. He fished in his pocket and pulled out a small object. "Here's our part of the deal," he told Ray.

He held up the piece as if he were about to toss it across the room, apparently changed his mind, and lowered it. He stepped closer and pressed it into Ray's hand.

Ray understood. People had shed their blood for this little piece of strangeness. No one should play catch with it. He stared a moment at the object in his palm before he closed his fingers around it. It was larger than Arthur's. Bluer. With the little figure-eight piece at one end.

Like Arthur's, the strangely textured surface seemed to suck the warmth and moisture from his skin.

"Where's Peta?" Frik asked, looking around.

"On her way." Ray jerked the thumb of his free hand over his shoulder. "Should be landing on the helipad any minute." *And won't you be surprised to see who's with her.*

"Good. Because we can't do anything without Arthur's piece. In the meantime . . ."

He set his briefcase on the coffee table. Ray noticed for the first time that it was cuffed to his wrist.

Frik unlocked the cuff and the catches. He lifted the lid to reveal a gray, foam-lined interior. Nestled among the egg-crate contours were three oddly shaped objects, similar to the piece in Ray's hand, yet distinct—distant relatives, but unquestionably members of the same family. A wire-frame stand lay in a rectangular cutout.

"Voilà!" Frik looked around. "Now, where's this lab you told me you set up to assemble our treasures?"

"Right through that door back there," Ray said without thinking. He'd been toying with Arthur's piece on the workbench when the call announcing Keene and McKendry's arrival had come from downstairs. He'd been trying to run a current through it, but not only was it non-conductive, it absorbed whatever he shot into it without altering its own temperature even a fraction of a degree.

Had he put it away?

"We should wait for Peta," he said quickly.

"We will," Frik said. He rose and carried the briefcase like a tray toward the rear of the penthouse's great room. "We have no choice. But why waste time once she arrives? We can assemble what we have now and be all set to go. When Peta gets here we'll simply have to plug in the final piece."

"I don't know, Frik," Ray said, trailing after him.

"I do. I've waited all year for this moment, and I'm not going to put it off a nanosecond longer than absolutely necessary."

Ray glanced over his shoulder. McKendry was close behind, but Keene remained slouched in his seat by the window. How was he going to steer this little procession away from the lab—at least until he'd checked it out to make sure that Arthur's piece wasn't visible?

He tried to scoot around Frik. "At least wait until I straighten up a little."

"Nonsense," Frik said, not even slowing. "We've known each other too long to worry about messy desks and overflowing wastebaskets."

He pulled the door open and stepped through, leaving just enough space for Ray to slip past him.

Ray made it to the workbench first and suppressed a groan—*You idiot!*—when he spotted Arthur's piece lying out there dead center for all the world to see. Wouldn't be the end of the world if Frik spotted it, but he'd promised Arthur and Peta not to assemble the device until they arrived, and he wanted to keep his word.

Pretending to clear a space for the briefcase, he swept a forearm across the scarred surface, effectively moving the piece to the side. Picking it up might be too obvious, so he brushed a sheaf of notes over it.

He turned to see if Frik had spotted it and barely suppressed a sigh of relief. The Afrikaner had stopped inside the door and was gazing at the equipment racked on the walls.

"What do you with all of this stuff?" he said. "Looks like an electronics store."

McKendry sniffed the air. "A temperature-controlled, electrostatic-filtered electronics store." He glanced at Ray. "Laminar flow?"

Ray nodded. "Just a hobby. Trying to build a better mousetrap."

"Forget mousetraps. Before the night is out you'll *really* have something to tinker with," Frik said.

He removed the wire-frame stand from the briefcase, followed by the three pieces, one by one. He handled them gently, as if they were fragile.

Ray knew that if these were related to the piece Arthur had given him, they were anything but fragile. He didn't know why, but his mouth began to dry as he watched Frik settle the largest of the three pieces into the base of the platform. After he'd snapped another, slightly smaller piece into the first, he held out his hand for Keene and McKendry's.

"Yours comes next."

Ray handed it over, reluctantly, but he had to marvel at how perfectly it fit into the other two.

"Which one is Simon's?" McKendry said. He stood behind Frik, watching over his shoulder. His voice was soft, almost hoarse. "The one he died diving for?"

"This one." Frik lifted the final, unassembled piece. He rolled it between his thumb and fingers. "Poor Simon. I miss him. He gave his life for this. I propose we name the device after him. The Brousseau Device, so that we never forget him."

"As if we need that to remember him," Keene said from the other room.

A grand gesture, Ray thought, but ultimately meaningless. What did Frik care who it was named after, as long as he controlled it?

"What about Paul Trujold? And Arthur?" Ray asked.

Frik glanced up, a sardonic smile twisting his lips. "Paul was my employee. I assume Arthur acquired *his* piece through the mail or via your friend Manny, and he died in a men's room. I think the device deserves a better pedigree than that."

He fit Simon's piece into the assembly, then jerked back his hand.

"What happened?" Ray asked.

"It . . ." Frik rubbed his fingers. "It felt like a shock, like a—"

"Holy shit!" McKendry rasped.

Ray didn't have to ask—he knew what the big man was talking about: the incomplete assembly was moving. It spun around so the gap where the last piece would fit faced the pile of papers Ray had just moved. Platform and all, it began sliding, inching its way across the workbench.

"What do we do?" Ray said. He felt his gut coiling into a knot. Objects didn't move on their own, a force pushed or pulled them, energy was expended . . . unless it was magnetic and being drawn toward a metallic—

Oh, hell! It was butting up against the papers covering Arthur's piece. Ray reached out to grab it, but Frik stopped him.

"Wait!" He gripped Ray's wrist with his good hand. "Let's see where it's going."

Ray had a pretty good idea: it was moving toward the rest of itself.

Sure enough, it kept moving, bulldozing the papers aside, until it straddled Arthur's piece.

"Where did *that* come from?" Frik frowned as he pointed. "That's . . . that's . . ."

"Arthur's," Ray said. No use trying to deny it. By process of elimination, Frik certainly knew what it looked like.

"It was supposed to be in New York!"

"*Supposed* to be. But it's been here all along."

"So Peta lied about—"

"No, she really thought it was there. By now she knows otherwise."

"I don't understand," McKendry said.

"It's a long story," Ray muttered, thinking that it was one he didn't want to tell. Not yet. Not until Peta and Arthur arrived.

He didn't have to worry about stalling. Frik was off and running. He picked up Arthur's piece and dragged the assembly and its frame back to the center of the workbench. "Right now it's show time."

"We should wait for Peta."

"What for? Peta is coming in empty-handed. As I said before, I've waited too long already."

He grabbed the pair of insulated gloves lying to his right and slipped a glove over his good hand. Before Ray could stop him, he had snapped the fifth and final piece into place.

A flash of brilliant blue-white light lit the room, knocking Frik backward. He would have fallen if McKendry hadn't been standing there. Ray too was staggered by the brilliance. He blinked furiously, trying to focus through the floating afterimages, but he could make out only shadows. He heard footsteps pounding in from the great room.

"What the hell was that?" Keene's voice.

"Look who decided to join the party," McKendry quipped.

"What are you jerks trying to do?" Keene said. "Wreck the thing?"

Finally Ray could see again. He focused on the workbench and saw the device jittering around as if in an earthquake, only the floor was still. And one of the pieces—Simon's, no Peta's, he thought—was smoking. The fumes stung Ray's nostrils.

"Something's wrong!" Frik yelled.

"How about telling us something we don't know," Keene said.

The smoking piece twisted and took off, hurtling across the room to shatter against the far wall.

Frik and McKendry hurried over to check out the fragments. McKendry, who had been closest to them, got there first.

"Nice work, Van Alman," Keene said, his tone verging on a snarl. "You must've put it together wrong."

"I couldn't have," Frik said. "The way they're shaped, there's only one way those pieces can interlock. I—"

"Face it, man," Keene said, keeping up the pressure. "You blew it. Whatever you did triggered an eject button."

"More like a *re*ject button," McKendry said, picking up a handful of fragments. "This piece was bogus, guys. The device spat it out."

"Peta!" Frik said, doing his best to ball his good fist within the heavy glove and pounding it on the table. "Damn her! She gave me a fake! When she gets here—"

"Watch out!" Ray's gaze had been fixed on the device. "It's up to something!"

They all watched as the device began to glow and a blue light enveloped it and its stand. The glow brightened and seemed to thicken—not a term Ray would normally apply to light, but the best he could come up with at the moment—and obscure the device within it.

Suddenly a beam of bright blue shot out, thick as a man's wrist and laser focused. It barely missed Keene's head as it lanced toward a spot on the wall just to the left of the door. Keene stared at it a moment before stepping through into the great room. "Get in here, guys. You've *got* to see this."

Ray led the way but stopped dead in the doorway when he saw what Keene was talking about. McKendry plowed into his back, propelling him into the room.

The beam of light had pierced the wall without damaging it—no hole, no burn marks. As far the beam was concerned, the wall didn't seem to exist. It traveled with undiminished brightness across the great room, through the outer wall, and into the night.

"Look," McKendry said, pointing. "It's moving, almost as if it's tracking something."

At that moment Ray became aware of a pulsating thrum.

"Do you hear that?" Frik said.

Ray nodded. He knew the sound. "That," he said, "would be Peta's helicopter heading this way."

42

"There it is," Peta said, pointing through the helicopter's bubble window.

Arthur grinned. "You're sure?" He sat to her left at the helm of the sprightly little Chief-8, his right hand firm on the stick. He winked at her. "It's so hard to tell Ray's casino from the others."

The wink said it all. Even among the gallimaufry of brightly lit, high-concept, high-rise casinos lining the Las Vegas Strip, ferro-concrete behemoths in drag watching the endless parade of tourists, Ray's wedged-shaped Daredevil Casino stood out. Maybe it was its shape, apex aimed like a spearhead at the sidewalk. Or maybe it was the space shuttle that appeared to be launching from the right side. Or perhaps it was the realistic Godzilla-like creature, with animatronic head and arms, bursting through the left wall.

She noticed a crowd beginning to gather around the monster and glanced at her watch; almost half past eleven. Ray's stuntmen-cum-actors must be about to begin their assault on the giant fire-breathing lizard.

"Anything wrong?" The flight had been glide smooth until a moment ago, when she'd noticed a little pitch and roll.

"Some strange updrafts around the casino."

The Daredevil's rooftop helipad loomed before them. Peta dug into her shoulder bag. She found what she was looking for but didn't remove it. "I want you to see something before we land," she said. "I didn't want to be the only one in on the secret."

"Maybe it should wait till after we land." Arthur kept his eyes straight ahead.

"I really think you'll want to see this now."

She opened her hand and held the piece up where he wouldn't have to turn his head too far to see it. After a quick first glance he stiffened and took another look.

"What in the world?"

"It's my piece, the one you gave me."

"But I thought—"

"I had Ralphie make a phony—and he did a masterful job. That's what I gave Frik."

"So he thinks he's got three but he's only got two. I love it! Doesn't Ray know—?"

"Uh-uh. At the time I wasn't quite sure about Ray. I mean, whether or not he had something to do with your, um, death, or if he and Frikkie were in cahoots. So I didn't tell him. I've learned the truth, but I haven't exactly had time to call him."

"So you and I will be the only ones who know." He grinned. "How do you want to work it? We can let them assemble it with the fake, and when nothing happens, pull out the real things and say, 'See if this works better.' Or we can—"

The interior of the cabin filled with a bright blue light. The helicopter dipped. Arthur fought the stick.

"Oh, God!" Peta cried. The light had centered on the piece in her hand, but it was coming from outside. When she looked through the window, she could follow a tightly focused beam straight back to Ray's penthouse atop the casino. "What are they trying to do to us?"

She saw four figures rush out onto the helipad. The one she recognized as Ray began waving at her. Was he warning her off or telling her to hurry in?

The chopper was bucking like a wild stallion. Arthur forced it into a stuttering descent toward the helipad. "It's that thing, that piece you've got there. Somehow it's set off something below that's affecting the controls."

"Should I toss it out?" Peta said.

"Hell no! We're not *out* of control, just having some difficulty is all."

"How much difficulty?"

A tight grin. "Oh, I'd say something akin to flying through a Midwest supercell."

"With or without tornadoes?"

"Without. But that could change any moment." He glanced at her. "Look. An actual touchdown might be too dicey with these controls the way they are. But I can get low enough so that you can toss the piece onto the pad."

"And then what?"

"Then we see what happens. If I get the helm back, we'll land. If not, we'll fly off and look for a place in the desert to put down. Either way, we'll know the piece will be safe with Ray until we make it back to the casino."

"Bring her down as low as you can," Peta said. "These pieces seem to be indestructible, but let's not take any chances."

Arthur fought the Chief-8 downward. When the landing runners wobbled between eight and ten feet above the helipad, Peta pushed her door open. Noise and wind swirled through the cabin. Looking below, she saw Ray, Keene, and McKendry backed against the wall of the penthouse.

Frik stood at the edge of the landing circle, where the tornadic downwash whipped his hair and clothing. Peta saw his face, his tight, angry posture. He knows, she thought. He must have tried to assemble the device with the fake piece.

Was that why the chopper was acting crazy?

She cataloged her options. Fast. The way she did during emergency surgery. She could toss out the real fragment, surrendering it to Frik, or keep it in the chopper and risk a crash. Or—

"Hold her steady!" She unclasped her seat harness.

"What are you doing?"

She tucked her piece of the device into her bra. The beam followed it, making her chest glow with the same eerie blue light. "See you below," she said.

Swiveling onto her belly, she slipped her legs through the door.

"Peta!" Arthur shouted, panic wild in his face. "Get back in here! You'll break your neck!"

Feeling nothing except the need to take action, Peta continued her outward slide. The vortex from the whirling blades tore at her skirt, whipping it above her knees. She wished she'd worn jeans—she'd have a better view of her feet. Inching down, she kicked back and forth until her boots found the landing runner. She hooked her heels on the steel tubing, reached down and grabbed it with her left hand, then her right. Finally she kicked her feet free and swung down to hang with her boot soles only three or four feet above the helipad. She was about to release her grip when the chopper suddenly veered up and away from the roof.

The beam of blue light followed her, targeted like a laser on her chest. She repressed a scream as she looked down through hundreds of feet of empty air at the top of the giant lizard monster's head. On the ground below, people in the gathering crowd began to look up and point. She wanted to shout, I'm not part of the damn Daredevil show! This is the real thing!

She felt her fingers slipping and tightened her grip, envisioning herself splattered on the pavement below while the onlookers applauded the realistic gore effects. The little chopper began to angle back down toward the roof. The parapet hove within reach, the chopper dipped, and Peta saw the upper edge of the wall rushing at her.

She cried out and nearly lost her grip as her right hip and thigh slammed against the concrete.

The chopper wobbled away and back again, ramming the small of her back against the edge of the parapet, twisting her body and tearing her right hand free of the runner. Clinging by one hand, she felt wind catch her skirt and wrench her back and forth.

With her free hand, Peta tore open the skirt's hook and loop closure, and the skirt dropped away. Arthur must have regained a modicum of control because the chopper lifted and angled back over the helipad, bringing her shoes to within a yard or so of the surface.

That was more than good enough for Peta. She released her grip and dropped onto the hard concrete surface.

The relief of feeling something solid beneath her gave way to a blast of pain as her right ankle buckled. Instinctively she rolled as she fell, and felt the piece slip from her bra and tumble away . . .

. . . to land at Frik's feet . . . almost as if it wanted to be there.

He snatched it up and raised it above his head. The beam of light focused on the piece, making it look like he held a blue sun against the night sky.

"You gave me a bad moment there, Peta!" Frik said, shouting over the noise of the chopper. "I thought we were going to lose this!"

He ran toward the penthouse, brushing past Ray, McKendry, and Keene, who were hurrying forward to help Peta. She struggled to her feet. Her ankle blazed with gut-wrenching agony. She glanced up and saw that Arthur had full control of the chopper now. Removing the piece had worked. She gave him a thumbs-up. He nodded gravely through the bubble.

She turned back to the other men and pointed toward Frik's retreating back. "Stop him!"

Her shout was lost in the wind and the engine noise, and she doubted McKendry and Keene would have been much use anyway. They stood frozen on the helipad, eyes fixed on the chopper, gaping at Arthur. She saw Keene grab Ray by his shirt and point to the chopper, shouting something she couldn't hear, doubtless something about a dead man piloting an aircraft.

No help there. Ignoring the stab of pain each step sent up her leg, she hobbled after Frik on her own. He had all of the pieces now. If she didn't do something right away, he would assemble the artifact and take possession of it. Too many people had died because of his obsession. She couldn't let him have control of it.

She stepped through the sliding glass door into the great room and stopped. Frik was nowhere to be seen. He had what he wanted. Could he already have gone?

A bright blue glow from the rear doorway answered her. She reached the lab and found Frik hovering over the four assembled pieces, guiding hers—the fifth and last—toward its position.

Her piece clicked into place. Immediately, the glow disappeared. The device sat cold and dark and apparently inert on the workbench, looking for all the world like nothing more than an oddly mottled Easter egg with an extra nodule on one side.

It was as if Frik had turned off a light.

He turned to face her. "What is this, Peta? Another goddamn fake?" He pulled over a metallic briefcase that sat open on the lab table. "I'll just have to take this back to my own labs and figure it out." He extended his scarred left hand toward the object.

She lunged, reaching for it with both hands. Though she did not yet fully understand why she felt so passionately about it, every instinct told her to stop Frik from removing the device. He grabbed her arms. She struggled to release herself from his grasp.

Suddenly, time seemed to slow down. She watched as if through a heat mirage as a ripple ran over the surface of the spheroid, followed by another and another, blurring the edges of the separate pieces. Fusing them into a single object.

At its center, a tiny spot of bright white began to glow, and then light was everywhere, blasting through Peta like a storm wind through a screen door, engulfing her in heat like the heart of the sun. Consuming her and everything around her.

43

When the white light faded and she began to recover her senses, Peta thought for a moment that the world had been turned on end. But the problem wasn't the world. She was the one who was upside down, lying on the floor of Ray's penthouse lab, staring up at the underside of the main table and the solid gray line of the ceiling beyond it.

Reoriented, she jumped to her feet. Her body responded at once, but she felt weightless, as if she had floated to a standing position in a flying dream.

On the table, the artifact had returned to a state she could only think of as dormant. It looked like nothing more than a chunk of rutilated quartz from somewhere in Arizona, or a pretty colored rock that some collector had picked up on Montserrat to remind himself that a sleeping volcano could look like any other mountain until it erupted.

"What the fuck?"

Frikkie's left hand appeared on the far side of the table as he pulled himself up off the floor. Staring at it, Peta flashed on what it had looked like minutes ago as he'd reached for the artifact: severely scarred from the fire that had killed Paul Trujold. Now, it wasn't scarred at all. The skin looked smooth and healthy.

No amount of plastic surgery or expert grafting could have achieved that result in so short a time, she thought, as Frik's head came into view.

Immediately, she noticed that the scarring on his face was gone too, as was the damage to his eyelid, which had given him the permanent sleepy-eyed look of a myasthenic in the throes of crisis.

That was when it occurred to her that she was standing with her full weight on her twisted ankle, but there was no pain. Her side and back, which should have been covered with cuts, bruises, and abrasions from her ride on the runner of the helicopter, felt fine. If anything, she felt as if she had just come from an hour with a masseur. She reminded herself that she was a physician, a scientist. Perfect cures didn't happen this way, in a split second. Miracles, as they said, took a little longer.

Reluctantly, she acknowledged the certainty that had been taking shape in her mind. It had to be the artifact. There simply was no other answer. They had both touched it; they were both made whole.

She shook her head at herself and her ridiculous willingness to believe in magic. Fact: Antibiotics and aspirin were miracles. Fact: People couldn't walk on water without webbed feet.

Fact: That thing over there was not God any more than Frik was the devil.

In the throes of intellectualizing, Peta almost missed seeing Frik reach out to grab the device. Using a reserve of strength she didn't know she had, she shoved him away from it. Taken by surprise, he staggered backward. His carotid pumped.

"Out of my way, bitch!"

Frik's rage at Peta's continued attempts to thwart him was palpable. She braced herself for his assault.

"I suggest you move away from the artifact, Frikkie." Arthur stood framed in the doorway into the lab.

Frik stopped in his tracks. Very slowly, like someone in an Abbott and Costello movie, he swiveled around. It occurred to Peta that the Afrikaner had been so busy grabbing for the piece of the artifact she had dropped that he hadn't taken the time to notice who was piloting the helicopter.

"I wish everyone would stop looking at me as if I were a ghost." Arthur stepped into the lab. "If you want to find out how alive I am, why don't you try to touch that device."

"Why don't you try to stop me."

Frik took a step toward the table. Arthur moved to intercept him. The Afrikaner spun on his heel and charged at his old friend.

Caught off-guard by Frik's change in direction, Arthur didn't have time to brace himself. The two men tumbled, ass over elbows, through the door and back into the great room.

Recovering his feet, Frik grabbed Arthur by the jacket and lifted him into the air. As he rose, Arthur thrust out his leg, catching Frik in the groin just as Ray and McKendry and Keene charged in from the helipad.

Arthur bounced lightly to his feet. "Stay out of this. He's mine."

"Don't be so sure," Frikkie said in a stage whisper.

It had become obvious to Peta that an all-out physical battle between Arthur and Frik was inevitable. Arthur was taller, Frik broader. They weighed about the same, and since the miraculous actions of the artifact, both were fit and hugely strong. Without intervention, it would be anybody's victory.

As if to prove her right, Frik rushed toward Arthur, who prepared to block the Afrikaner's charge. Too late, Peta noticed that Frik had grabbed a vase filled with roses and baby's breath and flung it ahead of himself. Arthur's blocking punch shattered the crystal, sending water and flowers and splinters of glass flying everywhere. And blood. Arthur's blood. Spurting from his knuckles.

That was enough for Peta. She wasn't about to let Arthur be annihilated. The others could stand by out of respect for his wish to deal with Frik on his own terms; she couldn't. There was no way that she could endure it—or live with herself—if he died again. This time for real. She dashed forward, ready to attack Frik.

And stopped.

The hairs on the back of her neck rose. She felt as if something had hit her at the base of her neck and a jolting shiver ran down her spine and up again.

Disoriented, she turned around.

The lab was bathed in an eerie glow, the way light looks from twenty feet underwater. She tried to call out to the men. No sound emerged. She faced them and tried again. This time her voice rang out loud and clear, but the fight claimed their full attention.

Pressing his advantage, Frik grabbed Arthur by the shoulders and spun, hurling his former friend over a plush leather chair and into an antique coffee table. He threw the chair out of the way and dove. Arthur was ready. Catching Frik with his feet, he propelled him through the air, to land with a thud by the sliding glass doors to the helipad.

With a handspring, Arthur was back on his feet, running toward his opponent. As Frik struggled to stand, Arthur kicked him in the chest, sending him crashing through the closed half of the glass door.

"That one's for Simon," Arthur yelled.

Cheering, Keene and Ray and McKendry moved toward the helipad. Spurred on by their support, Arthur started forward. Through the commotion and the shattered glass, Peta could see Frikkie roll to his knees and come up throwing something. The Grenadian shielded himself from a shower of pebble-sized chunks of glass.

Frik, backing up onto the wide roof, motioned for Arthur to come and get him.

Hoping that the other three men would have the sense to make sure the right man won, Peta started after them. Their attention was focused on Arthur and Frikkie, rolling near the low parapet at the edge of the roof, first one on top, then the other.

She looked back into the lab.

The artifact had transformed into a single brilliant, shapeless white mass. She saw what might be the outline of a face in the glow as the object left the table and began to float, infinitely slowly, toward the tall ceiling. The image of the strange mural in the undersea cave rose in her mind. Was this what the painter had been drawing?

Midway between the table and the ceiling, the device ceased its motion and hovered.

The lights in the suite flickered and went out, leaving only the green glow of emergency fluorescents. In the moment before their screens popped like balloons pricked by a dozen pins, she saw on the security monitors that downstairs in the casino, machines were wildly spewing out money.

Glancing to the side through Ray's wall of glass, Peta watched the city lights of Las Vegas blink out. A wave of black washed over the neon city, leaving Las Vegas Boulevard in darkness. An instant later, almost as if it had been timed, fountains of sparkling red and orange and yellow shot from the roofs of the other casinos, starting from the southern end of the strip at Mandalay Bay, rushing toward the Daredevil Casino and beyond.

In homage to the midnight hour and the start of 2001—the true millennium—the nine minutes of planned fireworks crackled and flashed and boomed from the Strip's megahotels.

Firework mines thundered in quick white bursts that deafened her and drowned out the sound of her shouts. Rockets rose into the sky, bursting into sparkling blue and red and gold and white star-flowers.

She looked up at the artifact.

As if it had waited for her attention, the glowing orb started to move again, this time toward her. Like a living thing, it floated inches from her face and, impossibly, passed right through the vast wall of windows. She turned to follow its progress and spotted it, one small, unblinking light against the backdrop of flaming, sparkling fireworks that showered Las Vegas. Traveling southeast, slowly at first but gaining speed, it left a trail like a miniature comet drifting through the desert sky.

Peta stood transfixed until she could no longer differentiate between the orb and the stars. When it was out of sight, she turned toward the door that led to the helipad. The Daredevils, their battle abandoned, stood in awed contemplation of what they had witnessed.

Characteristically, Keene was the first to break the silence. "I wish Selene could have seen that."

And Simon, Peta thought.

"Maybe she did see it, Josh," McKendry said. "Anybody want to take a guess at what it was?"

"It was mine, that's what it was," Frik said.

"By all means go and get it." Arthur's voice held no antagonism. His body language indicated that his desire to fight had left with the vanishing object.

"Do you think, maybe, this proves we aren't alone in the universe?" Ray asked, a surprising note of longing in his voice.

We had it in our hands—the cure for the ills of the world—and we let go of it, Peta thought as the lights came back on in the suite. She knew without looking that the monitors were back in operation, and that downstairs in the casino and out on the Strip, it was business as usual. "And so the world goes on," she said.

"Time for our meeting?" Frik was apparently trying to resume command of the situation.

"We'll meet, all right, but without you." Arthur took a step toward him. "You're out of here."

The others chorused their agreement.

Frik didn't move. Almost in pantomime, Ray walked over to Arthur's side. Frik backed up to the exit. "You'll be sorry, you bastards."

"Oh, I don't think so," Arthur said. "What do you think, guys?" His glance included Peta.

Reserving judgment on the issue of whether or not she wanted to be one of the boys, she joined the Daredevils as they walked Frikkie out of the penthouse.

EPILOGUE

At the base of the abandoned oil rig in the Dragon's Mouth, off the coast of Trinidad, Manny Sheppard cut his engine. In the absolute quiet of the Caribbean night, he watched a strange glow hovering over the water.

Beneath it, a rippling began, like waves from a dropped stone. Once, twice, and again, as if in a three-gun salute to Obeah, and to the dead and finally buried, the glow faded and returned. Then it began a slow ascent into the heavens.

ABOUT THE AUTHORS

Kevin J. Anderson has written twenty-six national bestsellers and has been nominated for the Nebula Award, the Bram Stoker Award, and the *Science Fiction Chronicle* Readers' Choice Award. He lives in Monument, Colorado. Janet Berliner, author of many novels, including the Bram Stoker Award–winning *Children of the Dusk* (with George Guthridge), lives in Las Vegas. She has also edited many anthologies, including *Peter S. Beagle's Immortal Unicorn.* Matthew J. Costello lives north of New York City. He is the author of numerous novels, including *Unidentified*, a recent Literary Guild Selection, and has teamed up with F. Paul Wilson on two previous novels. F. Paul Wilson has written more than twenty novels, including the bestseller *The Keep* and the Repairman Jack novels. Twice winner of the Prometheus Award for best libertarian fiction, he lives in Wall, New Jersey.